MURDER IN HASTE

Who is the stranger with the pale, expression-less eyes? And what is it that frightens "Lisa" —the shy, quiet girl with the appealing smile? To Gilly Amery, Sydney fashion reporter, these are idle questions arising from a chance encounter in a café. But within a few hours they have become of vital importance. This is the tense and dramatic story of how, at a smart cocktail party, Gilly stumbles upon murder—and finds herself involved in a series of blood-chilling events which threaten her own safety. The excellent characterization and the cleverly constructed plot combine to make this a sophisticated thriller of the best kind. Set against the bright background of society life in Sydney, it is a tale of mystery and suspense which will hold the reader enthralled.

MURDER
IN HASTE

HEATHER GARDINER

THE MYSTERY BOOK GUILD
5 & 6 ST. ANDREW'S HILL, CARTER LANE
LONDON, E.C.4

This Edition April 1955

*All characters and incidents in this novel
are entirely fictitious*

Made and Printed by Litho Offset in Great Britain at
GREYCAINES
(Taylor Garnett Evans & Co. Ltd.) Watford, Herts.

For
GEORGE

CHAPTER I

IT WAS a hot sultry afternoon when I met Lisa.

She was sitting at a small table in a café, staring out at the busy street as if the scene around her played no part in her thoughts. I don't think she was aware of the stream of faces passing the window or the endless flow of traffic along the hot bitumen road. She looked as if she'd stepped out of the world of reality into a word of fancy where time and space ceased to exist. The soft curve of her smooth red lips reminded me of the famous Mona Lisa smile.

I christened her Lisa. Idly I wondered what her real name was, and later I discovered it, but to me she became Lisa from that first moment, and I have never thought of her by any other name.

She wasn't well dressed, or smart or beautiful. She certainly wasn't the type of girl to figure in my daily gossip column in the *Sydney Daily Times*. There was nothing outstanding about her, yet her face will always live in my memory long after other more beautiful and more important faces have faded. I can still see her clearly, just as I saw her in the café, with that small half-smile touching her mouth. She looked rather sweet, rather shy and just a little sad.

I was on my way back to the office after reporting a fashionable but tedious luncheon party when I spotted the small café, and my feet—or perhaps it was Fate—led me in almost automatically. I knew the little café well, and Barney Blair and I had argued and laughed and gossiped over innumerable cups of tea at its check-clothed tables.

I was feeling sorry for myself when I pushed the swinging doors open and stepped in. It was a beastly day. I had a cocktail party to attend that evening; and all my friends seemed to have escaped the heat wave by taking themselves off, very sensibly, for holidays. Even Barney, the sports reporter and the Bright Spot in my daily routine, had wangled a trip to Melbourne to report the England-Australia Test, and I had a vision of him lounging around the M.C.G. or swilling beer with honey-haired blondes, while I sweated and toiled and attended maddeningly dull functions.

The café was almost empty. It was too early yet for the usual afternoon customers. Mabel, the waitress, moved towards me lethargically.

"I'm longing for a pot of tea," I told her.

She ran a languid hand over her platinum hair. "It's a stinking day, Miss Amery, isn't it?" Her eyes took in my white linen frock and big hat, and registered approval. "Sit over by the window. It's the only cool spot in the whole shop. You'll be right under the fan there."

I walked over to the table by the window. And there I saw Lisa. She was sitting very still, with an odd smile pulling at her mouth, and a far-away look in her blue eyes.

I sat at the empty place opposite her, and she turned her head slowly to face me, as if she were reluctantly abandoning her fairy-world and returning to the matter-of-fact things of everyday life. Wearily she picked up the paper that had been lying by her elbow and began scanning the news, but it failed to hold her attention. She turned over to the social notes and ran her eye down them.

I smiled a little. The paper she was reading was the *Sydney Daily Times*, and the column which seemed to absorb her far more than the leader on World Affairs was my own gossip page.

Mabel appeared with a tray which she set in front of me with a clatter. I took out my notebook and pencil and began jotting down a few notes about the luncheon party I'd just attended.

Lisa stirred her tea listlessly, and once, when I glanced up from my scribbling, I saw she was watching me with curious, interested eyes. I put my notebook away and lit a cigarette.

She pushed the ash-tray towards me, and when I smiled my thanks she looked straight at me as if she'd like to speak, but didn't know how to begin. It was then I realized she was lonely.

"It's terribly hot, isn't it?"

8

Her face lit up pathetically, and she answered quickly, as if frightened I might withdraw the conversational opening. "Oh yes! But I'm getting used to it. And it's ever so much better than the freezing cold."

Oddly, I wished she hadn't spoken. The common little voice dispelled the mystery of her haunting smile and robbed her face of its remote ethereal quality. The Mona Lisa touch had gone and in its place was a rather pretty girl, older than I'd first imagined her, with blue eyes and a Cockney accent.

I was so certain of the accent, that I began to say, "How do you like Australia?", then realized it was the sort of question English migrants get sick of answering, so instead, I asked her, "What made you decide to come here?"

She looked down at the wisps of steam rising from her cup. And for a second I caught just a glimpse of the secretive, far-away look that had aroused my curiosity and interest.

"It's hard to say." She shrugged. "My parents were killed in the blitz. There was just my brother and me. And Jock . . ." She paused. "When Jock . . . went . . . I wanted to get away. He was with the Air Force." There was pride in her voice. Obviously she'd adored her brother. "I always remembered," she went on quickly, "him saying Australia was a good place to live. He was with a whole lot of Aussies and he used to come home with tales about Melbourne and Sydney and big cattle ranches out in the country. Some of the stories were real funny and Mum and Dad they used to laugh and say one day we'd have to see it all for ourselves. I suppose that's why I'm here. It's a sort of promise I'm keeping."

Poor little Lisa.

"What a pity your brother isn't with you," I said softly, "but I'm sure you'll find lots of friends here." I hoped she would.

She glanced at me quickly, almost defiantly. "I'll be all right."

I wondered whether she'd mistaken the sympathy in my voice for the smug patronage of one who is securely placed towards one who is struggling to find a niche in a new country.

Perhaps she realized what I was thinking, because she smiled, suddenly, as if to counteract the bluntness of her

9

words. "I've only been here two months and I've been pretty lucky because I got a job straight off, working in a hotel in Melbourne. At St. Kilda it was, and close to the beach and everything! Only then the girl I was relieving came back and they didn't want me any more, so I thought I'd try Sydney." She gave a small shrug. "I can always go back home, I suppose."

"You were living with friends in England? Or with relatives?" I was curious to know just where home meant to a girl whose parents and brother had died in the War.

She shook her head. "I s'pose the Convent's sort of home now. Wonderful to me, they were. Took me in after the bombing and looked after me and didn't ask any questions. I was terribly sick."

I'm sure she didn't realize her fingers were straying to the little gold cross hanging from a thin chain round her neck. It looked as if the Sisters had attended to her spiritual as well as her physical well-being, I thought cynically.

And partly because I was touched by the depths of her loneliness, and partly because I wanted her to know that Sisters at a convent weren't the only people in the world capable of a friendliness to strangers, I took out my notebook, tore a page out and scribbled my name and 'phone number on it. I handed it to her.

"Do ring me and tell me how you get on. If you can't find a suitable job I'm sure I can help you. I know a lot of people."

She took it like a swimmer struggling to reach land and clutching at every stick floating in the water.

"Thank you. I'd like to do that." Her eyes lit up in a smile that turned mere prettiness into something rare and rather beautiful.

She opened her brown handbag and tucked my piece of paper in one corner. Then she hesitated, and when she withdrew her hand it was holding a big square envelope. She fished inside it, drew out a photo and held it across the table saying, "This is one of Mum and Dad and here's our old dog Toby. That was taken just before the War."

It was a coloured well-thumbed card showing her father and mother side by side on an old-fashioned sofa with a dog at their feet. I'm sure no eyes were ever as bright as the two pairs staring out at me, and I couldn't imagine any rug being as vivid as the red of the mat on which Toby reclined. I couldn't see much resemblance between Lisa and her parents save in the blue of their eyes—that seemed to be the only feature they had in common. But where the mother's nose had been long and thin, Lisa's was short, and where the father's face had been coarse, Lisa's was unexpectedly fine-boned. I thought they must have been proud of their daughter.

While I was murmuring the usual comments over Lisa's photo I had a sudden feeling I was being watched. I knew someone's eyes were studying my every movement as plainly as if a hand had touched my shoulder. I glanced up, quickly.

A man was sitting at the table next to us. I hadn't noticed him come in. For a second our eyes met, then I dropped my gaze to the photo in my hand. There had been something cold and rather frightening about those shallow blue eyes. I returned the photo to Lisa and she put it back in her bag.

"It's high time I got back to the office," I said, gathering up my purse and trying to catch Mabel's attention.

Again I could feel those unknown eyes watching me.

"Oh, you're going?" Lisa said, with a faint trace of disappointment.

I smiled at her, gently. "I'm supposed to be working. The longer I stay here, the longer I'll have to stay at the office to finish off my work. If I didn't there'd be no social column for you to read in the *Sydney Daily Times* tomorrow."

She glanced down at the paper on the table.

"Do you know all these people? She's lovely looking, isn't she?"

Her finger pointed to the rather smudged photo of the Welch family. It was one of a soppy series we were running under the headlines of 'Well-known Public Figures at Home'.

It wasn't a good photo, and yet, as I looked at it, I thought it caught the atmosphere of the Welch household rather well. Even a stranger could sense the pride and adoration in John's face as he gazed at his surprisingly young wife. And although the black-and-white print couldn't do justice to Miranda's lovely colouring, it showed the beautiful oval of her face, the high cheek-bones, the smooth, shapely head. She was looking at John, accepting the comparatively new, and rather exalted, role of Mrs. John Welch with poise and grace. Clare was the misfit in that picture, I thought, as I gazed down at the blurred faces in front of me. The smile she gave Miranda was too sweet, too sickly and too false. It was a defiant smile which was meant to assure the world that she and her step-mother lived in harmony and mutual respect. It was a shade overdone. Behind Clare, with one hand resting lightly on her shoulder, was her fiancé, Dr. Tony Cambray, a solid, dependable figure who wore his clothes with the casual ease and assurance of the man who has been brought up at the best schools, who has always taken his social position for granted simply because he happened to be born into one of Australia's pioneering families.

I smiled as I thought of Clare's rebellion when I'd first suggested that family group.

"But, darling," she'd said, screwing up her small face, "they're so utterly repulsive. Those dreadful photos, I mean. They look so artificial and everyone knows they've been posed and I think the whole idea's perfectly foul."

But eventually she'd given in.

And in a small café in one of Sydney's busiest streets an English girl who'd probably never heard of the Welch family before pored over the photo as if it were a newly released portrait from Buckingham Palace.

I looked around for Mabel, wishing she'd emerge from her hidden haunts. The man at the table next to us turned his head, sharply, and his flat blue eyes focused on the hand lying idly across the check cloth on his table. It was a firm, capable hand with square fingers.

He'd glanced away too quickly. I knew perfectly well he'd been watching us for the past few minutes, and if I'd turned a fraction sooner our gaze would have met again.

I was vaguely annoyed. I also began to wonder what was wrong with my face. Was it a black smudge on my nose, or a smear of lipstick on my chin, that drew his eyes the minute I turned away? I took out my hand-mirror, surveyed my face and decided it looked much the same, though a little more worn than when I'd set out that morning.

"She's like a film star!" Lisa said, with her eyes glued to the paper.

The remark was sudden and spontaneous. It was the remark of a small child making a discovery. In that instant I knew exactly how she'd spoken, exactly how she'd looked, when she was a plump toddling infant.

She was engrossed with the Welch photo, and there was a puzzled frown hovering between her eyes. Then her face lit up with the joy of recognition, and again I was reminded of the face of a child who finds that the strange and unfamiliar can be pigeon-holed in a half-forgotten, yet suddenly vivid, memory.

"Of course!" She was still looking at the page in front of her. "She stayed at the Oceana in St. Kilda. Ever so pretty she was and what lovely clothes."

I didn't know whether she was talking about Clare or Miranda. It could have been either of them. They flitted to Melbourne in much the same way as I took a ferry to Kirrabilli.

I tucked my purse under my arm and prepared to leave. I didn't want to stay and discuss the Welches with Lisa. It was enough that I had to attend a dreary, official cocktail party at their house in just a few hours' time. And on such a day, too! If only it were cooler!

I leaned across the table to say good-bye. But the words faded into the air because something about Lisa caught and held my attention. She hadn't spoken and she made no movement. She'd completely forgotten me. She'd receded from me as if a great engulfing wave had spread between us, and yet she was aware, terribly aware, of her own existence. There was a stillness about her as though she was holding her breath, listening. She was vividly, intensely, alive.

"Good-bye, Lisa!" My own voice broke through the barrier, softly.

She lifted her eyes but she didn't look at me. I don't think she heard me. Her head jerked round sharply, as though she'd become acutely conscious that we weren't alone, as though

13

she'd felt the presence of someone alien and in some way . . .
rather terrifying . . . right beside her.

The shallow blue eyes at the next table met hers, held them
for a second, then looked away. I watched the man fish in his
pocket for cigarettes and matches and hold them in his hand,
weighing them. Then he put them on the table in front of him
and appeared to forget about them.

I glanced back at Lisa. She was staring at the open newspaper in her hand, but she wasn't reading it, because the
flimsy pages were shaking like leaves caught in a quick gust
of wind. Only sudden illness or . . . fear . . . could make her
hand tremble like that.

"Lisa! What's the matter?" There was urgency and
alarm in my voice, and I was hardly aware that I'd called her
by a name she wouldn't recognize.

She looked up then.

"You're not sick?"

Her face was deathly pale and her eyes were round and
staring.

"Oh no. It's just the heat, I suppose."

She closed the open jaws of her brown bag with a sharp
click and folded up the newspaper.

"Oh no," she said again in a small thin voice. "I'm all
right."

She got to her feet jerkily and fled to the door, pushing
her way out on to the crowded pavement.

Her exit was so sudden, it took me by surprise. I stood up.
Something small and gold gleamed and winked against the
table-cloth and I paused to pick it up before I ran to the door
in a desperate, futile attempt to call her back. I felt I had to
know what was wrong with her.

But someone reached the door before me and slid out into
the street leaving me on the inside staring hopelessly at the
leisurely shoppers overflowing the footpath. Lisa had disappeared as completely as if the crowd had swallowed her.

I turned back to my table. Lisa wasn't the only person
who'd vanished. The table next to mine was empty, too, yet a
cup of coffee was almost untouched and a packet of cigarettes
and matches lay carelessly by the plate. A two-shilling piece,

gross over-payment for a single cup of coffee, perched precariously on the edge of the table, where the cloth was rumpled as though a hand had clutched at it hurriedly in passing.

The pale-eyed watcher had gone. He'd been in such a hurry that he'd left his cigarettes and rushed out, pushing past me rudely, with no apology.

How queer, I thought, that he should have gone tearing after Lisa like a hurricane. At the back of my mind was a vague uneasiness about the whole incident. It had happened so abruptly, so inexplicably.

I picked up my things and as I stood waiting for Mabel I glanced down at the small gold object still nestling in the palm of my hand. It was a tiny gold cross.

I popped it into my bag and hoped Lisa would ring me soon. Somehow I knew her little cross meant a great deal to her, far more than just a small piece of gold dangling on the end of a broken chain. And because it was important to her I was terribly anxious to return it. Perhaps I could put an ad. in tomorrow's paper. . . .

Mabel drifted over to me, her long red-nailed fingers sweeping up the two-bob bit as she passed with the ease of a bird swooping on a worm.

"He was a gentleman. Anyone could see that. Rather nice, I thought."

Mabel, I decided, had no discrimination. Any male over twenty-one looked good to her.

"She left in a hurry, didn't she?" She nodded towards Lisa's empty seat scornfully. "Didn't pay her bill, neither."

Mabel was never in evidence when wanted, yet she always knew exactly what was going on in the café.

"It just shows, Miss Amery, you can never tell with people. She looked a mild little thing——"

I cut her short because I wasn't interested in her opinion of Lisa. "I told her I'd pay for both of us. How much?"

Her eyebrows rose. "Friend of yours, Miss Amery?" Her tone was disapproving. Mabel was a perfect snob in her own way.

She handed me the bill and I paid her and walked outside into the hot street, pushing Lisa and the blue-eyed stranger out of my mind. They were none of my business, and anyway, I was overdue at the office already.

But I'll always be glad I obeyed the impulse that urged me to speak to Lisa and I'm glad, too, that I was able to perform the small service of paying her forgotten bill. . . . I hope, if she thought about it at all, that my friendship helped and encouraged her, because Lisa's world was hard and cruel and without mercy.

CHAPTER II

IT WAS even hotter than at midday by the time I left the office that afternoon, and the heat seemed a good enough excuse to treat myself to the luxury of a taxi.

I hailed a cab and sank into it thankfully, kicking off my shoes surreptitiously and wriggling my toes. The driver pushed his cap back on his head and scratched his unruly mop of hair. "Where to, miss?"

I gave him the address of the small block of flats that meant home to me, and relaxed against the cushioned seat.

I looked at my watch. Nearly five. In an hour I was due at Coolibah, the lovely old Welch homestead. I cursed myself for having accepted the invitation to 'cocktails, from 6 till 8'. But I knew I would have to be there. John Welch was managing director of one of Sydney's biggest concerns, The Stock and Station Co., and for some unknown reason his parties ranked as important events. No one really enjoyed them but, nevertheless, everyone of note attended, and women angled for invitations weeks ahead. To be seen at a Welch party was the first rung on the ambitious ladder of success. Wives pushed their reluctant husbands into new suits, donned their latest models, and set off with grim determination to mingle with the mighty.

Poor John, tied to a dreary round of entertainment and committee meetings. It wasn't as though he needed to work. It was simply that he couldn't get out of the habit, because it wasn't in his nature to relax and put his feet on the mantel. He'd inherited more than a mere fortune from his father—he'd inherited the same tremendous energy and drive, not for the sake of making money, but simply because work was the purpose and breath of life.

Perhaps if his first wife had lived, the pattern of his existence would have altered. She had been the daughter of a wealthy steel magnate, and John had been her childhood sweetheart. With that same singleness of purpose that coloured his every step, John had waited till Clarissa Bentley reached the final year of her teens, and then he had married her. She was the star that guided and lit his road. No other woman had any place in his life.

Then, when she was little more than a girl, Clarissa had died giving birth to her first baby. John had christened his daughter Clare, had engaged a competent nurse, and had flung himself into a maelstrom of work until his wounds healed.

When I was young, I'd been a little scared of John whenever he came to the house to visit my father. He'd always been kind and his birthday and Christmas presents were generous and often wildly extravagant. But to me myself he seemed a figure who lived in a world far removed from my childish vision.

Perhaps my father sensed this, and because he was fond of John and wanted me, as I grew up, to see what lay beneath that impersonal exterior, had told me the history of John's life. Since then my fear had given way to respect and affection.

Clare and I had been bosom pals at school, but later we'd drifted apart. It was inevitable. I had my living to earn and Clare's set was too wild and spendthrift for my limited means, and after a while she'd ceased asking me to her parties or to her riotous week-ends at the beach. Her circle of friends grew even wider when she came into her mother's money, and juicy tit-bits reached me from time to time of the sort of gaiety that would have made her mother's hair curl.

If John worried about her, he gave no outward sign of it. He and Clare had no common meeting ground. He'd devoted too much of his time to his job and too little to his own daughter, and by now it was too late to pick up the threads. It seemed as if he and Clare were destined to go different ways, bound together only by their mutual affection.

And then two things happened which left Sydney gasping. John, after twenty-five years of widowhood, married a girl who looked almost young enough to be his daughter, a serene, lovely girl called Miranda Grey, who fluttered her long eyelashes at him and proceeded to twist him round her slim little finger. And Clare startled her friends by falling in love with a suitable young man.

Coolibah had settled into a new routine, with Miranda fitting like a glove into the role of wife and hostess, and Clare, a strangely subdued Clare, contemplating respectable matrimony with Tony Cambray. Everyone was happy. . . .

I'd been so busy thinking about the Welch family that I'd ceased to notice the streets flying by. My driver turned his head. "Cottrill Street you said?"

I told him "Yes," and he turned off the main road and began climbing the steep hill that led to my flat.

I'd be glad, I told myself, when today was over. It had been a dreary day, and the short interlude with Lisa kept popping in and out of my mind, like a jack-in-a-box. She'd looked so white, so bewildered, when she rushed off, almost as if she'd had a sudden shock. Yet a few minutes earlier we'd been chatting quite calmly about her home and her job. If only I'd asked her where she was staying in Sydney I could have got in touch with her and found out whether anything was wrong. But there was nothing I could do now save wait and hope she'd ring me.

As for the man in the café . . . I shrugged. Just another wolf on the prowl, probably. Anyway, Lisa wasn't a child. She was old enough to take care of herself.

The car drew up outside the white gate, so I slipped my feet back into my shoes and scrambled out.

Home at last. I could see the curtains of the downstairs flat—Dawn and Blue Bailey's flat—hanging limply beside the open french windows. I was paying the driver when a voice hailed me, and I swung round to see Blue himself, enormous and amiable, leaning idly against the doorway, saying in lusty tones, "Hi, Gilly. Why don't you come on in and have a beer?"

He sauntered across the tiny strip of lawn and propped himself against the white fence. He was clad in a brief pair of swimming trunks and his skin was stained a deep, dark brown.

"Looks as though the Test's in the bag, doesn't it?" he said, opening the gate for me and ambling beside me up the steps and into the red-tiled lobby. "Stinker of a day. How about a swim?"

I groaned because it sounded so tempting. "I'm more or less on duty tonight. I've got to be at Coolibah at six. Thank heavens, it's only across the road. . . . Where's the brat?"

"Joey?" His face spread into a wide grin. "Mr. Welch offered him ten bob to cut the lawns ready for the party, so Joey nicked off early from school. You'll find him heaving the mower over there. He's saving up for a bike."

I grinned back at him. "Joey's nothing if not enterprising."

"Like his Dad," Blue said modestly.

Dawn poked her head round their front door and Blue put out his hand and ruffled her hair.

"Hullo, Gilly." She looked at me with her nice, steady grey eyes. "Why don't you come in and have a drink? And then come to the beach. We're bringing the gang back with us later."

Blue stretched lazily, like a great brown bear. "We've just been through that routine, hon. Gilly's off to the Welch party. Poor old Gilly."

Their faces were so full of sympathy I couldn't help laughing. Dawn and Blue were two people who hated formal gatherings in any shape or form. They were straightforward and honest and knew exactly where they were going—usually in a bee line for the nearest beach. They revelled in heat waves, the way people do who spend most of their lives in the water.

I put my finger on the lift bell.

"You'd better drop in tonight," Blue said. "After the Welch show it'll be a nice change for you to see how the other half lives. I wish old Barney were here."

He didn't wish it half as much as I did. I stepped into the ancient rickety lift.

"I'll put one on the ice for you," Blue called after me. "Come down and crack it when you get home."

"I might at that. Have fun!" A silly thing to say. My neighbours Blue and Dawn Bailey always had fun. They lived with terrific zest and energy. It was hard to believe they were old enough to be the parents of a boy of Joey's age. I loved all three of them, and even forgave Joey for the time when he planted a revolting, squat green frog right in the centre of my lounge floor.

20

The lift creaked wearily up past the Simpsons' empty flat and I thought how lucky they were to have flown to Brisbane, away from this dreadful, clammy heat. A sudden jerk made me realize I'd reached the second landing, and I slid the door open and stepped out.

It was good to get inside my own little flat and see my bits and pieces scattered all around me. I sank into a chair and looked out on to red roof-tops. Beyond them a clear stretch of blue water was peaceful and calm, and the sounds that floated up from below were the only reminder that the rush and bustle of life continued.

My lounge was attractive with its gay chintz covers, the little desk beneath the green-curtained windows and the cream coffee table strewn with magazines and books. I wish I could spend the evening quietly at home—and perhaps a quick drink with Blue and Dawn when I grew tired of my own company.

It was odd how singularly reluctant I was to attend the Welch party that night.

I lit a cigarette, with one eye on the clock on the mantel. It would take me half an hour to dress. There was time for ten minutes' relaxation. I toyed with the idea of ringing Miranda and telling her I had a headache, or a sudden cold, but I knew I daren't offer any such paltry excuse. Miranda expected me. Tomorrow she would read my column with satisfaction and later she'd say to John in her rich soft voice, "Gilly is really quite charming. We must see more of her."

I shut my eyes and pictured exactly what the party would be like—Clare, a little bored and longing for the moment when she and Tony could sneak off to more exciting places; Tony, well bred and polite, discussing the latest Test scores and speculating on Australia's chances; John, turning swiftly from the weather to the economic position as the occasion demanded; and Miranda, with her smooth hair gleaming like silk, moving in shining glory among her guests.

And when it was over, John would mop his bald head, thankfully, and retire to his study to wrestle with a pile of files.

I walked into the bedroom to consider what gown I would

wear. I knew all along it would have to be the grey, but it was nice to pretend I had a large extensive wardrobe like Miranda's or Clare's.

By the time I'd showered and dressed I was in a better mood. I studied myself in the mirror and decided the grey was well worth the month's pay it had cost me. It matched the colour of my eyes, and brought out the flashes of gold in my brown hair. And if my figure was just a shade too thin and my mouth a shade too large, I couldn't blame the gown for my defects.

One last look at myself and then I went into the lounge and began transferring lipstick, comb and compact from my big leather bag to my soft suède cocktail purse.

Suddenly I touched something small and cold and I hauled it out. It was Lisa's little cross. I held it in my hand for a second, then put it on the mantel where it would catch my eye should Lisa ring me.

It was just on six when I walked out of the flat and slammed the door behind me. There were sounds of activity from the Baileys as I passed, and I wondered from what secret source they drew their tremendous energy. How could Dawn bear to beat up a batch of scones on a day like today? And what could Blue find to sing about, in a queer cracked voice, when the temperature soared towards the century?

As I strolled down the path Dawn stepped through the french windows. "Gilly, you look lovely, darling. For heaven's sake send Joey home, will you? He should have been here hours ago. Tell him we're waiting to go swimming. That'll fetch him."

I smiled at her and crossed the road.

It took me barely a minute to reach the long driveway winding up to the gracious old Welch homestead. I could see signs of Joey's work in the neatly cut lawns, but here and there the smooth green surface was marred by brown patches—the result of prolonged heat—and by large tenacious docks. Once the garden had been a show place with carefully tended grass and brilliant flowers lining the drive; but the gardener had joined the A.I.F. and had never returned. John had been unable to find a man to replace him.

The big house looked solid and comfortable in the softening light. It was built on a high slope overlooking the harbour.
A wide verandah stretched like a connecting balcony between
the rooms facing the drive, and tonight the french windows
were thrown wide in the hope of catching some passing
breeze. On the other side, hidden from the driveway, the
land dipped sharply down to the water, and two flights of
stone steps led from the little sitting-room and the sun-deck to
a paved terrace below.

As I drew nearer the verandah I heard a radio blaring
from the lounge, and I could see Tony sprawled in a chair,
with a cigarette in one hand. In the big long drawing-room
a man and a woman were talking.

I waved—but the only response I got was from a small
figure lying full length beneath a gum tree, with his ear cocked
to the radio. It was Joey. He bounded up and came hurtling
over.

"Heard the latest? Poms're all out for 196. Vic Richard-
son's been giving the scores and summary."

And somewhere in Melbourne, Barney was eagerly
following the Test, I thought wistfully.

I grinned at Joey's rather dirty face. "I thought you were
supposed to be cutting the lawn."

"Aw gee, can't work all night, can I?" he said indignantly,
as if I were sabotaging the Gardeners' Union. Then he reverted
to the more important question of the Ashes. "I reckon," he
said pompously, "this Test's gonna be a walk-over. Lindwall
took 4 for 32; isn't he a beaut? And Miller collared two and
Bill Johnston got a couple. You should've heard about the
catch Neil Harvey took. It was a corker—threw himself full
length on the ground. Poor old Poms!" he added, with a
sympathetic sneer.

"Don't you worry about the Poms, they'll lick the Aussies
hollow. We'll never make 196 tomorrow!" I loved teasing him.

"Break it down! Anyway, women don't know." He was
full of scorn. "You wait till Miller gets in, he'll knock the tripe
out of the bowling."

"Your father's going to knock the tripe out of you if you
don't go home this minute."

He grinned at me, suddenly and engagingly. He was a miniature of Blue in that split second.

"Gertcha! Dad never does his block."

"He's doing it right now. You'll see. He's waiting to take you for a swim."

"He is? Why didn't you say? That's different. Ta-ta, Gilly."

He hitched up his short khaki pants with a quick characteristic gesture and made off down the drive—an untidy, shambling little figure with tousled fair hair and skin the colour of old mahogany.

Dawn certainly knew her own child, I reflected. The word 'swim' was like a magic charm. I watched him for a second, then turned towards the house again.

I knew I was early, because there were no cars in the drive, except Tony's big dark Bentley. It was the sort of car he would own—sleek and luxurious without being flashy. I hoped I wouldn't be the first arrival, but it was too late to turn back, and in any case Miranda would like me to note the flower arrangement and the colour scheme of the big drawing-room before it overflowed with guests.

I lingered for a minute in the garden, admiring the blaze of red and gold zinnias and the neat privet hedge that separated Coolibah from Finch Martyn's house next door.

Beside Coolibah it looked very small—an elegant cottage with gaily striped verandah blinds and a yellow door. Finch would be at the party of course. As an interior decorator he found the Welches' friends an invaluable source of income. I couldn't help wondering whether it had been sheer chance or sheer good judgment that had prompted him to move into Cottrill Street. It had certainly paid dividends. He'd been quick to see the opportunities it offered him—and with effortless ease and charm he'd cemented a nodding acquaintance with the Welches into a firm and solid friendship. He'd become an indispensable asset to their lives, an extra and distinctly eligible man who could be relied on to even up the numbers for dinner, to keep the conversation rolling, to spread his attentions equally among old and young alike—providing they were female sex and prospective clients. I had to hand it to Finch! He was likable but shrewd, attractive but business-like. The faint smear of scandal from his divorce had merely added glamour to his handsome profile, and even if men viewed him with suspicion, their wives found him enchanting.

I walked slowly up the big stone steps to the open front door, and put my finger on the bell. There was no answer except from a host of insects that rose like a cloud from the fly-wire frame in front of my nose, as if they resented this rude interruption of their afternoon siesta.

The house was strangely still. Even the radio was silent now. I stood at the door, waiting. The corridor stretching ahead of me was dark and shadowy against the glare of the light outside, but as my eyes grew accustomed to its duller shades I could see the wall table adorned with a bowl of roses and two delicate chairs standing on the soft blue carpet.

The whole place was quiet—much too quiet for a house that awaited guests on a hot summer's evening—and for a second a vague, unreasoning fear crept over me. There was an ominous quality about the silence all round me, as if the big house were watching and waiting—for what?

Even Joey had disappeared through the big iron gates at the entrance to the drive. There wasn't a breath of wind. Nothing stirred. Nothing moved.

I could feel my dress beginning to stick clammily to my back. Tonight, I thought drearily, there would be no relief from the sweltering heat that had suffocated Sydney for the past few days. The rain, if it came, would be heavy and sultry and tomorrow would be as hot as ever.

I turned back to the door listening for quick footsteps up the hall, for those small sounds that turn a house into a home. But Coolibah might have been empty and neglected. It might have housed only the dead.

I shuddered a little at my own flights of fancy and then smiled, putting my finger on the bell again.

This time there was an answer to my ring. An impeccably tailored butler came down the hall to open the door and take my invitation card. Obviously the arrangements for the party were in the hands of the expensive, capable Gerard, because only Gerard, at an exorbitant price, could supply a band of young men who looked like film stars on vacation.

I followed the elegant back of my escort down the corridor. On my right was the lounge, with a wisp of smoke still rising from Tony's cigarette butt in the ash-tray.

To the left, the door of the little sitting-room was open and I could see, at its far end, the big french windows leading to the terraced garden below, and on the horizon, leaden water merging with leaden sky. Then I stopped. Something on the table just inside the door caught my eye. It was a purse—a shabby brown purse with a gilt clasp. It was far too old and worn to belong to Clare or Miranda, yet there was a familiarity about its bulging sides and leather strap.

I paused. A haunting, elusive memory touched me and fled.

The elegant young man had stopped too, bored, patient and disapproving. His eye reminded me that the best guests do not pry into their host's private rooms. I walked on slowly, trying to resurrect and rationalize the will-o'-the-wisp link between memory and a brown handbag.

Then I heard Miranda's voice and the frail link fell apart. She came gliding towards me with her peculiarly graceful walk, dismissing the butler as she passed him with an eloquent gesture of her hand.

"Gilly! I wondered who it could be. But how nice of you, darling, to come early." She held out smooth red-tipped fingers and let them rest in mine for a second. "When I heard the bell, I wondered if it was Finch. He promised to drop in before the party began because I want to consult him about Coolibah. John and I feel it's time the poor old house had a few renovations. Finch is quite marvellous, isn't he? He's done wonders to that drab little cottage of his."

I was listening to the voice rather than the words. It was a warm, husky voice with an attractive way of picking out the main points in a sentence for special emphasis. It seemed to linger lovingly over its own speech, listening with satisfaction to its own lilting tones.

Tonight Miranda was wearing black—a deceptively simple model that must have cost a small fortune—and her pale yellow hair was brushed back severely into a big bun high on the nape of her long white neck. Her lovely wide-set eyes reflected the green of the emeralds in her small pointed ears. She looked cool, chic and charming.

"I'm so glad you're here, darling. I want you to meet Simon."

"Simon?" I searched in my mind, but the name meant nothing to me.

"Simon Ashton. He only arrived this afternoon. We've persuaded him to stay with us for a few weeks. His father is one of John's dearest friends. They met in London, during the War."

Her voice flowed on as she led me to the drawing-room.

"Clare and Tony only rushed in an hour ago. Poor dears, they've been looking at houses all afternoon, because they think Tony's flat will be too small. The wedding is so soon now —so much to be done."

She paused in the doorway, like an actress waiting for her cue to enter. John was pumping a stranger's hand up and down enthusiastically, saying, "So you're old Mark's son. Well, it's good to see you. Sorry I wasn't available when you arrived, but I haven't had a spare minute till now. We'll be seeing a lot of you, I hope."

Tony was standing a little apart. He looked up quickly, gave me a cheery grin, and raised his hand in a lazy greeting. I smiled back at him.

Then John saw me and strode over to take my hand in his. He was a little older, a little more tired than when I'd last seen him, and there were beads of perspiration on his bald pink head and on his upper lip. But his vitality was undimmed.

"Gilly dear, how are you? How's the working girl?"

I told him the working girl was fine, thanks, and he said with a twinkle, "Still slaving in that office of yours?" His tone implied that writing social notes was an amusing hobby that kept me out of mischief.

"Remember the time when you and Clare used to race round the house like a couple of wild young monkeys, always getting into scrapes?" His eyes flickered to Miranda, drawn irresistibly to her shining hair and soft white skin. "Where is Clare, by the way?"

Miranda raised her shoulders. "She flew to her room to change. She'll be here in a moment, I imagine. Gilly, you know Tony, of course? But I don't think you've met Simon Ashton." Her hand was under my elbow, edging me forward.

I glanced at the stranger in the room and had a swift impression of a dark-haired man who seemed to have taken up an immobile position by the hearth.

As I said "How do you do?" he moved, with a stiff inclination of the head that almost developed into a bow, but stopped short as if too much movement might ruin the cut of his superbly fitting suit.

And then I saw his eyes. They were as pale and shallow as the pools of water left on the sand by a receding wave.

I looked away in sudden, acute embarrassment. I'd seen those eyes before. I'd seen them just a few hours earlier when they'd stared at me while I spoke to Lisa in a small café in Pitt Street.

He was the very last person I'd expected to meet at John Welch's party. I looked at him again quickly and his gaze met mine coolly and dispassionately as if he were seeing me for the first time. If he remembered me he certainly gave no sign. Surely I wasn't mistaken. Surely he was the same man I'd seen in the café.

And then I realized Miranda was watching me, curiously. "You haven't met before, have you?"

He didn't give me time to reply. "I'm afraid I haven't had that honour. But I'm delighted to meet Miss Amery now."

He spoke in a cool, colourless voice that had no shade, no light, no depth—a voice that matched his eyes. A well-bred English voice.

I wanted to ask him if he recalled a small café with check-clothed tables and a platinum-haired waitress. I wanted to ask him why he'd ordered a coffee and hadn't stopped to drink it. And most of all, I wanted to know why he'd rushed after Lisa.

I looked at his blank eyes, hesitated, and my moment was gone, because Clare came flying into the room with quick impulsive steps. "Sorry I'm late, everyone." Her voice was slightly breathless. "I've had one hell of a day. . . ." She stopped short and glanced slowly round the room as if she were taking stock of those present.

John laughed and said to Tony, "Clare's never learnt the meaning of time. I've never known her to be punctual in her life. She'll probably be late for her own wedding."

"Most brides are these days. Isn't that so?" Simon's voice was smooth as satin, and he didn't look at John as he spoke. He looked at Clare. She was standing just inside the door with a queer little smile playing about her mouth, and her eyes as hard as marbles. A new Clare, a Clare I didn't know.

Then her face softened and she made a little dash towards me, holding out both hands. "Gilly, darling, how heavenly to see you! It's so ridiculous to think we live almost opposite, yet we hardly ever get together these days." I couldn't help noticing how cold her hands were, as though her brittle manner were outward only and hid a secret freezing process going on inside.

"Isn't the weather lousy? And what a divine frock, darling. Where did you get it? I never seem able to find anything I like in the shops these days."

She was talking too fast, stringing her sentences together so that they had to be sorted out by the listener. She was like a small gypsy, with dark hair cut in a thick glossy fringe and big luminous brown eyes that had a funny slow way of blinking as if, in twenty-four years, they'd never grown accustomed to the light. And I could have sworn there was a hint of fear in their depths. She glanced away quickly, as though she knew I was watching her, and plopped into a chair.

There was a queer, undefinable tension in the room. Tony seemed to feel it too, and his glance wandered to the bar as if he wished the party would get under way. Then he thought better of it and perched himself on the arm of Clare's chair and gazed down at her small dark head.

She smiled up at him. The fear in her eyes was gone. She seemed to find reassurance and comfort in Tony's face, in his broad shoulders, his light brown hair, his confident, easy manner.

He smiled back at her—a smile which ripped aside the air of pompousness and dignity that aged him beyond his years. There was so much of the small boy in that infectious grin, that I suddenly found it hard to believe he had settled to a medical course after the War—and even harder to believe that he was now a successful young doctor. He'd been so young when he donned uniform, and that grim year as a 'guest' of the Germans had given him an early maturity—until he smiled. It was a charming, youthful smile.

After the string of men who'd gone before him, he was certainly a refreshing change in Clare's life. I thought with a shudder of the dance-band leader with the long side-boards; the Yank with the phoney Southern drawl; and I remembered vaguely a long-haired artist . . .

I stopped reminiscing about Clare's love-affairs because I realized Tony was asking me had I heard the latest scores. I told him Joey had greeted me with the news.

He grinned and said, "Women have no soul where cricket's concerned."

"That's just what Joey said."

We all laughed.

Miranda turned to Simon. "Joey is a small urchin who's bound to succeed in life. One day he'll be a shining example of private enterprise."

John gave one of his bursts of laughter. "Everyone in this street knows Joey. I asked him yesterday would he like to cut the lawns and earn some pocket money, and the little devil said quite solemnly that he'd be prepared to take the job for half basic wage rates. That kid's got a business head. He'll go far."

In fairness to Joey, I said hastily, "He's saving for a bike."

"Bike?" Miranda raised her eyebrows as though a bike were a queer thing for a small boy to want. She was really rather stupid in some ways.

"Good God! Is that what he wants?" John was amused and delighted. "There's an old bike in the garage. I bought it for the gardener, but he'll never use it again, poor chap. We'll have to dig it out for Joey. Tell him he can come and look it over tomorrow and if he can ride it he can have it."

I could have hugged him. What a pity, I thought, he'd never had a son of his own.

Tony and John began a conversation about the chances of England snatching the Ashes from a tight Australian grip, but I gathered that the English players could only put their trust in rain, and now, even the rain had deserted them. Simon threw in his lot with the cricket discussion and announced in his clear, cold voice that Hutton was the best bat in the world.

"Now that Bradman's retired," Tony added slyly.

Clare and Miranda and I settled down to purely feminine matters—frocks and hats and wedding preparations.

We were a normal happy group of people chatting idly, waiting for the guests to arrive. And yet, there was an oddly strained atmosphere in the room as though our conversation cloaked secret, hidden emotions. Mine certainly did, and as I listened to a description of Miranda's latest hat I found my thoughts ranging from Simon Ashton to the brown bag I'd seen in the sitting-room.

And I wondered at myself for puzzling my brains over an old leather purse that probably belonged to one of the maids. Of course. That must be the answer. Yet I wasn't satisfied.

Miranda's voice pulled me up sharply. "Don't you adore Clare's frock, darling?"

I said quite truthfully that I did. It was a heavenly affair of layer upon layer of flame tulle swirling about her slim legs.

Clare made an impatient, deprecating movement with her hand, as if she were wearing a chain-store dirndl. "Pierre designed it for me. He always makes my clothes. He knows what suits me."

"It's a perfect colour for you," Miranda said in her lovely throaty voice. "Such a warm bright red."

Suddenly the frock looked too bright, too harsh for a hot summer's evening. Miranda's remark was the sweetest piece of cattiness I'd ever heard.

She hadn't meant it like that, I told myself. She was smiling at Clare with friendly, admiring eyes.

Clare shrugged her shoulders and stared back at her, and for a second I could have sworn that a swift, sharp antagonism leaped between them, like a tongue of fire, and then died.

31

Miranda said calmly, "Do tell me, sweetie, how you got on this afternoon. Did you like any of the houses you saw?"

And Clare smoothed the folds of her red skirt with restless fingers and began talking quickly about the big place at Mosman, the downstairs flat in a big block right in the centre of the city, the maisonette.

At the other side of the room I could hear John and Tony talking about cars. They seemed to have exhausted the subject of cricket.

Simon was still standing on the hearth half listening to John and half listening to Clare, as though he couldn't make up his mind which group to join. He seemed alone and apart, like a cat who walks by himself. I moved nearer to him.

It occurred to me it was after she'd seen Simon that Lisa had taken fright. Perhaps she knew him, and disliked him. Perhaps he terrified her in some way. She'd certainly bolted outside like a rabbit with the pack after her. I could almost be frightened of Simon myself, I thought.

But my curiosity was too strong to remain unsatisfied, so I gazed at him, trying to summon up any charm I possessed, and said, "Did I see you today, or not? It's been puzzling me."

I must have expected a cagey reply, because I was surprised when he answered quite frankly and openly, "You were in the café. I remembered you perfectly but I hardly liked to mention it. What happened to your friend? Was she sick? She looked as if she'd seen a ghost."

His smile even extended to his eyes. We were getting along like a house on fire.

"I'd never met her till today," I said chattily. "We began talking and she was busy telling me her life story and then she suddenly dived off and left me. I wondered whether you noticed."

He shook his head. "I had some crazy notion she was going to faint and I went after her. But I couldn't see her. Who was she?"

Obviously he hadn't known her after all. My intriguing mystery blew right up in my face and turned out to be an ordinary case of a girl who felt the heat and a kindhearted man who wanted to help. I was faintly disappointed.

32

"I haven't an idea who she was," I told him, losing interest in the subject and in Simon. "All I know is she's an English girl whose parents were killed in the blitz and whose brother died in the Air Force. I think she's looking for a job over here. She told me she'd been working at the Oceana in Melbourne—it's a pub in St. Kilda—and then she drifted to Sydney."

I broke off because I realized the men had ceased talking about miles per gallon and I was holding the centre of the stage.

Outside the cicadas had started their evening chorus, but here in the room there wasn't a sound. Time had suddenly stopped. Every tiny movement had ceased and even Clare's restless hands were lying limply in her lap. Simon was like a carved stone figure at my side, with only those queer shallow eyes alive in his face—moving slowly from John to Miranda to me.

Suddenly I was afraid, and I didn't know why.

Miranda's heavy white lids came down like shutters on her long green eyes.

"You were saying, darling?"

Her voice made my pause a mere fragment of time, the slight hesitation of a speaker who loses the thread of conversation. And yet it wasn't like that at all. I knew quite well what I'd been talking about. It was that hush, that air of strained expectancy, that had stemmed my words.

They were all watching me, waiting for me to continue.

"Simon and I saw each other in a café today," I said gaily, trying to instil a little party spirit into the room. "But we've only just remembered it."

"Then you've met before," Clare said breathlessly. And again I thought I caught a glimpse of fear in her eyes.

"Not officially," Simon smiled. "But we were both interested in the girl sitting at Gillian's table. One minute she was there and the next she wasn't."

John took out a snow-white hanky and mopped his bald patch. "The vanishing lady? Queer people in the world. We get a lot of odd customers in Sydney, but then, of course, it's a port and the sea always throws up strange dregs."

But Simon wasn't listening to John's clichés. He turned to me.

"What was it she left behind—something she dropped. Anything valuable?"

So he'd seen that, too. There seemed to be very little he missed.

I was conscious of the stillness of the room, of Tony's politely interested face, of John's puzzled eyes. Miranda was examining her long red nails, but I felt she was listening with every muscle in her shapely body. The room was uncannily quiet.

"Nothing of any value at all," I replied to Simon. "Just a small piece of jewellery." I could no more have mentioned the tiny gold cross than I could have flown to the moon. Religion in any shape or form is such a tricky, embarrassing subject to those of us who merely know a church as a spectacular setting for weddings.

Suddenly everyone began talking at once, as though they realized the conversation had become too spasmodic and disjointed. Miranda rose gracefully and switched on the lights, letting her satisfied glance wander from the thick Persian carpet to the big bowls of gladioli and the gleaming glasses ranged along the bar.

"I wonder if Finch is coming?" she said. "He's so naughty to be late."

Tony's mouth curved in a slightly mocking smile. "Oh, he'll come all right." His tone summed up Finch neatly—from a man's point of view.

He struck his hands in his pockets and stared out through the window on to the smooth green lawn which ran like a thick carpet down to the wrought-iron entrance gates.

"I think your guests are about to descend in droves. I can see the Fellowes' Buick and Tim Hunt's A40." His voice was light and cheerful, and the room was so vivid and gay that I wondered why I'd had that ridiculous impression of fear—and threat.

At the time I could only blame the heat. This heat, I thought, glancing through the open french doors to the heavy overcast skyline, does queer things to all of us. It heightens the

34

imagination and spreads an air of depression over the simplest words and deeds. If only a wind would whip the clouds into action—anything rather than this sultry motionless blanket overhead that grew thicker and thicker, hotter and hotter.

Then I heard the sharp crunch of wheels on the driveway, the banging of doors and voices calling to each other with the hearty good-humour party-goers always assume. A woman's laugh rang shrilly through the warm still night.

Gerard's band of discreet young waiters materialized like spirits at a séance, with trays of drinks and huge platters of cold chicken, lobsters, oyster patties, sandwiches, and salads made of lettuce hearts and tiny red tomatoes.

The party had begun.

I think I realized from the moment I set foot in Coolibah that something was wrong that night. I felt it before the party got into swing even stronger than I did later when we walked in a nightmare world of shadow—and terror. It was in the lovely flower-decked lounge that I first knew fear had somehow seeped in amongst us like an unknown, unexpected guest.

CHAPTER III

FOR an hour I circulated madly, filling the pages of my note-book. Women guests always like to know the Press is on hand to witness their finery, and besides, Miranda expected me to feature the party in detail in tomorrow's paper.

The room vibrated to the sound of high-pitched laughter, clinking glasses and booming male voices. After a couple of drinks I was ready to laugh at my earlier sense of uneasiness. Even my unreasonable dislike of Simon seemed to have dispersed like an early morning mist and I began to think he was quite distinguished-looking in his own smooth way. And I'd quite forgotten about the bag I'd seen in the sitting-room.

Women I barely knew paused to speak to me, with a covert glance at the pencil in my hand and a mental reservation to look for their names in my gossip page next day.

The room was getting unbearably hot and stuffy and I edged my way over to the windows and stepped through the french doors on to the verandah. It was good to smell the air after the heavy atmosphere of expensive perfume, cigarette smoke and liquor, and to get a moment's respite from the noise that rose and fell like the laughter of kookaburras.

Evening had descended, softening the harsh colours of day and touching them with magic. Age-old gum trees raised gnarled arms in silent supplication to the dark sky, and the winding driveway swept towards the gate like a black river running across the grass.

It was peaceful and rather lovely. Then I realized I wasn't alone out here. I caught a flash of red and someone moved from the shadow into the light. To my surprise, it was Clare.

"Oh!" She caught her breath when she saw me. "It was so hot in there, I just slipped out for a second."

She might have been hot, but she was trembling as though it were mid-winter. I wanted to ask her if anything was the matter, but she didn't give me a chance. She began babbling about Dawn and Blue—how were they? It was such ages since she'd seen them—and she didn't know why she never popped over to my flat these days.

"Come over any time," I said, trying not to look at her shaking hands.

She nodded her small dark head. "Oh, I will, Gilly. Truly. I'd better go in now or Tony'll be wondering where on earth I am. Have you ever met his people, darling?" She paused as if she'd run out of breath.

"No. They're buried in the country, aren't they?"

"Tony saw them last week-end. One day I suppose I'll have to go up with him—to the station, I mean. I hope they approve of me."

But I knew it wasn't the thought of meeting the Cambrays that had thrown her into a fit of nerves.

"Life can be so messy, can't it, darling? You think everything's under control and then you find it isn't."

"What's out of control?" I urged.

She was more gypsy-like than ever in the dim light, with that heavy mane of dark hair framing her white face. A beam of light caught the exquisite diamond wings of her brooch, the flashing brilliance of the big square-cut engagement ring that looked almost too heavy for her small finger. She stood there blinking at me.

"Out of control?" she repeated. "All sorts of things. Tony and I can't find a house we like, and I'm rushing round madly trying to get a few clothes together, and there's such an awful lot to do I simply don't know where to start."

I knew she was lying. It would take more than choosing a house to upset her. She'd see a place, like it and buy it. Clare was the perfect example of spontaneous living.

"If there's anything I can do, any way I can help——" I suggested hopefully.

She didn't let me finish. "Oh no, Gilly!" She sounded frightened. "Thanks all the same. I guess I'll work things out. There's nothing you, or anyone else, can do."

She touched my arm with her cold fingers and said, "We'd better get back to the bun-fight, I suppose."

But I didn't move.

She slipped past me and walked quickly into the crowded

room. Her red frock mingled with the dark suits and coloured gowns of the guests hovering about the windows, and I could see her hands making tiny fluttering gestures as she stopped to chat to people she knew.

She was her usual, lively self again. Yet I felt uneasy, and I couldn't get her face out of my mind.

I pulled myself together. Clare was right. Her affairs were no business of mine. Why should I be jittery simply because my imagination was running riot? All evening I'd been in a queer mood—dreaming up fears and tensions that didn't exist. I'd even tried to fit poor innocent Simon into the role of a dragon who chased girls from cafés. And now I was trying to make out that Clare was frightened . . . of what? I almost laughed. I'd never seen her frightened in my life.

But I was still watching her when a hand rested lightly on my shoulder and I swung round quickly, nervously, and looked up into Finch Martyn's amused eyes.

"What's on your mind, darling?" He peered at me, like a wicked, dissipated faun. "Too much hooch? You've got a start on me. You came early and I came late."

I smiled at him. "Miranda was hoping you'd come in time to discuss the renovations to Coolibah before the party began."

He spread out his hands. "Dear Miranda gets some odd ideas in her lovely head. She wants Coolibah turned into a sort of modern hotel with chairs on tubular steel legs, and futuristic paintings. I try to tell her old bricks and wide verandahs don't lend themselves to that type of thing, but what can one do with a wench as stubborn as Miranda? Darling, you look charming. You wouldn't like to have dinner with me, I suppose? No, I thought not. Still faithful to Barney. And I thought, perhaps, while the cat was away . . ."

I said quickly, "It's awfully sweet of you to ask me, but I really must hurry home. I've got lots of things to do. And I half promised Dawn and Blue I'd drop in. They've got a keg-party."

His face brightened visibly. "Do you think they'd like an extra guest? Me?"

The Baileys' flat was open house to anyone who liked to join in, but I wasn't telling Finch that. He'd be over like a shot, dragging me with him. So I merely laughed at him and said why didn't he ring Blue and find out.

"Are you sure you don't fancy a small dinner for two— just you and me in a cosy spot with soft lights? Why do my favourite girl friends always turn me down?"

I told him, heartlessly, that he'd recover. I never took Finch at all seriously. His brand of conversation was habitual rather than emotional. He was mercurial, attractive and unstable. I could only marvel at the way he'd managed to clamber into the Welch circle. It was so much easier to imagine him at pub crawls and wild week-ends than at fashionable, formal parties.

"You still haven't told me," he said, thrusting a battered packet of cigarettes under my nose, "what's on that funny little mind of yours."

I smiled at him. Nothing was on my mind—nothing that I could put my finger on.

"It's just the heat, I suppose." Then I frowned. Who else had used that very phrase today?

Lisa! I could picture her clearly standing by the table, grabbing up her bag, snapping it shut, saying, 'It's the heat, I suppose.'

A brown bag made of shabby leather. Something clicked in my brain and I thought of the bag I'd seen in the little sitting-room, and the memory which had eluded me became a vivid, startling recollection. Why hadn't I thought of it before? My mind flooded with light—and with bewilderment, too. I felt certain the bag I'd seen tucked beneath Lisa's arm was now lying on a table at Coolibah. But how? Why? What on earth would she be doing here? She certainly wasn't one of the invited guests.

Had she applied for a job as a maid? But Miranda hadn't advertised for domestic help. To be without servants would be the equivalent of a volcanic upheaval at Coolibah, and Miranda would have been on the 'phone about it to all her friends. Besides, Elsie and Nora wouldn't dream of leaving. They'd been with the Welches for years and were likely to end their days with them. And yet, if I were right, if that bag was Lisa's, it meant she'd been here, in this house.

How odd that Simon should be here—and now, Lisa!

I recalled that pause in the conversation when Simon and I had been talking about her, and about the Oceana Hotel, earlier.

Finch's voice startled me. I'd been lost in my own thoughts. "What's wrong with you tonight? You look almost fey." He was watching me with bright, inquisitive eyes. "I think you need a drink. Come on." His hand urged me forward into the hot, noisy scene. "Leave it to me, darling. I'll whip up something to shoo the blues. You look far too gloomy."

He turned towards the bar, but he didn't get far before female voices pounced on him with little cries of delight.

"Finch! Where've you been all night?"

"Miranda told me you were here."

"I simply had to see you and say hullo before I left."

He threw me an agonized glance over his shoulder and met the voices with a charming, delighted smile. I knew he'd be occupied for quite some time—he was much too popular to be left alone for long, especially now that his divorce had put him back on the market again.

The crowd was gradually thinning as I made my way towards the hall door. I don't know why it had become so urgent for me to see Lisa's bag again, but I knew I had to have two seconds alone with it. I knew I had to satisfy my aching, gnawing curiosity, and it never occurred to me that what I planned was completely unorthodox. I merely wanted to slip down the hall to the sitting-room and make sure I hadn't been dreaming.

But I was baulked by departing guests, laughing, talking, lingering over their good-byes, and telling Miranda and John that it had been a lovely, lovely party and thanking them so much. The gangway was successfully blocked.

I wended my way back to the open french windows. I could slip out on to the lawn, round the back of the house and up the flight of stairs to the sitting-room. I knew every inch of the way by heart.

I slid on to the verandah and began walking quickly across the grass, past the large well-lit kitchen, where a few men leaned idly on the sink, smoking, and waiting for the final guests to depart before starting on the mammoth job of clearing up. Gerard's select little band didn't look quite so impressive straddling the kitchen chairs and perched on the tables. They looked nice and human.

The light from the window threw the lawn and big Moreton Bay fig tree into startling clarity, then faded away. The night loomed ahead like sleek black velvet, but now, as I rounded the back of the building, the sombre cloak of darkness suddenly glittered with a hem of diamonds. I paused for a brief moment, staring out across the water to the fairy lights beyond.

The pause was long enough to make me realize, with a stab of shame, that I was behaving like a ninny. Nevertheless, I didn't turn back. I walked past the big stone steps from the sun-deck on towards the sitting-room.

Then I heard a noise and I stopped, listening. It was the noise of feet padding across the grass, cautiously, furtively. Someone was just behind me.

I wheeled round, and for some reason panic caught at my throat and I would have screamed, but a voice said, "Gilly! Good God! Have you got wanderlust or something?"

It was Finch's voice, very close to me. I let out my breath in a quivering sigh of relief. "You startled me."

He put his hand on my arm. I couldn't see his face, but I would have known the feel of those long skinny fingers anywhere, I thought. There was nothing restful or peaceful about his touch. It had an electric quality as if my arm had come into contact with a live wire.

"I sneaked after you because I wondered where you were going. The minute I take my eyes off you, you run away from me. I went to get you a drink, remember? What are you doing wandering round like a zombie?" There was an urgency behind his casual words.

I laughed, nonchalantly I hoped. "It's so terribly hot, I thought I'd like a walk in the garden."

"Alone? On a dark night? Come off it, darling. What's got into you?"

How could I tell him when I didn't know?

"Why don't we go in and say good night, because the

party's breaking up anyway, and then if you want air, I've got plenty of the stuff on my porch. I've got some comfy chairs there too, and a nice supply of beer on the ice." He sounded hopeful.

"Not tonight." I felt a little foolish in the face of his common sense. "Come on, we can get in this way."

I led him towards the sitting-room steps. Now that I'd almost reached my goal I wasn't going to be thwarted at the last minute. I was going to find out if it was Lisa's bag, even if it killed me.

He followed, hanging on to my hand, telling me dryly that I was a daffy female. I began to laugh, then broke off abruptly because my foot touched something soft lying on the path, and I drew back hurriedly, falling against him.

His arms closed round me with practised ease and his voice said mockingly, "This is awfully nice, darling, but awfully sudden."

And then he stopped fooling because he could feel me trembling.

"What's the matter, Gilly?" he asked sharply.

I couldn't speak. Something was there, at my feet—something black and shapeless like an old sack sprawling against the white steps.

He saw it too, and grabbed my arm, trying to hold me back as I bent and touched the formless mass. My fingers closed round what felt like a sleeve, then, horrifyingly, they touched human flesh.

My scream rent the air like the eerie wail of a banshee.

He clapped his hand over my mouth. "For God's sake, don't! It's probably only a drunk."

He leaped for the steps, skirting the dark bundle, and I stumbled after him, clutching wildly at him, crying, "Who is it? Who is it?"

We reached the sitting-room and I could hear him swearing as he tried to find the light-switch, then the darkness was torn aside by dazzling, blinding light, and his arm was round me as we peered down the steps to that object lying limp and sack-like on the concrete paving. But it wasn't a sack. It was a horrible, twisted human figure.

I was frozen to the spot in sick terror. I remember Finch's fingers digging into my shoulder and his voice saying, "God Almighty! It's the little brown mouse." Then he was galvanized into action and made a bolt for the hall. "Wait here. I'll get Tony."

I couldn't have moved an inch if I'd tried. I was petrified with horror. I studied the room in front of me, the pictures on the wall, the big chairs—anything rather than having to look outside. On the table I could see Lisa's bag, but I couldn't have taken a step towards it. The burning desire to examine it had gone.

It was only a few seconds before Finch returned with Tony, but to me it seemed a whole life-time before I heard their footsteps in the hall and saw Tony closing the door carefully behind him. He didn't look at me, but rushed down the stairs with Finch at his heels.

I forced myself to look at The Thing lying face downwards on the path. Tony was bending over it, feeling it with the quick, capable fingers of a doctor.

Slowly he moved the head and a small trickle of evil red wandered like a snail across the white concrete. Now I could see the face and my eyes were glued to it and I couldn't tear them away, although I knew in a moment I'd be sick. From her dreadful, ghastly resting-place Lisa stared back at me with unblinking, lifeless eyes.

"She's dead!" Tony's voice was loud and shocked.

The room seemed to sway around me, and then an arm supported me to a chair and Finch was saying, "Take it easy, darling. Don't think about it," and I wanted to cry, but instead I shut my eyes and tried to follow his advice.

But Lisa's face, so sweet and shy in life, so ugly and terrifying in death, filled every crevice of my mind.

CHAPTER IV

VAGUELY I remember John hurrying into the room, and the sound of voices on the 'phone.

And when I looked up the first thing I saw was Lisa's bag lying on the table exactly as I'd seen it—how many hours before? Hours and hours ago, surely, yet the clock on the mantel said 8.30.

"Thank God they've gone." Miranda's voice was low and strained and her face gradually swam into focus before me. "I thought the last guests would never go. I knew something was wrong the moment I saw Tony whispering to John—and then John hurried out, too, but I never dreamed . . ." The words faded away.

Clare was standing rigidly against the door, looking into space. Her red dress was in striking contrast to the pallor of her face, and she didn't move, even when her father came striding into the room. He went straight over to Miranda as though his eyes were blind to everything save her lovely, fair head.

She lifted her face and said softly, "Oh, John! What a shocking accident! She must have fallen down those steps. But what was she doing here? Who was she?"

John patted her hand. "We'll soon find out. The police are here now. Luckily they've sent McLean—quite a good man. It's devilish bad luck it should have happened here, right at this time, with the house full of people, but I'm sure McLean'll see reason. We'll have the whole matter hushed up. Don't worry, dear."

He spoke with the assurance of a man who is used to giving orders—even to the police. His vitality and confidence filled the room, making it seem too small for his personality.

He pulled out a hanky and dabbed at the perspiration on his bald pink head. "It's a most unpleasant business. Most unpleasant."

I thought he was putting it far too mildly and I felt a

prickle of anger. Lisa was down there—dead—and nothing could bring her to life again. John didn't seem to realize a girl had died here, in his own house. Didn't he care? What did the inconvenience and scandal matter compared with the fact that her life had been snuffed out, like a candle, almost before it had burst into flame? She'd been so young to die.

John noticed me for the first time. "Gilly dear, I think you'd better go into the lounge with Miranda. No sense in you girls staying here so close to the scene. Besides, the police will be invading this room. I've told McLean he'll find you in the lounge if he wants you. It may not be necessary."

He walked out with barely a glance at Clare, who stood like a flame-red pillar against the white walls.

Miranda said, "John's right. There's nothing we can do. For God's sake, Clare, don't look so tragic. It's simply awful of course, but it's not as though any of us knew the girl. She's a stranger. Dreadful things like this happen every minute, every hour—street accidents, drownings—but life goes on just the same. Come on, sweetie."

She led the way across the hall. I paused to let Clare go ahead of me, but she made no move. Her eyes were fixed on the back of Miranda's pale yellow hair and they were filled with such sheer, undisguised anguish that I felt my stomach turn over. I touched her gently.

Odd, I thought, that I'd never realized how fond she was of her father, or how much she resented Miranda's presence. I'd always known, secretly, that she didn't like Miranda. But I'd never known, till now, the depths, or the reason for that dislike. It had never occurred to me before that John simply didn't notice Clare when Miranda was around.

She came to life when I touched her.

"Miranda is being perfectly sensible about the whole affair," she said in a small voice, as though she were fighting an inward battle to be quite fair and honest, "but I can't get that girl's face out of my mind. I'll never forget it. I wish I hadn't seen it."

I followed her into the hall and across to the lounge. I felt exactly the same as she did. But Lisa's face had been with me from the moment I'd met her in the café. Every step I'd taken since then seemed to have brought her clearly before me . . . the little gold cross reposing on my mantel . . . meeting Simon Ashton again . . . seeing that brown bag. . . .

Clare threw herself into a chair and huddled against its broad back with her flame skirts spreading around her. "What I don't understand is what she was doing here."

I'd been asking myself the same question. Miranda shrugged her shoulders, impatiently. "At a guess, she might have realized there was a party and the front door would be open. She probably slipped into the sitting-room unnoticed, and then, before she could find anything worth stealing, someone disturbed her and she ran out of the door into the garden, as she thought. She wouldn't know there was a drop there, and she fell before she could save herself."

A logical, perfect explanation. But it had one flaw. Lisa would never steal. I knew that as well as I knew my own hand.

"No!" I was surprised at the firmness of my own voice. "Lisa wasn't a thief."

Miranda stiffened almost imperceptibly. Her eyes were very green, very alert. "Lisa?" she said slowly. "And how did you know her name, darling?"

Her gaze never left my face for a second. I stared back at her, noting, unconsciously, how exquisite she looked with the light turning her hair to gold, and the black of her gown revealing the soft whiteness of her skin.

"I don't know her name. I met her today in the café and I called her Lisa—to myself. I've no idea who she is. Simon and I were talking about her in the drawing-room earlier."

And while we were talking about her the conversation had suddenly dried up in other parts of the room. I remembered that awkward, embarrassing pause, that sudden feeling of tension.

"Simon?" Clare sat up very straight. "He knew her too, then?"

"He only saw her," I said stiffly. For some reason I didn't want to discuss Lisa. "I spoke to her for a few minutes and she told me, strangely enough, that she'd seen you before. You were staying at the Oceana Hotel when she worked there. She was looking at that photo in today's paper."

Neither of them spoke. They were gazing at me as if I'd just dropped in from Mars.

"Me? She'd seen me?" Clare's voice came in a breathless little rush. "Oh no, darling. I've never stayed at the Oceana in my life."

Miranda swivelled her eyes round to Clare. "Are you sure, dear? After all, you have stayed in some queer places. It's quite possible."

Clare screwed up her face in an effort to think, and put her hand to her heavy mane of hair. "No! Never at the Oceana!" She shot Miranda a glance of thinly veiled dislike. "It's nice to know you take such an interest in my past life." Her voice was sweetly malevolent.

Miranda dropped her gaze to the emeralds on her wrist. "But naturally. Everything you do interests me. After all," a faint sweet smile, "I'm your step-mother. We're related. And when one is fond of a person . . ." She let her hand trail gracefully over the arm of the chair.

At that instant they looked about as fond of each other as a couple of alley cats.

"What does it matter?" I cried impatiently. "Anyway, Lisa didn't say who it was she'd seen. I didn't know whether she meant you, Clare, or Miranda."

Miranda gave a small start of surprise, then smiled her lovely, slow smile. "When I stay at hotels, I never choose dingy little pubs. The poor girl must have been confused. She must have imagined she'd seen one of us—probably she'd merely seen photos of us at some time. After all, we're both rather well known." There was a hint of smugness in her tone. "But tell me, darling, how did you come to find her out there?" She waved her hand vaguely towards the garden. Streaks of green lightning flashed from her emeralds.

"Finch was with me. We were trying to cool off—it was so hot."

It was still hot, I thought, glancing at the motionless curtains.

I wasn't going to tell Miranda I'd been prowling round trying to identify an old purse I'd seen in the sitting-room. She wouldn't have understood.

Conversation ceased after that, and Clare became absorbed in pleating her red skirt, scraping her nail down each fold until her forty-guinea model resembled a tattered mosquito net. Once, Miranda shot her an amused, patient glance, and said, "You'll ruin your frock."

Clare lifted her brown eyes and studied Miranda coolly, then resumed her occupation. "It doesn't matter. I'll never wear the damn thing again, anyway."

It was a relief when Tony walked in. There was no trace of the small-boy smile on his face now. He was wearing the professional, rather pompous manner of a doctor about to interview nervy patients. Clare sprang up and threw herself at his chest.

"Have they gone yet? The police, I mean. Have they found out who she was? Tony, isn't it ghastly to think it happened here, right in this house. Gilly and I used to run up and down those stairs hundreds of times when we were kids, and the worst I ever got was a sprained ankle. I simply can't imagine how she could have fallen."

He stroked her shining black hair and pushed her gently back into her chair. "These things happen every now and then, darling. It's no use worrying about it. There's nothing we can do."

His face said quite plainly that even a doctor can't raise the dead.

"Inspector McLean will be here in a minute. I imagine he wants to ask you a few questions."

Miranda stirred in her chair. "But surely John told him we know absolutely nothing about the girl. What on earth does he want to ask us?"

"He's trying to find out when she arrived, whether anyone saw her." He spoke calmly, but I caught a hint of worry behind his voice, as though he were trying to conceal some small fact which puzzled him.

Clare caught the faint undertone, too, and she gazed up at him, frowning. He ignored the questioning look in her eyes and proceeded to hand round cigarettes. His face was a little too bland, a little too expressionless—the face of a doctor who calms a patient before telling her she has cancer.

In the hall outside the door I heard John's voice saying, "In here, Inspector. This business has been a dreadful shock for my wife. I know you'll realize that."

A slow, rather nasal voice replied, "I'll make it as brief as I can," and I found myself imagining the shrug that accompanied the words.

Then I was looking at a tall, loose-limbed man who ambled into the room as if he were joining his pals at the bar. He wasn't my idea of a police inspector. He looked casual, lazy and typically Australian. His eyes were blue and I couldn't help wondering whether they were suffering from a first-class hangover or whether they always wore that tired, faded look.

John performed the introductions. We might have been starting on a party all over again—save that no one smiled but Miranda, who rose to the occasion magnificently and even managed an expression of polite yet sad welcome.

Simon and Finch trailed in, belatedly, like stray sheep reluctantly joining the flock. I was glad when Finch came and sat on the arm of my chair. I felt the need of moral support, and his hand on my shoulder was firm and comforting, as if he knew exactly how I felt. But then Finch had a positive flair for reading the female mind.

Over in a corner a man was settling himself in a chair, pulling out a notebook and pencil. He was evidently lesser fry because no one bothered to introduce him. He was a ghostly figure in our midst and we ignored him as if he were invisible save to those with the psychic eye. I smiled at him to see if he was real, but he seemed embarrassed, so instead I concentrated on Inspector McLean, who was saying in his slangy drawl, "I'd just like to get a few facts straightened out. Did any of you see this girl or speak to her when she dropped in this afternoon?"

There was a stony silence, before John said in a rather irritable voice, "I think I made it quite clear we none of us have the slightest idea who she is, or why she came."

Miranda took up the thread, giving McLean the full impact of her lovely, clear eyes. "If only we could help—but we know nothing about her. One of the waiters must have let her in."

I thought the Inspector lost a little of the tired, faded look as he absorbed her shining hair, and I found myself thinking irrelevantly that there is always something about a blonde.

"I've checked with Gerard," McLean went on, "and none of the staff had ever set eyes on the girl. I'm quite satisfied about that. And Mr. Welch tells me your two maids had the afternoon off. So either she walked in off her own bat or someone in this room is lying."

John glared angrily until Miranda put a restraining hand on his arm. "I'm sure none of us would have any reason to lie to you, Inspector. Obviously the girl was selling something and when she found the door open the temptation was too strong for her. She must have heard someone coming and tried to slip into the garden, and then, of course, the stairs . . ." She gave a small shrug.

"It could be that way, Mrs. Welch. It's a good theory. But it doesn't quite fill the bill."

I saw Tony stare at him and make up his mind to speak. "Inspector," he began, but got no further because McLean silenced him with a hand that requested him to be patient a little longer, and to let matters take their course. Tony sank back with a worried frown.

Then I forgot about everything except the object McLean had produced from nowhere like a conjuror, and which now reposed on the table beside him. It was Lisa's bag. "If she were trying to escape without being seen, surely she wouldn't leave her bag behind," he said, letting his tired gaze flit from face to face. "It's still possible she may have been a thief, of course."

"Oh no! Not the little brown rabbit!" Finch bit off the words as if he regretted them, as if they'd poured out involuntarily.

"You knew her, Mr. Martyn?" The question was polite, almost bored.

Finch drew his hand away from my shoulder and fished in his pocket for cigarettes. "No, I didn't. But I remember seeing her scuttle up the drive and I wondered who she was. I live next door and I happened to look out of my study window and saw her." He sounded selfconscious, a strange state of mind for Finch.

"Surprising the things neighbours notice," McLean said dryly, taking in Finch's handsome, slightly effeminate face. It was a face that had misled even his best friends. It was the sensitive face of an artist. It gave no indication of the toughness that lay beneath it. And yet Finch had been a fighter pilot with an impressive War service to his credit.

"I'm afraid I didn't watch her, so I can't tell you any more. I merely caught a glimpse of her, that's all." Finch carefully lit two cigarettes and pushed one into my hand. "And I really can't see where all this is leading."

Tony sat up straight as if for once he agreed entirely with Finch, and it was time to get down to brass tacks. "How exactly did the girl die, Inspector?"

McLean picked up the bag and put it on his lap. "She was struck on the back of the head and pushed down the steps. She was murdered, of course."

I felt as if I'd received a blow right in the pit of the stomach. I couldn't believe my ears. I sat there, staring at the Inspector, telling myself that it couldn't be true. It was terrible and shocking enough that Lisa should have died. But murder! Horror and fear and pity surged through me at the thought of a poor, lonely girl—murdered—far from home, with no one to mourn her, no one to weep over her. And somewhere, perhaps close at hand, a murderer lurked in the garden, a maniac, waiting to strike again. I thought of the way I'd crept past the kitchen with the dark night closing in on me and I shuddered. It could have been me lying there instead of Lisa.

It was so quiet in the lounge you could have heard a pin drop.

The faces that stared at the Inspector were blank and uncomprehending, with fear rising to the surface as the meaning of his words penetrated the aura of disbelief, of bewilderment.

Tony nodded, almost I thought with relief at having his own judgment confirmed. "I saw the body and the way she was lying. It didn't add up to a fall down the stairs. But it wasn't my place to say anything till you'd seen her and drawn your own conclusions. She could have knocked the back of her head on the window-frame and then toppled down the steps, I suppose." But he didn't sound convinced.

Nor did McLean. "We've found the weapon," he announced in matter-of-fact tones that clinched the whole matter finally and dreadfully. "That large fancy poker in the empty grate. Wiped clean. We'll test it for prints nevertheless."

"Murder!" Clare's hand flew to her throat and her eyes were huge with terror. "It's not true, Tony, is it? It can't be true?"

He held her hand tightly and gazed at her with infinite compassion, but he didn't speak. His glance told her all too plainly there was nothing he could say, nothing he could do.

Her eyes flickered back to the Inspector. She was frightened but she was angry too. "Why are we sitting here talking if there's a maniac in the neighbourhood? Why don't you do something? Why don't you catch him?"

"Steady, Clare! The Inspector knows his job. He knows what he's doing." John's face was impassive and I had the idea he'd known all along that Lisa's death wasn't an accident. Just as Tony had known. "I imagine you're quite certain it was murder, Inspector? You've got grounds for the statement?"

McLean didn't speak for a moment. The pause was nerve-racking. "Oh yes. I don't think there's the slightest doubt. And, Miss Welch, I assure you we're doing everything possible to find out if there's an escaped lunatic in the district."

He didn't sound hopeful of the result of the search.

Clare collapsed in her chair like a doll whose springs have given way. She was so white I thought she might faint. "We always leave our doors open," she said miserably, "and anyone can walk in any time. It's so ghastly to think of a murderer, probably in the garden right now." Her voice rose alarmingly.

"I can assure you there's nothing in the garden now—but a few trees and grass," McLean said imperturbably. "You didn't happen to notice a stranger lurking around earlier, did you, Mr. Martyn? You seem to know a lot that goes on around here."

Finch ignored the sly dig behind the words and took them at face value. "The house has been full of strangers for the past two hours. Most of them were strangers to me, anyway. Didn't someone tell you there was a party here tonight?"

"You're not suggesting, I hope, that one of our guests was a maniac in disguise." John glared at him, and his voice was steely with reproach. "The people in this house were well known in public life and I can give you a list of their names, Inspector. That should satisfy you." His words were becoming staccato with irritation and annoyance. "I think you'll discover some shady character was roaming about while we entertained our guests. Perhaps the girl was seeking shelter in this house, and he followed her. They could both have slipped in unnoticed while the party was in progress."

"Quite," McLean said, "save that the girl was dead before the party began."

There was a stunned, breathless silence. I shut my eyes and thought of that moment when I'd stood alone outside the front door. I'd smelt death then! My sixth sense had suddenly come into operation, but I'd refused to heed its warning. When I opened my eyes the Inspector was looking straight at me.

"You came very early, Miss Amery. You were the first guest to arrive—apart from Mr. Ashton, who's staying here, and Dr. Cambray, who came in before you with Miss Welch. You didn't notice anyone hanging about?"

I shook my head numbly. "Not a soul. Only Joey. He was working in the garden and I know him well, because he's a small boy who lives next to me, and I stopped to speak to him for a moment. He's sharp and he's no fool. If there had been any suspicious-looking character hanging about I'm sure Joey would have seen him and would have told me about it. There wasn't a sign of anyone. I'm sure there wasn't."

The silence seemed to deepen after I'd spoken. Everyone was staring at me. Simon stopped contemplating the knife crease in his Savile Row trousers and gave me the semblance of a smile, just a quick twist of the corners of his mouth; like birds taking flight, Clare's hands began to move, plucking jerkily at her skirt; Miranda lay back in her chair with only her watchful eyes and the rise and fall of her breast to show she was still in the land of the living; even John was looking at me queerly, with a warning frown I couldn't interpret.

"Darling Gilly. Determined to hang one of us," Finch said softly.

I didn't grasp his meaning at first, then it dawned on me. The very ground seemed to fall away beneath me and I felt myself suspended in space, oblivious of the faces around me.

If a tramp hadn't killed Lisa, that meant—one of us. One of the people sitting in this very room. One of my friends. It had never entered my mind. Even now, I couldn't grasp it. It was too monstrous, too absurd. No one had known Lisa. And murderers don't kill without a motive.

Miranda plucked the thought from my mind, and her low sweet voice turned it into a deadly shaft. "It's odd that Gilly was the only one who knew the girl—the only one who'd ever spoken to her."

Nothing more. Just those few damning words.

No one moved by as much as a flicker of an eyelash, yet I felt a strange withdrawal away from me as if I'd developed leprosy. McLean was watching with fascinated interest. He did nothing to relieve the tension. Then it broke.

"You knew this girl?" John was shocked. "Why didn't you mention it?"

"I did. In the drawing-room before the party began." My lips were dry and stiff. "I met her today in a café. Simon happened to be there, too, and he can tell you I'd never seen her before in my life."

I glanced at him hopefully, but he resumed the study of his immaculate trousers and didn't look at me as he said, "It's true I saw her with Gilly in the café, but I'm afraid I was sitting rather far away. I can vouch for the fact that the girl left in a hurry. She was as white as a sheet and I went after her because I was worried about her. But I didn't find her."

"Surely nothing Gilly said could have frightened her?" Miranda suggested, wide-eyed. "I can't imagine anyone being frightened of Gilly. The idea's quite ridiculous."

The idea hadn't existed until she put it into words. At that moment I think I almost hated her. And so did Clare.

There was hatred and contempt written in every line of her small furious face as she leapt to her feet in a gust of temper. "What a bitch you are, Miranda! I know exactly what you're thinking. You're afraid the police will think one of us— yes, of us—is a murderer and you'd sooner it was Gilly than anyone else, wouldn't you, because you don't want the name of Welch fouled in the mud! It would never do for Mrs. John Welch to be mixed up in——"

"Clare!" John's voice was a lash. "How dare you! I think you owe us all an apology for behaving like a child. No one has suggested Gilly or anyone else in this room is capable of murder. I'm afraid I've spoilt you all your life. You've never learnt control. You've always had too much money." He was trying to be calm, but Clare had touched him on the raw, and it looked as if they were heading for a ding-dong row.

She faced him. "It's not your fault I've always had money. You had nothing to do with it. Blame my mother. It's a pity, isn't it, Miranda? So much less for you to play with." Her mouth curved in a contemptuous smile.

"For God's sake, shut up, darling." Tony tugged at her arm.

I'm sure she'd forgotten everyone save Miranda and her father, but Tony's touch brought her sharply back to her surroundings, and her flaring outburst subsided abruptly. She wrenched her arm free and sank back in her seat, looking miserable.

John was white with rage. At that instant we were a nice civilized group of people ready to scratch each other's eyes out.

I thought Simon must have been embarrassed, because he rose and wandered to the window. But then I caught a quick glimpse of his face, and to my amazement I saw that he was grinning like a Cheshire cat. I couldn't help thinking it was a strange time for mirth. When he turned and resumed his seat, however, his face was perfectly composed again.

I realized Miranda's soft, penitent voice was saying, "Gilly, I didn't mean to suggest for a moment that you had anything to do with . . . murder. I'm so terribly sorry if you misunderstood me."

I murmured, "Of course not."

And then she spoilt it by adding, "We all know what a filthy temper poor Clare has."

She gave a martyred sigh and let her eyes wander back to McLean.

He seemed disappointed that the enthralling little scene had finished so tamely. Perhaps he'd been hoping for another murder, right here in front of him.

"Suppose you tell me what you know of this girl, Miss Amery," he said calmly, and the attention of the room riveted on me again and I found myself absurdly nervous.

"But I've told you all I know. I've no idea why she came here tonight. I called her Lisa because the name seemed to suit her. She'd been working at the Oceana Hotel before she arrived in Sydney. She talked about her parents and about Jock—her brother I think—and I gathered they'd all been killed in the War and Lisa decided to emigrate to Australia. She rushed out of the café and that's the last I saw of her."

Until tonight. Until my foot had touched something soft at the bottom of the stone steps, and a stream of blood had trickled slowly across the white concrete.

"You're quite sure you didn't see her when you came to Coolibah?"

I shook my head. How could I have seen her?

"She was dead." Was it my own voice speaking? I wondered. It sounded hoarse and croaky.

"Dead?" McLean repeated. "And just how did you know that?"

"I saw her bag on the table, but there was no sign of Lisa. The sitting-room was empty. I stopped to look."

"But, darling, she may have been somewhere else in the house," Miranda said sweetly, with the same tone she might have used to discuss a misplaced brooch.

I shrugged because there seemed no answer. But I knew, deep inside me, that Lisa wasn't wandering round the house when I arrived. She was already lying at the foot of those wide stone steps.

"Odd she should turn up here so soon after you'd met her today." McLean leaned forward and his eyes were unwavering. "Miss Amery, whom did she want to see in this house?"

I stared back at him.

"I don't know," I said quickly.

"Who was she trying to blackmail? You?"

I caught my breath in utter astonishment. "No, of course not."

How could I make him understand what Lisa had been like? Certainly not like a blackmailer.

He opened the brown bag and drew out two folded pieces of paper, which he spread on the table beside him. One was the slip on which I'd written my name and 'phone number. "Is this your writing?"

I nodded dumbly.

"Are you in the habit of giving your name and number to strangers you meet in cafés?"

My lips were dry and I wanted to keep licking them. "No, of course not. But somehow, she seemed young and sort of defenceless, and I thought I might be able to help her." As I said it I thought how lame and weak it sounded. And yet, it was the truth.

"She wasn't as young as all that," McLean told me, brightly. "She was well over twenty-five."

I was surprised. I would never have guessed it.

"Perhaps you can explain this, too," he continued, holding up a cutting from a newspaper.

I didn't have to look at it twice because I recognized it immediately. I'd written it myself. It was the feature article on the Welch family—the article Lisa had been reading.

"Did you give her this, too? You're a helpful person, aren't you? I hope I run into you if ever I'm out of a job. . . . You wrote it, of course." He spoke mildly, but the eyes which I'd labelled 'faded' were glinting dangerously. "Why was she interested enough in this," and he tapped the paper with a thin forefinger, "to cart it round in her bag?"

I couldn't find an answer. "I don't know," I said desperately, "she was reading it and she thought Miranda—or Clare—was very pretty."

They were all watching me as though I were a new rare specimen at the Zoo. I could feel the iron bars of the cage closing round me, shutting me off from friendship and reality. I'd stepped into a world where I was alone. Then Finch put his hand on my shoulder again. I've never been more grateful in my life than I was for the hard, reassuring pressure of those fingers.

McLean's voice cut the silence. "Women don't usually use photos of their own sex for pin-ups." But he dropped the subject and I breathed a sigh of relief when he turned his attention to John, and I heard John answering his questions in a clear, unhurried voice that brought a little sanity back to the room.

But at the end of it all we were none the wiser, and I doubt if McLean was, either. No one had seen Lisa, no one had entered the sitting-room.

"If she arrived about five-thirty—as Finch says—I know where I was at that time," Miranda said helpfully. "I was in my room dressing. And John was probably in the study. Where the others were I'm afraid I can't say." She glanced quickly at Clare. "You took ages to change, darling. Whatever were you doing? We were waiting hours for you!"

Clare gave her a look that should have turned her to stone, and lifted a trembling hand to her head. I couldn't guess whether she was shaking with temper—or with swift, devouring fear.

"I couldn't think what to wear." Her voice had a queer catch to it. "I just sat in my room, thinking, and I forgot it was getting late. There didn't seem any reason to hurry. Tony was listening to the cricket and Dad was working and it was so hot I didn't feel like getting dressed. I put on a green frock and then I took it off again because it didn't look right. I honestly didn't know I was taking so long. You know how it is, Gilly." Her brown eyes appealed to me and I nodded. "My step-mother," she pronounced the words bitterly, "is trying to tell you, Inspector, that my room overlooks the drive."

"Clare, darling, what a shocking thing to say!" Miranda lifted injured, innocent eyes. "I really don't know what's come over you today. Surely there's no need to be so . . . sensitive. The Inspector's quite capable of working out for himself that most rooms in this house overlook the drive. Not just yours. Any one of us could have seen the girl, I suppose, if we'd happened to look out. But we didn't."

McLean turned to Simon. "And you, Mr. Ashton?"

Simon knew what he meant, because he answered without a moment's hesitation, "I was in the sun-porch for a while writing a letter, and then I went to my room."

I'm sure McLean was far from satisfied, but he stood up, reluctantly, and a ripple of relief went over us like a soft, soughing wind.

"I guess there's nothing more I can do at present till I find out who she was. There's a lot of routine to be covered. Don't worry, we'll find out everything in time. However, it seems she must have been killed between the time Mr. Martyn saw her on the driveway and the moment Miss Amery passed the sitting-room—though we only have Miss Amery's word that the room was empty." He eyed me dubiously as if gauging whether I would have had time to slip into the sitting-room and kill Lisa before ringing the front bell. "We'll know very soon whether there's been a break from any of the jails or asylums. That angle will have to be investigated." He paused. "There were five people in the house, apart from the caterers, who could have seen the girl when she arrived. Someone showed her into the sitting-room before she had a chance to ring at the door, someone who knew she was walking up the path and wanted to reach her before she could open her mouth. When I've found that person I'll be a lot closer to solving the murder. Five people. Mr. Martyn franky admits he noticed her and his house is only a second from here. Six. And you, Miss Amery, make seven."

The silent ghost in the corner folded his notebook and turned into a solid, stocky man as he stood up. But I didn't hear him speak once, and to this day I often suspect he was a figure in my imagination rather than a creature of flesh and blood.

He followed the Inspector out of the room, leaving us to digest the notion that a murderer sat in our midst, talking, smiling, holding a cigarette in one hand, and giving a perfect imitation of shock and bewilderment at tonight's events— someone whose mask was so well controlled that it gave no sign of evil, secret knowledge. Not the slightest flicker, not a wrong word, betrayed its owner's identity.

And Lisa was dead.

"Thank God that's over. I need a drink. I thought he was going to keep us here all night."

Finch had spoken too soon. McLean poked his head round the door and asked if Mr. Martyn could spare him a minute.

Finch got up slowly, with an exaggerated sigh. "Should I make a farewell speech, I wonder? Oh well, on with the hand-cuffs."

He walked across the hall in the wake of McLean's gangling figure.

Miranda's eyes followed him, then she rose, with one hand clutched to her head. "I feel so dreadful, John, I simply can't stand any more tonight."

She took a step towards him, and with the same grace that characterized her every action, she fell against him in a crumpled heap.

CHAPTER V

"MIRANDA darling. . . ." It was pathetic to hear the strangled terror and anxiety in John's voice. He carried her over to the couch and bent over her. His face was ashen.

"That damned Inspector," he growled. "Miranda's not strong enough to go through an ordeal like this."

Tony was already at her side, pushing John gently out of his way, and feeling for her pulse.

"She's all right. She's only fainted. She'll come round in a minute."

The rise and fall of her breast was perfectly even. John, I thought, looked in worse shape than Miranda. He was hovering over the couch like a bodyguard, and as I seemed to be in the way and there was nothing I could do I wandered aimlessly back to my chair.

Simon had vanished and I wondered whether he'd followed Finch and the Inspector into the sitting-room, but the door was firmly shut to ward off intruders so there was no way of telling what was taking place in there.

Clare was still sitting in the same position with her knees drawn up beneath her and one silver slipper peeping out from the folds of her skirt. She hadn't budged an inch when Miranda fainted. She lifted her big brown eyes and blinked at me solemnly. "Life's bloody, isn't it, darling?"

The choice of word was unfortunate.

I tried to think of a comforting remark, but my mind remained obstinately blank, and the best I could do was to say, "You're as white as a ghost, Clare. Why don't you try and get some rest?"

"I'm as strong as a horse!" she replied flatly. "I never even do anything as dramatic as fainting." She began fidgeting with her skirt again, watching her own fingers as they moved restlessly in her lap. "Gilly, who killed that girl?"

I don't think she expected a reply, but I said, "I don't

know. Try not to think about it." Fine advice that I was incapable of following myself.

She gave a wan smile. "Miranda'll never forgive me for what I said about her tonight. I make the most awful fool of myself, don't I, with my lousy temper." She lowered her voice almost to a whisper and darted a glance at the busy scene around Miranda's limp figure. "I don't give a damn what she thinks, but Tony'll be furious with me. He loathes scenes."

"Nonsense!" I said, in the conviction that men in love don't bother about small details like outbursts of temper. "Everyone lets go sometime. Even Tony, probably."

She gave the vestige of a grin, and in it I caught a flash of the old unpredictable Clare who'd never cared what the world thought of her, and it warmed the cockles of my heart. She was so much more attractive that way than when she was trying to be sedate and respectable.

The smile faded. "God knows what Tony's people are going to say about all this."

"Does it matter?" I asked, a little coldly. No one seemed to be upset about the fact that a girl had died, tragically and needlessly. The only important aspect seemed to be the inconvenience she'd caused by getting herself killed on the wrong doorstep. "You've been jittery all night, Clare," I added more gently. "What's the matter?"

Her hands stopped their weaving motion. "Matter? Murder's enough to make anyone jittery. You don't look exactly calm yourself, darling."

But Clare had been a bundle of nerves long before she knew about Lisa's death. She must have read the question forming in my mind, because she jumped up and fled from the room.

I stood up, too. I'd had enough of Coolibah to last me for a life-time and my one desire was to get back to my own flat. If only I'd accepted Dawn and Blue's invitation to go swimming! I thought of them returning from the beach with a crowd of noisy, cheerful friends, and Dawn trying to hush them saying they'd wake Joey and the neighbours.

"John, I think I'd better go," I said hesitantly. "I do hope Miranda will be all right in the morning."

He swung round. He'd forgotten I was still in the room.

"What a dreadful night it's been for you, Gilly. Be a sensible girl and try and get a good sleep. In the morning you'll find the police have rounded up some known criminal on the loose. Everything'll turn out right."

I hoped his prophecy would come true.

"You can't go home alone," he said anxiously. "Tell Simon to get the car out."

Tony looked up quickly. "If you like to wait, I'll drive you."

I shook my head and assured him with false courage that I'd be quite safe and I only had to cross the road.

But John was tenacious. "I won't have you walking alone. Simon'll be glad to go with you."

At that second Miranda's eyes fluttered and she struggled to sit up. She looked straight past John and Tony at me.

"Gilly darling," she said, in a faint soft voice, "we'll see you again soon, won't we?"

I smiled at her and said I hoped so. It wasn't a true reflection of my feelings. If I had any say in the matter I wouldn't visit Coolibah again for years. I was quite prepared to be the rat deserting the sinking ship. A lovely-looking girl like Miranda, I told myself, had plenty of devoted friends and an adoring husband to support her without my feeble aid.

I walked out into the hall. There was no one about so I made for the front door. It was open and through it I could see the garden, black as pitch, and my courage began to ebb. Perhaps I should have waited for Tony after all. I closed the fly-wire door gently behind me. In two minutes I'd be home.

But something stopped me. It was the low murmur of voices from the far end of the verandah, and as I peered into the darkness a thin beam of light flashed across the red of Clare's skirt. I didn't mean to listen, yet I paused, straining my ears for a familiar word. I could hear Clare's voice, but it

63

was so soft I couldn't make out what she was saying. Now I caught a single breathless phrase.

"You're not going to stay here?"

A man replied, and what he said sent a cold chill through me.

"Why not? I've accepted Miranda's invitation. I've no intention of leaving—unless you're prepared to pay my price. And you know what that is!"

I was rooted to the spot. I knew that voice. There was no mistaking Simon's calm, well-modulated tones. A faint rustle and movement sent me scurrying back into the hall. I didn't want to be caught eavesdropping. I was just in time, because Clare came hurrying through the door and pulled up short when she saw me.

"I must go," I told her, trying to sound as if I'd only emerged that very second from the lounge. "Miranda seems better, and there's nothing I can do."

"Of course, darling," she said absently. "I'll tell Tony to drive you."

Simon stepped from the verandah into the lighted hall and stood behind her. To my amazement he said pleasantly, "I'll walk with Gilly—that is if she doesn't mind walking."

Clare made no objection. She simply blinked at me thoughtfully, then with an effort pulled herself from her own private world back to the hall where we stood facing each other.

"I'll ring you in the morning, Gilly."

Simon put his hand under my arm and propelled me swiftly out on to the verandah before I could say another word. He was the very last person I would have chosen as my companion, but there was nothing I could do about it without being churlish, so I allowed myself to be led away.

When I glanced back at the lighted hall, Clare was standing in the same spot staring after us, and conflicting emotions chased across her face like featherweight clouds across a windy sky. One of those emotions looked uncommonly like fear. Fear and indecision.

I felt I was beginning to have an inkling about the cause of her fear. She was afraid of Simon. And so was I. For all I knew, I told myself, I was stepping out blithely and carelessly with a murderer!

The piece of conversation I'd just heard was still ringing in my head and I tried to sort it out and make sense of it. One thing seemed clear—Clare was desperately anxious for Simon to leave Coolibah. And yet she'd treated him as she would a comparative stranger until they were alone together, unseen, unheard. But somewhere in her varied career her path must have crossed with his. And though he knew his presence was unwelcome, he had no intention of removing himself until Clare made it worth his while. If he'd met her before, he'd know she was rolling in money—and he meant to cash in on it.

But why should Clare be so anxious to be rid of him? Unless—and the more I thought about it, the more likely it seemed—unless Simon knew something Clare was anxious to keep from Tony's ear, a small indiscretion which she preferred to keep buried in the past. She'd never shown any signs of remorse or apology for her behaviour even in its wilder phases, but perhaps now she'd developed a sense of responsibility fitting to her 'engaged' status.

Whatever it was, it had nothing to do with Lisa's death, because Clare had been frightened long before the ghastly moment when Finch and I had stumbled over that inert, limp figure.

I shuddered, and Simon's hand closed tighter round my elbow. I hoped he didn't know what I'd been thinking about.

He must have felt me quaking, because he said, with a touch of amusement in his voice, "Why are you afraid of me?"

I was glad he couldn't see the surprise on my face.

"Don't be silly." I tried to make it casual. "I'm not scared of you—I'm scared of everything and everyone. I'd run a mile if I saw my own shadow."

After I'd spoken I became more conscious than ever of the darkness, with not even a friendly moon to light our way. Tonight our figures cast no shadows.

"You're perfectly safe, you know. The police are within a stone's throw of here. Didn't you notice the driver sitting in the car as we passed? He'd hear you if you yelled."

How could I have noticed when I could hardly see my own hands in front of my face? How could Simon have noticed? It confirmed my suspicion that he had eyes like a cat—eyes that saw everything, even in the dark. There was something cat-like, too, about the way he walked, quietly, with no ringing footsteps.

He was good-looking in his own fashion, but, I told myself in a queer flurry of panic, I didn't like smooth black hair and shallow blue eyes and feet that made no sound on the hard, dry pavement. I didn't like the feel of his hand on my arm, either. His fingers were firm and hard. Strong, perhaps ruthless fingers.

His voice flowed on suavely. "I hope I didn't force myself on you. But I didn't like the idea of you walking by yourself. Clare tells me you live just across the way. Besides, the Welches may want to go into a family conclave, so it seemed a good idea to leave them alone for a while."

I mumbled politely. The only person I wanted at that moment was Barney, and he was miles and miles away in Melbourne. Useless to think of him.

"It was quite a shock seeing you again tonight, because, of course, I had no idea you were a friend of the Welches. My father and John have known each other for years and when I decided to come out here, Dad wrote and told John about my arrival. And then when I finally did turn up today, Miranda was simply wonderful and insisted I stay with them. You know her rather well, don't you?"

No one, I thought, ever really knows Miranda. It's difficult to tell what goes on behind those heavy-lidded eyes.

But I said, "Yes, I suppose I do. Everyone knows her. She's far too lovely to be overlooked. You hadn't met her before?"

"No. But then, I'd never met John either. You see, I was pretty busy during the War and I didn't get back till the show was well and truly over and John had come back here. But I've heard Dad speak of him often. He did a magnificent job in England—he was chief amenities officer to the Aussie troops."

And then, abruptly, he switched the conversation.

66

"Rotten business tonight. Not very nice for you to be mixed up in. If I were you I'd try to keep out of it. Stay away from Coolibah if you're wise."

My heart began beating like a tom-tom, and I found myself looking for the lurking threat behind his words. A hidden warning? Or merely polite conversation?

"Why?" I tried to say calmly.

"Because, my dear Gilly, I've an idea you know too much about this Lisa, as you call her. Knowledge can be dangerous if a murderer catches up with you. McLean's right. Someone in that house killed the girl. It does look as if she were trying her hand at blackmail."

"She wasn't like that at all," I said, angrily; "I'll swear she wouldn't have known how to go about blackmailing anyone." It was the least I could do in her memory, and somehow, I had to make people see her as she really was—rather shy and lonely. "I've told you everything I know about her."

"I hope so," he said. "For your sake, I hope so. You should be quite safe if you've told the truth and the whole truth."

His queer, colourless voice made me feel anything but safe. It summed him up far too clearly—cold, competent and intelligent—and, perhaps, dangerous?

I began babbling about the weather, the heat and the chances of a storm, but eventually I exhausted every possibility of the barometer and ran out of conversation.

His hand tightened on my arm. "For heaven's sake, don't be so nervy."

Just then I saw the blaze of light shining on to the pavement from the lobby of our flats and I could have shouted with joy. I'd never realized before how dark and creepy Cottrill Street was. It had always seemed so friendly in the past.

With home in sight, I grew bolder, like a swimmer who had crossed a treacherous current and suddenly reached safe waters.

"What are you doing over here? In Australia, I mean? Or shouldn't I ask that?" I was prepared to be chatty now that I had one hand on the small white gate.

In the half-light he looked down at me with the hint of a smile curling the corners of his mouth. "I'm a Russian spy. Didn't you guess?"

I pushed open the gate, but he pulled me back.

"I'm sorry. I couldn't resist teasing you. I wish I could tell you I'm attached to the Secret Service on an important mission, but I'm afraid I can't. I'm over here on holiday, studying Australian conditions. And what I've seen of the country so far intrigues me. Especially Australian women."

I didn't know whether that was a compliment or an insult, and I didn't wait to find out. I squeezed through the gate before he could stop me and from the other side of the low, white palings I told him how sweet he was to walk home with me, and that I'd be quite all right now, thank you very much.

He was laughing. "One day, Gilly, you'll settle down and marry and have children and all this horrible business will be behind you—if you watch your step in the meantime."

He strode off into the darkness and I ran up through the big doors into the lobby. It was nice to think of his suggestion that one day I'd settle down, and the prospect assumed rosy proportions although that day seemed far off—with Barney, the Man in My Life, calmly studying a cricket ball while I was in the midst of a terrifying nightmare that had probably turned my hair grey in the last few hours.

The door of Blue and Dawn's flat was open and a lot of uninhibited noise issued forth cheerily. People were spilling in and out of the lobby and one of them saw me and pounced.

"Gillian Amery! Come on in before the keg runs dry." A brown hand clutched me.

But one party for the night had been quite enough, and I pulled myself free, saying, "Honestly, I'm too tired. I know Dawn'll understand. Tell her I'll be down to see her in the morning."

I began slowly mounting the stairs. I passed the darkened landing by the Simpsons' empty flat, where shadows reached

68

out and plucked at me, and I quickened my steps, hastening up the second flight of stairs, and switching on the light that illuminated my own landing.

The voices from downstairs became fainter and fainter, and I was almost tempted to run back. But I plodded on wearily, telling myself that soon I'd clamber between nice white sheets and put the whole dreadful night behind me. I'd forget about everything till morning. Things always seem better by daylight. Tomorrow I'd start thinking, but not tonight.

Usually I turned the landing light off once I was inside my own flat, but now I gave way to my hatred of the dark and decided to leave it on.

I walked into the lounge, shutting the front door firmly behind me. I sat down and looked around me. My small clock ticking away merrily, my little writing desk with the typewriter standing open, the photo of Barney on the low cream table. The sight of familiar things helped to make the night seem normal and serene, almost as if the past few hours had only taken place in my imagination.

I made myself some tea and sat in the biggest chair, riffling through the notes I'd made on John's party. Murder or no murder, my column would have to come out tomorrow just the same as any other day. In one page of the paper there'd be a juicy account of the sensational evening at Coolibah— that was Ned Cawley's department, he covered crime—and on the social page there'd be my description of the party. The one would add colour to the other.

I was trying to think of suitable adjectives to describe Miranda's frock—a black sheath?—when the 'phone rang.

Barney, I thought, and leaped to it like a spring lamb.

But it wasn't long distance. It was Clare Welch.

"I just thought I'd 'phone and make sure you were all right. It must be so miserable for you, darling, all alone over there."

I told her Blue and Dawn were right below and there was no need to worry. "It's not as if I'm alone in the building," I assured her.

"If you're nervous you could come and stay here. There's plenty of room and I don't know why I didn't think of it before. Such a lot seems to have happened tonight I've gone woolly in the brain. But I really should have thought of it."

I said quickly, because the last place I wanted to stay was Coolibah, "Thanks awfully, Clare. But I wouldn't dream of troubling you. You've got enough on your hands. You've already got one guest."

"But Gilly, you're like one of the family. You wouldn't be any trouble, darling. Besides, we've got Elsie and Nora to cope. And the place has been simply swarming with police, and a couple of reporters got wind of things, and poor old Finch had a gruelling time with Inspector McLean." She paused for breath, and I could almost see her screwing up her funny little face and jabbing her cigarette in the air to give emphasis to her words.

"What did McLean want with Finch?" I asked.

"Oh, mainly about how you both came to find—the girl—and everything you'd said to him. And Finch was absolutely livid when he found you'd gone without him, and I told him Simon was with you and you'd be quite safe I was sure, but he said you should have waited for him. I think he's developing a crush on you. He's rather a honey, isn't he? And such fun. I adore him."

Clare would, I thought. She and Finch were alike in some ways—restless, turbulent and gay. Or at least, I'd always thought of Clare as gay until tonight, when she'd been oddly reflective—a side of her character that usually remained hidden.

I laughed outright at the idea of Finch entertaining any amorous notions towards me. I'd known him too long and too well.

Clare said, "What was his wife like? Did you know her?"

"Only what Finch told me, and that isn't much. They couldn't get on and it seemed easier to live apart. Then she fell for someone else, so he gave her a divorce."

"It must be awfully lonely for him," Clare said sympathetically. "I do wish he'd find himself a girl-friend."

70

"But not this girl," I smiled into the 'phone. "Don't let him fool you. That orphan-in-the-storm look doesn't mean a thing. It simply makes the women wild about him."

I heard her sigh sentimentally, and I thought it was rather sweet—and also rather trying—the way engaged girls try to foster matrimony among their friends.

"Anyway, darling, it's nice to know you've got Finch to look after you," she said, reluctant to abandon the idea of blossoming love. "Dad's quite sure McLean's barking up the wrong tree if he thinks the murder was committed by someone we know. He says the whole idea's moonshine."

It was comforting, but not wholly convincing. John might be a Big Noise in the business world, but as far as I knew, this was his first glimpse into the realms of homicide, and I wasn't prepared to take his word as final.

I remembered then that I hadn't asked about Miranda.

"Oh, she recovered." Clare sounded faintly sarcastic. "McLean actually apologized for worrying her, and he didn't ask her any more questions. Apparently even Police Inspectors have notions of chivalry towards beautiful blondes. She offered me the hand of friendship and retired to her room. And then I thought of the way we'd let you go off without even asking if you'd like to spend the night here, and I knew I'd just have to ring you, and here I am. Simon says you're awfully nervy, darling."

"Do you like him?" I asked impulsively, before I could stop myself.

The pause was infinitesimal.

"Oh! Simon, you mean?" She didn't answer my question. "Why do you ask?"

A new note had crept into her voice, and the chatty atmosphere seemed to have evaporated.

"I just wondered," I said weakly. "I got the idea you knew him quite well."

Again there was a breathless, silent second.

"I ran into him a while back, but I didn't realize he was Mark Ashton's son. It was just one of those meetings."

"I thought he'd only arrived recently?"

"Oh no!" For some reason she sounded flurried. "He's been

in Australia for a few months. In Adelaide and Melbourne. I met him at a party in Melbourne and when he landed in today Dad was bucked to find we knew each other. But I hardly know him at all. You know how it is at parties."

She knew him well enough to want him to leave Coolibah. That rather furtive conversation on the verandah hadn't been the idle chit-chat of two people who merely had a nodding acquaintance.

But, I reminded myself, if Clare didn't want to confide her worries, I could never hope to make her change her stubborn little mind. So I thanked her for ringing and she hung up hurriedly as if to ward off any further questions. I would have given my best hat to know what was going on in her mind. I tried to settle to my notes again, and rapped out a lot of stuff almost unthinkingly. I ended the rave by describing Miranda as one of Sydney's smartest matrons. I wondered whether she would like the word 'matron'. It conjured up a woman past her first bloom of youth. And Miranda's bloom would never fade. She was ageless as Cleopatra, as full of charm as the Lorelei. I wondered how old she was. Thirty at the outside?

And while guests laughed and chattered and lifted their glasses to thirsty lips, a figure lay in solitude in the dark garden, with only the cicadas to raise their voices in a mournful dirge for the dead.

I wandered over to the mantel and stared at the gold cross lying where I'd left it. Poor Lisa would never ring me now. I'd never be able to return her symbol of faith and hope, and I had a horrible feeling that in some way I'd let her down.

It seemed a long, long time since I'd spoken to her in the café. I tried to piece together the little I knew about her. I went over our conversation time and time again, but it got me nowhere. It had been the ordinary, everyday chatter between two ordinary, everyday strangers meeting for the first time. Yet something monstrous had penetrated Lisa's mind and had sent her flying out into the street. But what? She'd been reading the paper and then she'd seen Simon. Nothing else.

I was left with an unanswerable puzzle. Either the sight

of Simon or the innocuous words in my article had transformed her from an ordinary girl to a creature fleeing from her own bewildered thoughts. Simon swore he'd never seen her before, but I suspected he might be an evasive, accomplished liar if he set his mind to it.

I took out my copy of the paper and re-read the article that had interested Lisa. It was a dull account of John's importance in the world of affairs, with a few lines on the beauty and charm of Miranda, and a mere mention of Clare and Tony.

Then a short paragraph I'd forgotten struck my eye. Immediately beneath the blurb about the Welches was a tiny note about Finch Martyn's return to Sydney after a brief holiday in Melbourne. I remembered writing that piece—partly because Finch was well known and partly because the publicity was good for his business and I like to help my friends.

I started at it, wondering if it could possibly have any hidden significance. Then I relaxed.

It was odd, of course, that Lisa should have cut out the social notes and carried them round with her, but it didn't mean there was anything sinister in the printed page. I certainly couldn't see anything sinister enough to send her flying off in a panic. Perhaps I only imagined she'd been in a panic. Perhaps she'd merely remembered that she'd forgotten to turn the iron off and had hustled away with visions of a burning house.

John, I persuaded myself, was right. Lisa's death had nothing whatever to do with anyone at Coolibah and tomorrow would bring welcome news of the arrest of some loitering criminal who'd yielded to the crazy urge to kill for killing's sake. There was no other way to explain the death of an unknown girl.

I lit a cigarette, then put it out because it tasted like burnt straw, and switched on the radio. But I found I couldn't bear the noise and turned it off again.

Sleep was what I needed. In the morning everything would slip back to normal and McLean would round up his quarry and I'd stop my wild imaginings. Simon would seem an ordinary, nice man and Finch would dine out on the story of the murder, and Clare would lose her wide-eyed, frightened look, and Tony would grin again in his carefree fashion.

But there was one thing I'd never forget. Lisa's death. I glanced at her little cross with the broken chain. It shone dully, a reminder that just a few hours ago she was walking, and talking and breathing.

I sat still, listening. The lift was climbing slowly upstairs. I could hear its groaning clatter as it reached the first floor, and I frowned, because I knew there was no one in this small block of flats between the Baileys and myself.

Then I sighed. Blue or Dawn or perhaps some of their friends were coming to fetch me, to insist that I go down for a drink before the keg dried up.

The creaking grew louder, and with a rattle I knew well the lift came to a halt on my landing. I heard the door slide open, quietly, and I waited for the sound of voices or for Blue's mighty fist to thump on my door. Nothing happened. Up here, all was quiet as the grave. Only the sudden, erratic beating of my heart broke the stillness of the room.

Then a board creaked—the loose board outside on the landing—and I knew I wasn't alone. Someone was standing just a few yards away from me, with only the white panels of the door between us.

A burst of laughter from downstairs drifted through my open windows like a ghostly echo. A flying ant hurled itself against the light. Then silence again.

My heart leaped to my throat as I stared at the door in fascinated horror. I tiptoed over to it and stood listening in an agony of suspense and dread.

Again the board moved, as though someone were standing out there, pausing, making up his mind about something. But why didn't that person knock or ring my bell?

Fear came crowding in on me, blocking out every other thought.

In a tiny voice, no more than a whisper, I said, "Who's there?" But there was no reply.

Then I heard the faint scratching of fingers against the white panel, a soft flurry of noise like the scampering of mice behind the wainscoting. Rat-tat-tat. The knock was gentle, secretive and frightening. Not Blue's knock. Not Dawn's. With a hand that trembled so much I could hardly find the knob, I drew the door open, cautiously, and peered through the chink.

I don't know who or what I'd expected to find out there, but I know my mouth fell open in sheer astonishment when Miranda's eyes peered back at me.

CHAPTER VI

She stepped past me into the lounge.

"Miranda!" I couldn't keep the bewilderment out of my voice.

The last time I'd seen her she'd been lying wanly on a couch. Now she was gallivanting about the neighbourhood, still in her party frock, with a green chiffon scarf draped over her head. She looked amazingly healthy and quite unbelievably beautiful. I was suddenly suspicious of that fainting fit, earlier, but if it had been a successful ruse to end any further inquisition, I felt I could hardly blame her.

"I was hoping you wouldn't be in bed, darling," she said. "That's why I didn't knock loudly in case you were asleep."

She pulled off the scarf and threw it on a chair.

"It's late to come visiting but I knew I couldn't sleep and the house was so utterly dismal. John's shut himself in his study and Clare won't speak to anyone and Simon——" she lifted her shoulders expressively— "Simon, after all, is a stranger. One can't talk to him about family matters. Once Finch and Tony left I felt I'd suffocate if I stayed indoors a moment longer."

So she'd come rushing over in the dark to see me! I knew I was gullible, but even I couldn't swallow that yarn. Miranda had seldom visited me in the past and never at eleven o'clock at night.

"I'll make some tea," I said, because I could think of nothing better to say.

She shook her head. "Not for me. I need a stiff drink and you look as if you do, too."

I glanced at myself in the mirror and my eyes gazed back at me with a startled stare. It was a face I'd never seen before. Surely not Gillian Amery's face. I walked over to the wall cabinet and poured two drinks and handed one to Miranda.

"Are you sure you should be out?" I asked inanely. "Does John know?"

"Of course not. He'd only worry, poor darling. . . . I felt so rotten earlier. It's been such a ghastly night." She lowered her thick white lids. "If only the weather would break. One feels abnormal in this sort of heat at the best of times."

It wasn't the heat that made me feel abnormal. It was the whole horrible chain of events leading up to this cosy little visit, with Miranda and myself sipping whisky and gossiping about the weather like old cronies with time on our hands.

"It sounds quite a party downstairs." She twirled the liquid in her glass, watching it splash round the rim. "The Baileys live there, don't they? Joey's parents?"

I nodded and wondered when she'd come to the point of her strange desire to see me.

"Clare knows them, I think, but then, Clare has quite a wide circle of friends. John and I are glad she's decided to settle down at last. Tony seems to have the knack of managing her, which is quite a feat." She gazed at me over the top of her glass. "Clare isn't always an easy person to live with. We seem to rub each other up the wrong way, quite unintentionally."

I could believe that. They were both highly individual, both used to commanding attention. But Clare's impulsiveness and Miranda's calm assurance could never live happily side by side. I was sure she hadn't come to discuss personalities and the difficulties of family life, and because I couldn't stand this polite preliminary skirmish a moment longer, I blurted out suddenly, "Why did you want to see me?"

Her eyebrows arched a little. "Simon said you were in quite a state when he saw you home. I was a little worried about you, darling, and I thought perhaps you needed company. I'm afraid we all neglected you tonight. We forgot how awful it must have been for you to stumble over that girl the way you did, specially when you knew her. But you mustn't bottle things up inside and brood over them. It's so much better to talk about them and get them out of your system. Have you any idea, any weeny inkling, why your Lisa came to Coolibah tonight? You can tell me about her quite safely, you know. I'm not the police."

"I don't know anything I haven't told you," I said wearily, wondering why everyone assumed Lisa and I had been bosom pals. "And I can't even guess what she was doing at Coolibah."

She stood up and walked over to the mantel, leaning against it to survey her reflection with a queer smile, as if she liked what she saw.

Suddenly I was afraid of her—afraid of those long shining eyes and that unshakable poise and that low husky voice. I was afraid, too, of the lurking vitality and energy behind the graceful, flowing line of her body.

The 'phone rang and I jumped, quite literally.

Miranda stopped smiling. "Oh, lord! I hope that isn't John, he'll fuss so if he finds I'm gone. Tell him I'm just leaving."

The clanging, jarring noise filled the room.

"Answer it!" she said impatiently.

Who could be ringing at this time of night? Surely nothing else had happened? Normally I rush to answer the 'phone at any hour, but now I paused, with overwhelming premonition. Fear makes you like that.

I lifted the receiver and a voice said, "Darling, where've you been all night? I've been ringing every hour."

And my heart bounded with joy at the sound of Barney's voice and I clung to the 'phone as if it were his hand. I could imagine him lounging in a chair with his long legs stretched out in front of him, gangly, loose-limbed and casual. Dear Barney!

"Aren't you pleased to hear me?" I knew he was grinning, and I grinned back at him.

"Of course. It's wonderful."

"Here, what's the matter? You sound out of this world. You're not sick? Just pining for me, I hope."

He knew every inflection, could interpret every mood in my voice.

"I've only arrived home a short while," I told him, wishing with all my heart that Miranda would go so that I could pour out my woes to his sympathetic ear. But she merely moved to the window and stood looking out on to the dark waters of the harbour. I was terribly conscious of her standing there. "I've been to a party at John and Miranda's."

He gave a mocking groan. "The usual show?"

Usual?

"Not quite," I said, non-committally.

He picked up my tone sharply. "Anything wrong?"

Miranda was facing me now and for a flash I thought she must have heard Barney's side of the conversation until I realized his voice was too faint.

"Not really, I hope." I couldn't talk to him, not with her eyes watching me. "Lots of people you know were there . . . Tony and Clare, of course, and Simon Ashton—but I don't think you know him—and Finch . . ."

His voice rumbled like distant thunder. "Finch? Is he the trouble? You can tell that wolf from me to keep his hands off or I'll knock his bloody teeth in when I get home."

"Don't be silly, darling," I said weakly. "It's nothing like that. Finch has been perfectly sweet. How's the Test going?"

I asked for it, of course, so I couldn't complain when we swung into an animated patter about the prospects of the game, Bill Johnston's left-arm swingers, Neil Harvey's brilliant fielding, and the Miller brand of dynamite with the new ball. Barney warmed to the subject in the fond belief that I was keyed to excitement pitch about it all, and I tried to listen intelligently to a lot of guff that never has, and never will, make sense to me.

"By the way," he said, when he'd finished a brief discourse on the virtues of silly mid-ons and leg traps, "I've got those autographs for young Joey. You might tell him. Give him a smack on the rump for me."

"I will," I told him, "Miranda's here. We're having a drink and then I'm going to bed."

"Miranda?" He was vaguely surprised. "I didn't know you were as matey with her as that."

"Nor did I."

And then the exchange announced in a heartless voice that time was up and did we want an extension and I replied "No" rather quickly, and Barney said, "Have it your own way. But clear the decks tomorrow night when I ring. Just you and me. You can tell me then what's on your mind."

He hung up and reluctantly I pushed the 'phone back on the desk. Even the sound of his voice had done me good.

Miranda was gazing out of the window again.

"Barney is rather a sweetie. I do think you could do much, much worse, darling."

I resented her interest in my matrimonial prospects, so I said nothing.

"I hope I didn't cramp your style."

"Of course not."

"I do think you were wise not to mention . . . tonight. He might get the crazy idea you were in some sort of danger and come rushing home."

The very thought of it gave me a rich, satisfied glow.

"I did wonder, darling, whether you were falling for Finch. It's none of my business, of course, and I hope you'll forgive me, but I wouldn't want to see you hurt. We're devoted to Finch, but he's not the steady type, is he? John's awfully fond of you, Gilly, and he'd be so worried if he thought you and Finch . . ."

"He happens to be an old friend of mine, and that's all there is to it."

Funny how I hated discussing my friends and my private affairs with Miranda.

She perched on the arm of the chair and touched me with her long red-tipped fingers. The eyes that looked into mine were clear and smooth as the sea on a sunny day. Yet I had the feeling that, like the sea, they were full of unknown ripples and movement beneath the surface. She wasn't as calm as she made out.

"Don't worry too much about tonight, Gilly—about what happened. It's all too dreadful, of course, but it'll blow over in a few days. John's quite sure the police will find some poor insane creature wandering around the district. In the meantime we must simply try and keep our names out of it. For John's sake. Publicity of that sort would be so bad for a man in his position."

I couldn't see that it was worse for John than for the rest

of us. He was better fitted to weather the storm than any of us. With his money and prestige he could afford a little adverse publicity, but a poor gossip writer on a daily paper has to mind her p's and q's.

"Then, too, there's Clare," Miranda said slowly.

"You mean . . ." I was thinking of Simon and that hurried conversation I'd overheard on Coolibah's verandah.

I hoped Miranda was about to tell me why Clare was scared of him. Then I realized Clare would never confide her private worries in Miranda. She'd never go running to her step-mother. Miranda didn't inspire confidence—not from her own sex.

"Tony's people are very conservative," she was saying, "and they'd hate to find Clare's name splashed all over the papers in connection with a murder case."

She sighed and stood up. I was glad to have her at a distance. I didn't like the touch of those long cool fingers or the probing of those lovely green eyes.

"There's nothing, absolutely nothing, to connect any of us with that girl. But it was rather queer she should be carrying that cutting from today's paper, wasn't it? Are you sure, darling, you've no idea why?"

"Only what I've told you. She thought she knew you—or Clare. I didn't bother to find out which of you—it was merely a remark in passing."

Again I thought I detected a tiny ripple of emotion, perhaps fear, behind her eyes.

"I'm glad you didn't mention it to the Inspector. God knows what he'd make of it—and he'd start jumping to all sorts of wild conclusions. Clare and I are both quite certain we've never stayed at the Oceana, so I don't see how the girl could have recognized either of us. But convincing the police would be another matter. They'd find out we were telling the truth in the end, but until then they'd drive us mad with questions."

"But I thought I'd told McLean."

"Oh no, darling! And I hope"—she slid me an oblique glance—"and I hope your conscience won't find it necessary to tell him. We're in a bad enough mess already, without putting false notions in McLean's head. It was so unwise of Clare to give a display of temper tonight. I don't always see eye to eye with her, but that doesn't mean I'd want her to stick her neck out. I wouldn't like McLean to get any wrong ideas about her."

Like suspecting her of murder? I wanted to laugh. Clare couldn't kill a fly. I'd seen her burst into tears when a dog was run over.

Miranda was busy arranging her scarf round her head again. The movements of her hands were lovely to watch——strong, slim fingers that knew exactly what they were doing, tucking in the stray edges of chiffon, smoothing the sleek hair above her brow.

"We must stick together till this business clears up," she said, "and I know we can count on you, Gilly. You will be careful, won't you, what you say to the police? For John's sake. And Clare's. We want to keep the name of Welch out of it——"

I stood up. Perhaps I'd misjudged Miranda in the past, because I'd always thought she was wholly concerned with herself. It had never entered my head that she entertained protective instincts towards Clare, whom I suspected she disliked, or towards John, who was quite capable of looking after himself. The idea of her racing over to plead with me to keep Clare and John out of trouble suddenly seemed as phoney as Miranda herself. And I didn't know what it was all about.

Her eyes were watching me. They were long green slits as hard and brilliant as the emeralds on her arm, and I wondered, quite suddenly, why I'd ever thought she was beautiful.

She gave me one of her slow, dazzling smiles calculated to melt the heart of the devil—but it left me cold, and just a little frightened. Her face was still a perfect oval and her skin was still petal-smooth, but in that second I saw her loveliness as a rather too perfect mask which hid the personality beneath it. I didn't know whether I liked or disliked her, because I didn't know her.

"Poor Gilly." She reached for her big, black antelope bag.

"I've kept you up far too long. I only hope John hasn't missed me and I can slip back before he discovers I've gone. There's no need to mention my visit to anyone, is there, darling? We're all so fond of you, Gilly, you know we'll be standing by you if you need our help at any time. You can rely on us to help any way we can."

I walked to the door with her. I seemed to have lost my power of speech.

"I'm glad I came to see you, I feel so much better now. We must see more of you. Perhaps, later, you'll come and stay at our Palm Beach Cottage and bring that amusing Barney of yours with you. He's such an attractive man."

I smiled and thanked her for the invitation.

She opened her bag and rummaged in it, producing a tiny pencil torch.

But it wasn't the torch that interested me. It was the small revolver nestling against the satin lining that made me recoil with shock—and horror. She turned her head sharply and looked straight at me before I could wipe the surprise from my face.

Then she laughed and patted the black antelope bag. "Don't be so startled. You don't think I'd wander around at night without some form of protection, surely? I'm not a fool. John bought it for me during the burglary scares last year, and from now on I intend to carry it with me. And I'd certainly use it if I had to." Her eyes were amused.

If anyone had told me, two weeks ago, that Miranda Welch toted a gun I would have laughed my head off. But now I was prepared to believe anything. I'd discovered that, despite her charming smile and flower-like face, Miranda was no fragile, fairy princess. She was alarmingly tough and mortal. It was more than a shock. It was a revelation.

I watched her walk over to the lift door and slide the grill aside. She raised her hand in farewell and then, slowly, the lift moaned into action. Her black gown, her exquisite smiling mouth, her long slanting eyes and, lastly, her sleek hair bound in the green scarf, disappeared.

I shut the door and sank into the nearest chair with utter relief that she'd gone. Just why, I asked myself, had I been honoured tonight, of all nights, with a social call? It didn't add up! Miranda wasn't given to spontaneous action. She always knew exactly what she was doing and why. Yet if there'd been a purpose behind her visit tonight, I was darned if I could find it. Apparently she'd merely felt the need to warn me to be careful what I said to McLean, which was rather silly, surely, because I had nothing more to tell him.

Nothing—but the fact that Lisa thought she recognized Miranda or Clare as a former guest at the Oceana! And Miranda was anxious I should suppress that very fact!

If I'd been wearing a hat I would have clung on to it with both hands at that minute, because the idea which swept into my mind was as startling as a sudden gust of wind in my face. Miranda didn't want me to tell McLean about that part of my conversation with Lisa for the simple reason that it happened to be the truth!

I recalled the certainty in Lisa's voice when she pointed to the photo in the paper, when she said in her thin little voice, 'Ever so pretty she was, and what lovely clothes.' She'd been referring to Miranda.

I lit a cigarette to help me to think. The theory building up in my mind belonged solely to the category of Cat, but I couldn't resist following it up. Suppose Miranda had stayed at the Oceana? Why should she be so anxious to keep it secret?

The answer was obvious. It was also rather nasty. She didn't want McLean to start investigating that angle because John might discover that his beautiful idol had feet of clay. And above all things, Miranda would be anxious to preserve her marriage, outwardly anyway, because money and luxury were the breath of her very existence. So she'd braved the dark and come flying over to me to make sure I kept my silence.

But even if I'd hit on the truth, it still didn't explain Lisa's death. Perhaps if she'd been a blackmailer she might have seen a way to make money out of the situation, but it was as inconceivable that Lisa should attempt blackmail as it was to imagine Miranda wielding a poker lethally.

And then the whole crazy idea of Miranda sneaking off for a quiet week-end at the Oceana came crashing to the ground. It takes two to make an illicit outing, but as far as I knew, there was no other man in her life. Only John. If there'd been the faintest whisper of scandal about her I would have heard it. But she was pure as the driven snow. Even the most persistent Sydney gossips, who'd waited like hawks for Miranda to make her first slip, had been forced to admit, reluctantly, that John's marriage had turned out much better than they'd expected. Miranda, they said, was young to be the wife of such an important man, but she really did seem to be making a success of the job. Who would have thought she'd settle for a staid, elderly type?—not that John wasn't a perfect dear in his own way. And if they added that it was lucky he was so wealthy, there was no real malice in the statement. Rather, they implied, it was a satisfactory arrangement whereby John had acquired a lovely wife and Miranda had acquired a good, steady husband—one of the necessities of life—and lots of clothes and jewellery and trips in luxury liners.

If the seasoned gossips couldn't find an extra man in her life it meant he simply didn't exist.

I stubbed out my cigarette, picked up the empty glasses and took them through to the kitchen, feeling disgusted with myself for having thought up such a ridiculous, horrible accusation against Miranda. And that left me exactly where I was before she popped over to pay me such an unexpected visit. I could only assume she'd felt the urge to sample the night air and a little light conversation.

I went through my nightly chores of cleaning the kitchen ready for morning, and by the time I'd hung the tea-towel to dry on the rack behind the door I was calmer than I'd been all evening. There is nothing as good as a steady routine for settling the nerves, I told myself, as I rinsed the milk bottles and tucked them under my arm. If I wanted a supply in the morning I'd have to take the empties down and leave them outside the lift on the ground floor. The milkman wasn't accommodating enough to clamber up the stairs. It was an arrangement I'd become used to, grudgingly, and normally I regarded the trip downstairs as my constitutional before bed.

But tonight I couldn't face the long climb with the Simpsons' flat in empty loneliness beneath me, so I put the catch on the lock and pressed the button for the lift. The lower landing was dark as I passed it, and I thought of Miranda hurrying home in the dimly lit street with a little revolver tucked in her bag. She was much braver than I. I wouldn't have walked to Coolibah alone that night if I'd been armed with a machine-gun.

The laughter from Blue and Dawn's flat rose in sweeping gusts as I reached the ground floor. It sounded hilarious and gay and deliciously remote from sinister, evil things like . . . sudden death . . . a quick blow on the back of the head . . . a push . . . a sprawling figure at the bottom of white stone steps.

I put the bottles in their place and stepped back into the lift quickly. Weariness swamped me and I found I was longing to sink into the bliss of sleep and forgetfulness. Dreamless sleep. And tomorrow Barney would ring and by then McLean would have solved this dreadful tangle that had closed like a web around me, and I'd be able to tell Barney about it and wallow in his sympathy and alarm.

The lift came to a halt at my floor. I was glad the landing light was on. I wouldn't turn it off tonight. It would burn cheerfully like a beacon outside my door until morning crept in and flooded the building with the brilliance and comfort of day.

I was too tired, I told myself, to think any more about the terrible hours I'd lived through. I was filled with the false calm that fatigue brings, when the brain is too weary to grapple endlessly with problems that are beyond its reach.

I closed the lift grill and walked towards my neat front door. It was slightly ajar, just the way I'd left it.

Then I stopped. Something was wrong and I couldn't think what it was. But I knew the scene was different in some tiny detail from how it had looked when I'd carried the milk bottles to the lift.

Then it hit me! The lounge was in darkness! That was the difference!

I stared at the front door in rising panic. There was no friendly light showing through the crack, only a black and frightening pool with the reflection from the landing casting a thin amber streak across the carpet. I stood still in utter terror. Who had turned out my light? What a fool I'd been to leave my door unlocked even for a few seconds!

I listened with every muscle taut. Only the distant hum of noisy cars and faint, far-off laughter disturbed the serenity.

I felt my body relax as I suddenly hit on a perfectly logical explanation of the darkness inside. Of course! The bulb had gone!

How silly of me to be jittery! I'd been as nervous as a kitten all evening, nervous of Simon walking home with me, nervous of Miranda paying me a call, and now I was standing in a state of quivering alarm because my light had chosen tonight to peter out. It hadn't been replaced for months, and even the best of lights doesn't last for ever. Like the human body. Like poor Lisa's body—snuffed out, quickly and finally.

Don't think about Lisa, I told myself. Her death had turned me into a spineless coward, suspecting every shadow of hiding a maniac.

I was trembling as I forced myself towards the door. Slowly I pushed it open so that the light from the landing flooded the floor. There was no movement, no sign of an intruder. I'd been right! The bulb must have gone. I knew exactly where the light switch was, and I put my hand round the door with the certainty that I would find the small catch still pressed down.

At first I could only feel the smooth wall, cold against my warm, clammy hand. A little higher. Now I could feel the bottom of the square white guard, and my nail clicked against its surface. My finger found the spot where the small switch should have been. But instead of the switch my hand brushed against something that sent my blood racing with fear and horror.

My finger met the warm familiar touch of human flesh.

A hand was resting on the switch and its fingers moved and twined like snakes round mine.

I hurled myself away from the door. I didn't give a thought to the lift, but careered down the stairs, stumbling and tripping, gasping for breath. I didn't dare look back. I didn't want to see what was there, behind me. All I wanted was to reach the brightness and comfort of the Baileys' lounge and to throw myself against Blue's broad shoulder.

Past the eerie, silent flat on the first floor, where shadows lengthened and grabbed at me and the big banister post loomed suddenly out of the darkness like an evil, waiting monster.

Down the last few steps, with the Baileys' open door in front of me—a shining goal of safety and light. I fell into the room—sobbing, shivering—and landed against a couple of men who swayed beneath the impact.

They grabbed me by the arm, saying, "Here, what's up? Why the crying jag?"

I wasn't crying. I was trying to breathe. Then abruptly someone began to laugh and I found it was me.

It was the relief from passing out of blackest night into brilliant sunshine that struck me as funny. The room was distorted and unreal, like a scene from a canvas in which the painter had over-emphasized the brown limbs of sun-worshippers and had added inches to the physique of men. Everything and everyone seemed much larger than life. Gay, happy, fearless. But I didn't have time to stop and gaze at it. I wanted Blue.

A girl with corn-coloured hair and scarlet toe-nails abandoned her attempt at hula as I pushed past her, and a couple dancing in bare feet in the middle of the floor stood aside to let me through.

"Just another crazy woman," a voice said.

No one else took much notice of me.

"Where's Blue?" I was shouting now.

And a voice shouted back at me. "Where do you think he is while the keg lasts?"

I dived for the kitchen. Blue was leaning against the sink, with his shirt hanging outside his khaki shorts and his feet thrust into old, battered sandals.

"Blue!" I flew at him, and he put his great paw on my shoulder to steady me and peered down into my face. His smile faded.

"Here, hang on a moment. What's wrong? . . . Dawn, come here."

Dawn seemed to appear from nowhere and took my hand in hers, very gently. A few people crowded round, curious and interested, as though I'd added excitement and novelty to their evening. Dawn shooed them off, saying, "Get her a drink, someone. No, not beer, you fool—she's had a shock," and Blue looked at me with puzzled eyes, waiting.

I searched for words like a child learning to speak. "There's someone in my flat. There's someone in my flat."

Bewilderment gave place to angry determination on Blue's face. This was something he understood and knew how to deal with. He made for the door like a hurricane, scattering his guests aside. Some of them trailed after him eagerly, scenting blood in the air. Dawn tugged at my arm, pulling me back, but I dragged her with me, out through the lounge door, into the lobby where Blue's large form was leaping up the stairs.

She dropped her hand suddenly and went white round the mouth. "Joey! I must see he's all right. Gilly darling, wait here. Don't go up. Leave everything to Blue. He'll fix things."

She fled back to her own flat. But with people all round me I'd become brave and fearless and I began running up the stairs.

From somewhere below me a voice called sharply, "Gilly!"

I stopped. I knew that voice. I turned and stared down into the lobby. Finch's eyes stared back at me.

"Finch! How long have you been here?" Suspicion flooded me.

But it couldn't have been Finch standing there silently by the light switch, waiting for me to enter the room. Not Finch. He would have spoken, would have made his presence known. He had no reason to cower in the dark like a thief and a criminal.

He bounded up the stairs and caught my arm.

"Darling, you look queer. Has anything happened? I've only just come. I knew Blue wouldn't mind if I dropped in. It seemed a better way to spend the night than staying home brooding, going round in circles. God knows we need a little cheerful humanity after what went on at Coolibah. And humanity's one thing you always find at the Baileys'—in all shapes and sizes,"

I wasn't in the mood for a discussion of our mutual friends and I pushed on, leaving him gaping after me.

"Gilly!" he said again, and I found him by my side, clinging like a leech.

We reached the second-floor landing together.

Blue was standing in the doorway scowling with disappointment. His eyebrows rose a little when he saw Finch.

"There's no one here, Gilly. Your door was open and the light on, but not a sign of a burglar. However, you'd better come in and make sure nothing's missing."

I walked into the lounge with Finch at my heels. He didn't say a word as I glanced round hastily, assuring myself that everything was in place—just the way it had been when I'd last been in here. My clock was still on the mantel, my typewriter open with the sheet of half-written notes stuck beneath the roller, the big cloisonné ashtray full of cigarette stubs. I went through the bedroom and kitchen and even peered into the bathroom. Nothing had been touched.

When I returned to the lounge, Finch was propping up the wall saying in a bored voice, "What goes on?"

But his eyes weren't bored—they were wary beneath their absurdly black lashes, and his cheeks were sunken and hollow as though he were recovering from a long illness. Beside Blue's bulk he looked effeminate and frail, and even the pipe he pulled out of his pocket and stuffed between his teeth failed to give him masculine solidity.

Blue answered him, shrugging a little. "Gilly thought she had a burglar, but I guess she must have been mistaken. . . . What made you think someone was in here? Did you see the bloke?"

I shook my head, feeling a little foolish in the face of his obvious scepticism. "I felt a hand—just here—inside the door. It moved. Its fingers curled round mine."

Blue was grinning now and his eyes met Finch's above my head. "I have this sort of trouble with Dawn. She hears things in the night. She sees strange shadows. She knows someone's robbing us the minute I get comfortably settled in bed. I search the flat any time from midnight to sunrise. But I've never found her burglar yet."

I had a sudden thought. Perhaps one of Blue's guests had a perverted sense of humour. Perhaps Finch . . .

"It wasn't you?" I asked him. "You weren't playing a trick—a sordid joke—on me?"

He looked a little hurt before he laughed. "I always hide behind doors waiting to carve up unsuspecting females."

"Why don't you forget it? Come on down and have a drink," Blue said sensibly. Obviously he'd dismissed the whole incident as a mere figment of my vivid imagination. It would take a cartload of thieves—or even murderers—to frighten Blue, I thought.

Dawn joined us then. "Joey's still asleep, thank God. Gilly, you should have waited downstairs. What's happened? Did you find anyone here, Blue?"

He shrugged. "Everything seems to be in order. Gilly's caught your complaint, hon. She's started seeing things. God knows where you'll end up if you both keep carrying on like this."

Surely I hadn't imagined those vicious curling fingers closing round mine. If I'd stepped into the lounge instead of groping for the light. . . . I shuddered.

Dawn was watching me closely. "There's more to it than this. Spill it, darling."

I flopped into a chair. "A girl was killed at John Welch's party tonight."

They stared at me as if I'd gone crazy.

Finch said quickly, "Don't start hashing it over, Gilly. What good can it do?"

But I wanted to talk. I felt a weight lift as I told Blue and Dawn how Finch and I had been walking in the garden, how I'd stumbled and almost fallen over Lisa's body. And as I talked Lisa's face swam before me in a nebulous haze and I forgot I was here in my own flat. I was in the sitting-room at Coolibah staring down at the broad steps, watching Tony and Finch crouching over a limp, crumpled figure, and Lisa's eyes were gazing up at the sky—not in reproach or anger or fear, but in death.

And then Blue brought me back to the present. "Poor kid. No wonder you're imagining hands behind doors."

Dawn turned to him and said softly, "What she needs is sleep. She's almost out on her feet. I'm going to stay and see that she gets into bed. And you two can go and shut the gang up. Tell them to go home. Tell them anything, only keep them quiet."

They went like lambs, but at the door Blue turned and gave me a reassuring grin.

Finch wasn't smiling. He looked back at me and said, "Why didn't you wait for me to walk home with you to-night? Why did you go with Simon? Darling, for God's sake, be careful in future. Don't trust anyone."

Dawn pushed him out and shut the door.

"And now," she said in a brisk, businesslike manner, "you're going to bed. I think, Gilly, you've worked yourself into the sort of state when you're seeing things that don't exist, and you need a good long sleep and then you'll be yourself again."

I was more than content to sit there and let her do my thinking for me. I watched with dull, unseeing eyes as she hustled about the flat, making me a drink and standing over me while I forced it down my throat. It was strong but it tasted good, and suddenly I felt drowsy with a delicious numbness as though nothing mattered any more.

She led me into the bedroom, talking to me as she used to do to Joey when he was sick, folding up my clothes, taking the blankets from the bed and putting them in a neat pile.

"You'll only need a sheet tonight, darling. There's not a thing to be frightened about, remember. You're quite safe now. You're home—and Blue and I are only downstairs."

Nevertheless, when she thought I wasn't looking, she

peered into cupboards and wardrobes and I saw her jump a little when my slacks swung towards her on their hanger.

"I'm going to sit up here till you drop off, and then I'll put the safety catch on your door before I slam it, so you'll know you're quite safe. No one can possibly get in. Blue will be watching too, to make sure no strangers are lurking about. 'Night, darling."

She turned off the light and I heard her pad into the lounge.

I'd always been fond of Dawn, but I'd never loved her as much as I did that night. My own mother couldn't have done more for me. Dawn and Blue—I'd spoilt their party but they didn't gave a damn about that. Staunch, loyal, true, the sort of friends to cherish. Two sane people in a crazy world. Dawn and Blue. . . .

And somewhere in Melbourne Barney was sleeping soundly with not even a bad dream to warn him that I'd stepped out of my normal happy rut into a twisted path of shadow.

Gradually my eyes closed. In that period of half-sleep, before I lost touch with the world, Lisa joined me, and I sat again with her in the little café, listening to her small voice saying, 'She's like a film star,' and I followed her finger and saw that it was pointing not at Miranda but at Clare, and I cried, 'You've made a mistake. You mean Miranda.' Then the figures faded and Lisa's voice grew farther and farther away and I blacked out, mercifully, into peace.

CHAPTER VII

THE day had begun long before I woke the next morning. I stirred and opened my eyes, listening to a blowfly bashing itself at intervals against the ceiling and the ceaseless drone of traffic drifting through the windows.

The clouds seemed to have lifted a little because I could see a patch of encouraging blue sky—a welcome change after the sultry, heavy heat of the past few days.

I lay in a happy stupor thinking of the week-end ahead. A swim, perhaps. A lazy, chatty time with Blue and Dawn, enlivened by numerous cups of tea and glasses of iced beer.

Dawn and Blue. . . . Dawn had put me to bed, surely, and had tucked me in? Why? I wasn't sick?

And slowly, like the creeping tentacles of an octopus, the events of last night crawled through my mind, jerking me awake as effectively as a cold shower. The week-end which had loomed so cheerfully now stretched before me like a great yawning abyss, dark and frightening.

Sleep was impossible, so I got up, turned on the shower in my white-tiled bathroom, and laid out a seersucker sundress.

I was making tea when the bell rang—three short rings, the special signal between the Baileys and myself. But it wasn't Dawn or Blue. It was Joey. He was carrying a tray set out with toast and marmalade and a grapefruit soaked in sugar.

"Mum sent this. She says you gotta eat it."

I took the tray from him hastily. He was so pop-eyed with excitement I was afraid he might drop it.

"Thanks, Joey. It looks lovely."

He wasn't interested in expressions of gratitude. He had other things on his mind.

"Gee, Gilly! The papers're full of it this morning. There's a photo of that girl and all the dope about it. But they haven't copped him yet—the bloke who did it, I mean. Mum told me I wasn't to talk about it to you, but I guess you don't mind, do you? You're not a cissy."

I grinned at him and walked through to the kitchen and plonked the tray on the table.

"Help yourself. I'll never eat all this."

"Honest?"

"Honest," I told him gravely.

We sat down together like an old married couple. I hadn't thought about food and I was surprised to find I was hungry.

"Fancy you finding the body! Cripes! Wouldn't rock you, would it?"

I hastened to assure him it had rocked me considerably.

"An' fancy me being an eye-witness, so to speak. Saw her come in, I did, when I was pushing the blooming mower." He chewed thoughtfully. "The papers don't mention me." Obviously it was a big disappointment. "You couldn't do anything about it, could you? You work on a paper. You might be able to put in a word for me."

"I'd get turfed out if I interfered in the crime department. I only write fashions."

He made a deprecating noise. "The kids at school won't believe me—they'll reckon I'm laying it on when I say I was right there, right on the spot." He licked his fingers. "Whitey Gordon was mixed up in a case last year—'n he got his name in the papers and everything, and all because his Dad—Whitey's I mean—pinched a bloke trying to get in the windows. Nothin' at all, really. An' Whitey used to skite about it for months."

I reflected sadly on the modern child.

"Got any ideas?" He put his head on one side like a sparrow eager for crumbs.

"None," I said firmly, confirming his opinion that women never knew anything.

"I bet ole Mac's got his own ideas. Only he won't let on. He's the best cop in the whole force and he's caught lots and lots of murderers. He's famous. He's my godfather, too."

"Mac?"

"Inspector McLean, silly. He's a bonzer old stick. He's

been here this morning talking to Dad, and he asked me all sorts of questions about what I saw. He says there's no secret about the fact that it really and truly was murder. But," he added gloomily, "I didn't see anything funny going on. Clare and the Doctor bloke got out of the car and went inside—don't think they saw me 'cos they were too busy yapping to each other—and then that girl came, and I didn't see another soul till you passed. Except Mrs. Welch when she picked a couple of glads, but she didn't speak to me because I was over by the fence. Pity I didn't go round the back. Might've picked up a clue round there. But I was stuck at the front all afternoon."

Three short rings at the door sent him bounding to his feet.

"That's Mum. Gilly, you won't tell her—that I've been talking about the murder? She'd be hopping mad. And quick, what do you want down the street? I've got to go down for Mum and I was supposed to ask you."

"A loaf of bread and a dozen eggs," I replied with rapid co-operation.

I went to let Dawn in. She was spruce and fresh in a blue cotton skirt and white blouse. She might have been Joey's big sister, but she certainly didn't look old enough to be his mother.

"Hello, darling. Did you sleep?"

I tried to thank her for being a light in my darkest hour, but she waved me aside.

"Is Joey here?"

He came to the doorway and stood grinning at her. He was the image of Blue.

"I was just going," he told her. "Dad says he'll come with me. Has Mac gone yet?"

Dawn turned to me. "Inspector McLean wants to see you, Gilly. I stalled him off till you'd had breakfast. He's talking to Blue."

Joey gave another broad grin with a hint of admiration in it. "Mac reckons Mum and the Commissioner are the two bossiest people he's ever known."

"I only wish I could learn to boss you and Blue around," Dawn said. "I've been waiting hours for the meat."

"Okay. I'm going." Joey turned in the doorway and said slyly, "If I had a bike I'd get the messages done much quicker. Ever thought of that, Mum?"

Dawn laughed. "If I win a lottery I'll buy you a bike, and that's a promise."

"Pooh! I reckon I'll have one by then. Gilly, you know Mr. Welch pretty well, don't you? Do you think you could sort of drop the hint that I didn't get paid yesterday? With all this other business going on, he might forget about me. And I'm trying to save up."

Dawn threw her hands up in despair. "What can I do about a monster like Joey? Of course Gilly can't mention it. You'll have to wait. I'm sure Mr. Welch won't forget."

I smiled at him confidentially, because I'd just remembered a piece of news that would please him immensely. And I didn't see why murder and tragedy should interfere with Joey's pleasure. "Mr. Welch told me he had an old bike in the garage and he wondered whether you'd like it. He said you could take a look at it and if you wanted it you could have it."

He jumped in the air like a dervish. "On the level?"

"On the level," I told him solemnly.

His eyes were wide with delight. "Gosh, he's a good old codger. I'll settle for a bike any day instead of ten bob. Do you think I could slip over right now and get it? I don't want him to change his mind."

Dawn was frowning, doubtfully. "If he heard you calling him a 'good old codger' he probably would change his mind. Gilly, we can't possibly accept a bike. Not without paying for it."

"I think you can," I told her, watching Joey's anxious face. "No one ever uses it and John liked the idea of giving it away. It'll probably be miles too big for Joey yet, and it may not be in good condition, but John would be hurt if you didn't accept it. He's rather taken with Joey."

She still hesitated, so I plunged on, "I'll go over and talk to Clare about it this morning before I set out for the office. And then Joey can collect it this afternoon. I'll take

him over myself," and before she could reply I turned to
Joey and said, "By the way, Barney rang last night. He's got
those autographs you wanted."

He beamed. "Trust Barney. Gee, I reckon this is my
lucky day."

He bounded out, then suddenly poked his head round
the door. "Any little thing you want done, Mum? Apart
from the shopping?"

It was such blatant soft-soaping, and his face was so
strangely angelic, that I burst out laughing. Joey was taking
no chances. He was determined to have his bike.

I heard him clatter happily down the stairs and I wished
I could settle my own problems as satisfactorily as Joey's.

Dawn was laughing, too. "I'll bet he was goggle-eyed
about last night. I told him not to talk about it, but I knew
that was a fat hope. I couldn't keep it from him because it's
in the papers and he'd be bound to hear about it, anyway.
Then Mac arrived and that capped everything. How're you
feeling? Got over the heebies?"

I felt a touch of shame as I thought of the way I'd behaved
last night. It was impossible to feel scared this morning,
with the whole place buzzing with life, and Joey running
up and down the stairs and the sound of children's voices
in the street and dogs barking.

My courage always rises and sets with the sun.

"I'm fine. Quite ready to face your Mac."

"He's a pet, Gilly. Blue's known him for years, from the
time when he was just a plain copper. After your scare last
night, Blue got on to him and told him about it. I think
there really was someone in your flat, darling. You didn't
imagine it."

I blinked. Last night everyone had been eager to impress
on me that I'd dreamed up the whole affair.

"Blue didn't say anything about it to you," Dawn went
on, "because you had a bad attack of jitters. But, you see, the
lift was on the ground floor when Blue came up to investigate.
You'd only just used it, so it should have been standing at
your floor. But it wasn't. Blue thinks your burglar jumped
into it the minute you started running downstairs. He and

Finch searched the building, but there was no one hanging about. Whoever it was, he got away."

I'd known all along that I hadn't imagined that hand behind the door.

Dawn walked calmly into the kitchen and picked up the tray.

"I'm glad you ate your breakfast—with Joey's help. You don't have to tell me. I know my own offspring. Anyone'd think I half starved the little devil."

Her practical, everyday manner was inspiring.

It was no more than a minute or two after she'd gone that I opened the door to Inspector McLean. Joey's godfather! Mac! He looked more tired and lazy than ever. Not surprising, as he'd had far less sleep than I during the past twelve hours. He sank into a chair and stretched his legs out in much the same manner as Barney or Blue might have done.

"I've been hearing a lot about you in a short time," he said amiably, as if he'd dropped in for a chat over morning coffee. "I believe you had a spot of bother here last night. Nice flat you've got. Better than Blue's because you get a view of the harbour. Nice and peaceful. Much safer than the ground floor too."

"It didn't feel very safe last night," I told him.

"I've had Blue's version of what happened. But I'd like to hear yours."

I told him about my trip downstairs with the empty milk bottles, my discovery that the light in the lounge was out, the hand that touched mine as I groped for the switch, and my hurried flight to find Blue. I tried to convey the idea that I'd acted with a presence of mind and sanity that had been conspicuously absent. I saw no reason to mention that I'd been nearly out of my wits with sheer terror.

He gave me a fleeting grin, and I grinned back at him. Blue, I thought, would have given him an accurate description of the state of my nerves.

"And you had no further disturbances? You slept the sleep of the just—or should I say of the innocent?"

I told him I thought quite enough had happened for one night, and I was satisfied even if he were disappointed.

He stopped smiling suddenly and leaned forward. "Miss Amery, why should anyone bother to break into your flat and take nothing?"

He'd dropped his casual role. Even his eyes had lost their rather faded expression. They had a hard, diamond glitter.

"I don't know," I told him.

"Think! Was anything missing? Something you've overlooked perhaps?"

"Nothing that I know of."

"If the story's true, Miss Amery, there has to be a reason. People don't break into flats aimlessly. I believe someone was in here last night and I want to know what he expected to find. Letters? Papers?"

I shook my head hopelessly. He lolled back in his chair again and remembered to be the man from Sleepy Hollow.

"Well, perhaps you'll recall it later. We'll forget about it meantime, because I want you to tell me everything that happened to you from the moment you met that girl in the café yesterday. Try and think carefully. I want every word that was spoken, every move and gesture. You're in quite a spot, you know, because you're the only link we can find with her. Your name and address were in her handbag and she thought enough of that social guff you write to cut it out of the paper. You arrived at the Welches' shortly after she did, and what's more you discovered the body. Every path from that girl leads right back to you. But I'm an open-minded bloke and the story you told about meeting her in the café is crazy enough to be true. I'm prepared to believe it. And in return I expect you to help me. I want you to tell me every detail you gleaned about the girl. A woman may lead an ordinary, dull life with nothing of interest in it, but once she's been murdered it's often those ordinary facts about her that become important. You can live in obscurity with no hope of ever hitting the headlines, but get bashed on the head and every tiny action of your dreary existence becomes far more significant than the latest Hollywood romance." He grinned and handed me a cigarette. "So don't think you're boring me by telling me she had callouses on her hands or drank her tea out of the saucer. I'm a good listener."

At first I was glad of the cigarette, because it gave me something to do with my hands; but gradually I lost every shred of selfconsciousness; I began to enjoy telling my impressions of Lisa and I tried to build up an accurate picture of her, exactly the way I'd seen her.

McLean didn't watch me. He stared out of the window as if his thoughts were at least ten miles away.

I told him how Lisa had been sitting at the table, smiling a little, and how she'd seemed glad when I spoke to her. I told him, too, about seeing Simon quite close to us, and the queer feeling I'd had that he was watching us. The conversation with Lisa came easily to my mind. I'd been through it myself so many times that I knew it by heart, and I was ready to swear I hadn't left out a single word. I'd just reached Lisa's rush for the door, when McLean's voice broke in on me.

He wasn't satisfied. He wanted every word of that conversation over again, so I gave it to him, and it didn't differ by one word from my first version.

He nodded then. "She disappeared into the street. What next?"

Simon, I told him, had gone too. And I'd discovered I was holding Lisa's cross in my hand, wondering how I could return it to her. I stopped talking. McLean was looking at me as though I'd handed him the Koh-i-noor.

"Where is this little gadget now?" he asked in a rather strangled voice. "And how many people knew you had it?"

I stared back at him, wondering whether I was following his train of thought correctly. "I mentioned it in the drawing-room at Coolibah. Mr. and Mrs. Welch and Clare and Tony heard me. Simon asked me what Lisa dropped when she ran out of the café. But I didn't say what it was. I simply said it was nothing valuable."

"God preserve me from women," he breathed. "And you wonder why you had a burglar?" His voice sharpened. "Where is it? Get it!"

I stood up shakily. I half expected to find it had vanished into thin air, and I was so surprised to see it still gleaming innocently on the mantel that I couldn't speak.

I picked it up and handed it to McLean. He examined it carefully, then put it in his pocket.

"Why didn't you tell me about this before?"

"I didn't think of it. It slipped my mind."

He sighed patiently, then smiled to take the sting out of his sigh. "I hope there aren't too many other things that've slipped your mind."

He took me back then, to the café, and how I'd paid Lisa's bill and returned to the office.

"We can skip the rest of the afternoon. Pick it up from where you arrived home and began to prepare for the Welch party."

My voice droned on interminably as I set the scene at Coolibah. Told in everyday language, with the sun shining outside, it was hard to resurrect the atmosphere I'd felt in the big drawing-room last night, and it all sounded rather melodramatic and silly. So I stuck to bare facts and tried not to colour the story with my own emotions and feelings. I skipped quickly over the finding of Lisa's body, and was glad that he didn't pull me up and ask for a repetition, but merely glanced at me sympathetically and allowed me to go on.

No detail was too small or too insignificant for him; and occasionally he stopped me and wanted to know the exact words Miranda or Finch or Tony had spoken. What, he asked me, had Simon talked about on the way home?

"Mainly about John and his father being friends and how kind Miranda had been and how she insisted that he stay at Coolibah."

"Mrs. Welch seems more pleased about his visit than Clare, at a rough guess." He hit the nail on the head so accurately that I was startled.

My face must have given me away, because he added with a twinkle of humour, "Even plain cops notice these things."

I was glad to hurry off the subject. I didn't tell him about the conversation I'd overheard between Clare and Simon, because, I argued, McLean had already formed his own opinion of how the wind lay in that quarter. Besides, Clare was an old school chum, and loyalty forebade me mention-ing her confidential conversation—which, in any case, had nothing to do with murder. But I gave him a résumé of Miranda's visit, right down to the natty little gun she carried in her purse.

I racked my brains to see if I'd left anything out of my monologue, but no, I'd laid my memory bare. And at the end of it I felt like the worst sort of traitor—a police spy, a pimp, who is ready to tell tales about his friends behind their backs.

When I'd run dry there was a hush in the room that sounded queer after the monotonous prattling of my voice.

Then McLean said, "My God! You do pick up a lot of bits and pieces, don't you? No wonder you're a good gossip writer." He was eyeing me with interest and alarm. "Perhaps it was lucky Barney rang while Miranda was with you. Did you know then that she was lugging a revolver around with her?"

I shook my head.

He seemed amused, because he gave a short burst of laughter. "Miranda Welch has a nice line in drama," he said. "In fact, she's got a nice line. I hope she's got a licence for the gun, but I suppose her husband would see to that if he bought it. He's a wily old bird, John Welch."

He heaved himself to his feet and leaned against the back of the chair. "You've got a load of dynamite tucked away in that brain of yours. You must be causing a murderer quite a bit of anxious thought. Well, you've been a help, Miss Amery."

"I can't see it gets us anywhere," I said dejectedly.

He ran his hand through his hair, making it stand up like a fuzzy hedge.

"It gets us right back to your friends—that is, of course, if the people connected with Coolibah are your friends."

"Of course they are." I felt a little sick. "You don't mean——"

"It looks like it, doesn't it?" he said brightly. "But don't quote me on it. I've had trouble enough with one of your reporters as it is—Ned Cawley. I hope some day I'll find an excuse to slap that young man into jail. Do him good."

I smiled politely at the joke, but my heart wasn't in it. If the long rigmarole I'd just spilled to the Inspector had helped, I felt I had a right to know how and why.

He was smiling at me in the friendliest way possible. He looked rather pleased with himself. "Burning with curiosity, aren't you?" he said with nasty accuracy. "It's dangerous to have a face like yours. Much too easy for a murderer to read. The less you know the better. For your information, though, the idea of an escaped jailbird or a loony wandering around this area is all my eye and baloney. We've got to concentrate on this street—on Cottrill Street—if we want to get anywhere. But you've probably worked that much out for yourself. Tell me, didn't it strike you as odd that Miranda Welch and Simon Ashton should be seeking your company so soon after the murder? I'm not underrating your charms, of course," he added with a wicked grin. "What do you think of those two?"

What did I think of them? Last night I'd seen Simon as a new suave type of Dracula, and Miranda had resembled a highly coloured version of Mata Hari. But today they'd slipped back to their less spectacular roles. I shrugged. "I barely know Simon. And Miranda is very beautiful."

He gazed down at me with a hint of indecision on his face, as though he were trying to make up his mind how much or how little to confide in me.

"I want you to be careful, Miss Amery," he said slowly, "and for God's sake don't go around talking too much. If you've got anything important to say, remember there's only one safe person for you to bare your heart to—and that's me. I rather think you've been chatting to a murderer recently, and whoever killed that girl has a quick, agile mind. You're no match for someone like that. You're charming and you're pretty and you're not very logical, and if you stay that way you should be perfectly safe, and you'll probably live to a ripe old age. But don't trust anyone."

"That's what Finch said." My voice wasn't quite even and my legs felt shaky.

"Oh, he did, did he? Well, I wouldn't trust him too far, either."

"I've known him for ages," I cried. My whole world was toppling about me.

He gave me a fatherly look. "Murder pops up even in the

best circles," he grinned engagingly. "It's just a matter of opportunity and motive. Push a man—or a woman—too far, and the urge to kill gets the upper hand—especially if he thinks he can get away with it."

"But there's got to be a motive."

He pushed his hand through his hair again. "I can think up a dozen motives for killing that girl. Perhaps she was one of Finch Martyn's former wives who was getting in his hair, or perhaps she was having a baby by John Welch."

"Don't be horrible. John's the most respectable person I know." My gorge rose before I realized he was pulling my leg. I couldn't get used to conversation with McLean, because one minute he was serious and the next he was poking fun at me. It was like watching a chameleon continually changing colour.

"You must admit," he said with his head on one side, thoughtfully, "that he's got a distinct taste for women much younger than himself."

"Only Miranda," I said coolly. I wasn't going to fall into the trap of rushing to John's defence again.

"Never judge a book by its cover. Never trust the eminently respectable. As for Miranda Welch and Clare, there's just the possibility that one of them did stay at the Oceana, and that brings up a new train of thought, doesn't it?"

It may have done so for him, but it left me as blank as I'd been from the beginning of this hopeless mess.

He walked to the door and stood leaning against it. He never seemed to stand straight if there was a convenient prop.

"Don't let anyone pump you for information." He was deadly serious again. "Remember you know nothing. If anyone visits you, ring through to Blue or Dawn, make any excuse, and tell them who's with you. Don't be alone with one person unless someone else knows you're with that person, and remember there's safety in numbers. You're a lucky girl, Miss Amery. I don't think your burglar intended to kill you, but you came back too soon and surprised him, and if you'd walked into your flat like a lion, instead of scuttling off like a rabbit, well . . ." He let the sentence fall ominously into space. "Go on being a rabbit. I don't want to frighten you, but believe me, I'd be willing to scare the daylights out of you if I thought it would make you realize you've got to hold your tongue and watch your step."

Right then he had me so scared I wouldn't have said boo to a goose.

"You know more about the murdered girl than you realize—and that's your danger. I'll look after you, but I can't if you don't help too."

I hoped I was looking calmer and more dignified than I felt, because my knees had turned to water and I found I had to cling to the back of the chair for support.

As I look back I can see that already he knew far more about Lisa than I did, despite the fact that I'd been in contact with her and knew how she'd looked, how she'd spoken and how she'd acted. His information was secondhand, yet I think he understood, even at that stage, something of the turmoil in her tortured mind, and the glimmer of an idea was beginning to take shape and substance. Perhaps if I'd been built on brighter, more intelligent lines, I too would have been able to sort irrelevant facts into a logical pattern—but God knows, I've never been noted for the brilliant functioning of my grey matter.

He opened the door and stood silhouetted against the landing. "Don't let it get you down," he said cheerfully. "Just be yourself, and you'll stay in one piece." He gave me a gay smile and stalked out.

CHAPTER VIII

I sat down again because it's difficult to stand when your knees are knocking. And mine certainly were.

Why, I wondered, should these awful things be happening to me? I was a peace-loving citizen, and if I'd complained in the past about the boredom of a suburban existence, it was only because I'd never realized till now how wonderful it was to go to the office, to come home and cook a meal, to wash up and to listen to the radio with a clear, untroubled mind—with no ugly thoughts of a murderer stalking my footsteps. A sublime, happy world. And the pity of it was that I'd never fully appreciated its finer points.

I'd jumped headlong into a whirlpool. And all because I'd stopped to speak to a lonely girl in a café.

I brooded for a while on the injustice of life, and then decided my thoughts were getting me nowhere, and anyway it was time to go to the office.

I packed my notes together and decided to wear my new shantung and wide-brimmed hat. It would be a shame, I told myself, if death caught up with me before I'd had a chance to air my latest outfit. If I were doomed to die, at least I would meet death proudly, smartly dressed for the occasion.

It wasn't till my heels were click-clicking down the stairs that I remembered I'd promised to remind Clare about the bike. And a promise is a promise, especially when it is made to a small boy. It was just as well I remembered, because Joey and Blue were lumbering up the path as I reached the lobby. They were laden with parcels.

"Hiya," Blue greeted me. "We've got some eggs and bread that belong to you. I'll give them to Dawn and you can collect them when you come home. You're a ball of style this morning. Where are you off to?"

I paid him for my purchases and remarked, scathingly, that some people had to work on Saturday despite the forty-hour week. He merely grinned and offered me the advice that greater effort during the week might result in free Saturday mornings, and why didn't I try it?

Before I could think up a suitable retort, Joey piped up anxiously, "You haven't forgotten about you know what?"

He winked at me and I winked back at him.

"What's going on that I don't know about?" Blue demanded.

"Gilly's promised to write Barney and ask him about those autographs. Gee, just imagine it, Dad. Keith Miller, Neil Harvey, the whole team. Maybe he'll get some of the Poms too."

I was always impressed by Joey's flair for improvisation. Apparently Blue wasn't to know about the bike until it was a *fait accompli*, and then it would be too late for objections, especially with Dawn on Joey's side.

"You won't forget, will you?" Joey frowned, wondering whether I'd cottoned on to the stratagem.

To show that I had, I said calmly, "No, of course I won't. But I've got to rush over and see Clare now, and I'm running late."

He nodded delightedly, and as I trotted down the path I could hear his non-stop chatter punctuated by Blue's deep laugh as they carried their groceries into the flat.

I walked quickly over to Coolibah.

The clouds had rolled apart and the street was bathed in sunshine. It wouldn't last, but the hot dry heat was a nice change after the sultry days we'd just endured. A crowd of sightseers had gathered outside the entrance gates to Coolibah, gazing at the big house with morbid curiosity. A policeman in uniform was moving them on. He stopped me when I tried to push through.

"My name is Gillian Amery," I told him, "and Miss Welch is expecting me."

He hesitated a moment, then decided to let me pass.

As I walked up the long drive it flashed through my mind that unseen eyes were probably watching me, just the way they'd watched Lisa yesterday from the windows of the big house.

As if to prove my point, John stepped on to the verandah and came down the path to meet me.

"Gilly dear, this is a nice surprise. You're in time for coffee. Miranda's rustling some up and we're having it in the sun-room."

I could imagine how much Miranda was doing towards making coffee. She wouldn't know how to boil water, and even if she'd known once, before the palmy days of Coolibah, I was quite sure she'd made a point of forgetting such mundane accomplishments.

John and I walked through the front door together.

I was a little shocked at his appearance. The bright light revealed him, mercilessly, as an old man, and there were tired lines round his mouth and eyes. It seemed ludicrous and just a little indecent that he should be married to a girl as radiant, young and vital as Miranda.

"Tony arrived a while back," John said, ushering me into the hall, "but he says he must go to town. Doctors don't have much time to call their own—as bad as journalists, eh?"

"How right you are," I told him emphatically. "I really can't stay because I'm on my way to the office."

He laughed. "Nonsense. A cup of coffee won't take more than a few minutes. You won't get the sack for being a bit late for once," he teased me.

John had always been his own boss, making times and arrangements to suit himself. He didn't seem to realize that I couldn't do the same.

I could hear voices from the sun-room and Tony stood up when I entered, and Clare ran towards me impulsively, saying, "Darling, I'm so glad to see you. This place has been like a morgue all morning." Then she bit the words off, as if she realized they were far too appropriate. Clare always spoke first and thought afterwards. "Simon had to rush off to town and now Tony's going, too. I don't know what to do with myself. Why don't you come for a swim with me?"

Whether it was the result of Simon's absence or merely the effect of a good sleep, I don't know, but she was a different girl today. Her strapless white cotton frock showed off the lovely even tan of her arms and shoulders, and contrasted with the glossy blackness of her hair. She was as lively—and as restless—as a grasshopper.

Miranda was sitting beside a tray of cups, pouring coffee from a big silver percolator. She was wearing a cornflower blue linen dress and a sweet, innocent smile.

"I've been quite worried about you, darling." She flashed me a warning glance, then lowered her black lashes demurely. "After you'd gone home last night, I nearly rang to see if you'd arrived safely, but then Simon came back and said you were tired and nervy, so I thought it best to leave you in peace. I hope you slept well?"

Obviously she'd managed to slip back to the house unnoticed. I took the cup Tony handed me, and told her I'd slept much better than I'd expected.

"No nightmares?" Tony smiled down at me like a mischievous small boy.

I shuddered a little, and he added quickly, "I'm sorry, Gilly. I shouldn't have said that. Last night was rather a nightmare in itself, wasn't it? But if you don't snap out of it, I'll start prescribing a tonic to settle your nerves."

"Me and my nerves are used to each other." How easy to be flippant with the sun outside and people around me.

John pushed a chair towards me. "Why don't you sit over here, where you can get a view of the water. You know, I always think this is the best room in the whole house."

But I didn't take the chair he offered me. I wasn't particularly keen to face the garden and the terraced lawn where Finch and I had found Lisa. So instead I sat with my back to the long windows and answered queries politely about my health and wondered how soon I could get down to business and escape.

The fuss they made of me was flattering. I might have been the last surviving member of a distinguished, titled family. Yet I didn't feel wholly at ease. I was too conscious that they were playing a monstrous game of pretence—pretence that Lisa's death had no connection with Coolibah, pretence that the dreadful events of last night had left no ripple, no mark on the smooth surface of life.

"I've been longing to see you," Clare said, sitting on the arm of a chair and swinging one slim brown leg. "Finch was over this morning and he had some jumbled story about a burglary at your flat last night after you left here. I'm bursting with curiosity."

Miranda glanced at her sharply. "I didn't know Finch had been here."

"It was shortly after nine. Much too early for you to be up and about, darling. Practically the crack of dawn." Clare smiled wickedly. "You should remember the old saying about early to bed and early to rise. But tell me, Gilly, what really did happen? Finch made it sound too awful, and he said you were flying up the stairs like a ghost and positively flapping. And I wondered how he knew about it and he said he'd popped over to see Blue and there you were in a state, and he and Blue searched the whole house and couldn't find a soul. You know what Finch is like. I didn't know whether he was making the story up or not."

John managed to drag his eyes away from Miranda. "Don't talk about it if you'd rather not."

I smiled at him. "There's not much to tell. I thought I had a burglar, but Blue couldn't find him."

"But darling, why on earth should anyone break into your flat?" Miranda's eyes, I noticed, were blue this morning, as if to match the colour of her frock. "Thieves don't as a rule choose small places like yours. They'd know you had nothing of value. It's not as if you've got masses of jewellery. Whatever did he take?"

I could have slapped her, because her tone implied quite clearly that there wasn't a thing in my flat that couldn't be picked up at a junk-shop.

"Nothing was taken," I told her sweetly. "Perhaps he looked around and decided it wasn't worth the trouble."

"Do you mean to say someone broke in and then didn't touch a thing?" Tony was grinning at me, incredulously. "Gilly, I don't mean to be rude, but it does sound rather extraordinary."

Miranda gave a low, trilling laugh. "It sounds as if you had a ghost—not a burglar. Much more exciting. I'm crazy about spooks. I just adore those films about clanking chains and hands in the dark. But your flat hardly seems the right setting."

Hands in the dark? How odd she should have hit on that phrase.

"I would never have expected you to be the hysterical type," she said, "but you never know how people will react. Not even one's closest friends."

She leaned back languidly and I thought, with a stab of envy, that she herself certainly had the knack of remaining calm and civilized and beautiful in all circumstances. John was gazing at her with besotted eyes, and I suddenly had a dreadful feeling of pity for him. Miranda wasn't worth all that devotion. John should have kept it for some nice, homely woman of his own age.

"The imagination can play strange tricks at times," Tony said rather pompously. "There have been many cases where it leads to actual illness. . . ."

I stood up, a little angrily. Obviously I was the victim of an over-developed imagination.

"I promised Joey I'd ask you about the bike. I really didn't intend to entertain you with my own mythical adventures."

"Bike!" John's face was blank, then he smiled. "Oh yes. The bike! Tell Joey to come over and get it. Bring him over yourself."

"His mother has doubts. She doesn't know whether he should accept it or not."

"What nonsense!" John said in his determined fashion. "Tell her I'll be glad to get it out of the way. She's doing me a favour by taking it."

Dear, nice John, I thought, in a burst of affection.

"After lunch? I've got to dash to the office now."

"Any time you like. Clare or Simon can look it out. Tell Joey it's waiting for him."

"You're not going?" Clare wailed. "Aren't you going to come swimming with me?"

Tony linked his arm through hers and grinned at me over her head. "Poor Clare can never understand why some folk have to work. Can you, darling?"

"It's too nice a day for work." Miranda stretched lazily like a lovely, sleek cat. "A swim sounds rather heavenly. Or I wonder if I should see about those garden chairs I liked.

Where were they, Clare, can you remember? Was it David Jones'?"

I bestowed my sweetest smile on her and sauntered out into the hall, leaving them to discuss the problem of how to spend the day. It might have been an ordinary Saturday morning at Coolibah. Lisa's death was being carefully ignored —now that the initial shock had passed away.

John accompanied me down the hall. "I don't like the idea of your staying over in that flat on your own and I'd be much happier if you'd move in with us." He was frowning. "I didn't want to say anything in front of Miranda to frighten her, but I think you should tell McLean about your intruder."

Apparently he was the only one who'd taken my burglar alarm seriously.

"It seems strange it should happen so soon after that unfortunate business over here," he went on anxiously. "I've known you since you were a brat and I'd never forgive myself if anything unpleasant occurred to you."

"I told the Inspector about it this morning."

He looked vaguely taken aback and patted me on the shoulder.

"I'm glad you had so much sense. Leave these things in the hands of the police. That's their job. I'd be glad if you'd think about shifting, though. It's not that I imagine you're in any sort of danger. The fellow who killed that girl last night isn't likely to be hanging round waiting to be caught. He's probably miles away by now. But it's lonely for you being on your own. Come over here where you can be with Miranda."

Every road leads to Rome. Every sentence led right back to his wonderful Miranda.

I looked into his kind grey eyes and assured him I'd come bolting over if I felt the slightest cause for alarm.

Tony came down the hall with Clare behind him.

"Don't run off," he said to me, "because I'm going to drive you in. I pass your office."

Clare and John walked to the car with us and watched us set off. They were standing side by side and I was struck by the father-daughter resemblance between them—the same shaped head, the same mobile mouth, the same sharp thrust of the chin. I'd never noticed it so clearly before.

Then the car swept down the drive and Clare fluttered her hand in farewell and turned and walked inside. I wound the window down to let some air in and leaned back against the padded seat, clutching at my big hat to keep it in place. The battle became too great and I took it off and tossed it on the back seat. It was good to feel the wind blowing through my hair.

Tony wondered how the weather was in Melbourne and asked me whether I'd heard from Barney.

"He rang last night," I told him, "but he didn't mention the weather."

"It's quite important," Tony said, as he swung the big car round a corner.

I couldn't see, for the moment, just how Melbourne rain or shine affected our immediate future, and Tony must have noticed the puzzled look on my face, because he laughed.

"For the Test."

I couldn't think of anything better than, "Oh yes."

I envied Tony his ability to concentrate on the outcome of a mere game of cricket when there were such hideous events as murder clouding our lives.

"Barney's a lucky bloke," he said enviously. "He's got the right sort of job that takes him to the right sort of places. I hoped I'd be able to see this Test, but then at the last minute I couldn't make it. Now I'm glad, in a way. I couldn't bear to think of Clare going through that ordeal last night and me in Melbourne. It's a wonder you girls aren't screaming lunatics. Miranda, of course, never loses her head and J.W.'s a tough bird. You wouldn't think it to look at him. But I guarantee he'll outlast the lot of us. He's got a constitution of iron. But it was dreadful for you and Clare."

A thought struck me. "Tony, how did you know it wasn't an accident? What made you so sure?"

"Wound on the back of the head. If she fell she would've been alive now probably, because a blow on the front isn't so dangerous. Besides, you don't fall backwards and end up lying on your face. McLean spotted it straight off."

114

It was as simple as that, I told myself.

He switched quickly to another topic. "You're one of Clare's oldest friends, aren't you? She always says you're one person who understands her, although she doesn't see much of you these days. I wondered whether you thought she was . . . a bit worried or upset about something."

I told him I hadn't a clue, but that it was highly probable she was very worried after last night. Just as I was. Just as we all were.

"Of course," he said quickly, then grinned. "It's a tricky business trying to follow the workings of her mind. Rather like trying to climb a greasy pole. She's very highly strung and she's a complete extrovert. You've probably found that out for yourself."

I'd never thought about it before, because Clare was simply Clare. I stole a sidelong glance at Tony, noting the firm jaw, the nice, clean profile, the well-set ears. No wonder Clare had settled for the altar. He was distinctly eligible. I liked him best, though, when he was smiling. That happy grin had an attractive touch of devil in it, and dispersed the rather dull, rather solid air that always seems to linger round the well bred.

But I wished he wouldn't talk about Clare as though she were a guinea-pig whose emotions and reactions were professionally fascinating. Doctors are all alike, I thought.

"Clare has always been the same," I said brightly, "and her spontaneity is her charm."

"I didn't like leaving her this morning. But I've got an appointment for lunch and I couldn't break it, even for Clare, because it happens to be with Dr. Kennedy and I couldn't afford to turn it down. I think—though it's not definite as yet—that I stand a chance of becoming his junior partner, and it'd be the chance of a life-time if I land it. I haven't said a word to Clare about it in case the whole thing falls through, but J.W.'s in on the deal because he's a pretty good friend of Dr. Kennedy."

I murmured suitable phrases and for a while we talked about Tony's ambitions and hopes, and it wasn't till we'd almost reached the city that Clare's name cropped up again.

"I'm rather a dull sort of bloke," Tony said with a charming smile that made the statement a distinct lie, "and I never dreamed Clare would look at me. It only shows miracles still happen."

It was nice, I thought sentimentally, that a few people were happy. Joey with his bike; Tony with the prospect of a partnership with Dr. Kennedy and a marriage ceremony with Clare. I asked him whether his family would be coming down for the wedding and he replied vaguely that he supposed they would.

"They're getting on and they hardly ever come to town, but for an occasion like that they'll stir themselves. Mother wouldn't miss it. They haven't met Clare, but I know they'll love her."

"Clare thinks they mightn't approve."

He grinned quickly. "They admire John tremendously and they'll adore Clare. They'll probably tell her she's throwing herself away on me and warn her I'm not good enough. They think I'm quite insane because I refused to go on the land. But believe me, I had enough of country life when I was a child, and I always wanted a career of my own and I stuck out for it. They're reconciled to the fact now, of course, because there was nothing they could do about it when they saw I'd made up my mind. But they think it proves I've no common sense. Dad's got the firm belief that Australia rides on the sheep's back."

I smiled and reached for my hat. "He's not far wrong, judging by the wool prices."

He admitted there was something in that.

"When the family read what happened last night, it'll confirm their opinion of city life." He grinned. "Perhaps I should've settled for sheep after all. Thank God the papers played the whole affair down—McLean's doing, no doubt, with a little pressure from J.W. I must admit I was glad our photos weren't adorning the front page."

I thought of Joey's disappointment at the lack of enterprise on the part of the Press and I laughed.

"Joey was furious because he didn't get a mention. He seemed to think it would give him terrific prestige at school if he was named as a witness."

I expected Tony to laugh, too, but he didn't.

He said anxiously, "What a ghastly experience for a kid—to be mixed up in a case like this. There'll be an inquest, you know, and it'd be shocking if young Joey was called. It could have a marked effect on a sensitive child."

I hadn't thought of that aspect and a quiver of fear shot through me. Then I remembered that Joey was a sensible, normal child, and already the thought of owning a bike had assumed far greater importance in his mind than the sensational events at Coolibah.

I said as much to Tony, and he gave a sigh of relief.

"Thank God. He's a bonzer little kid and he does seem to have his head screwed on the right way. John gets a real kick out of him. I think he would have liked a son himself."

I'd often had the same impression. John was no different from other human species of the male sex, and the most flagrant example of man's egotism is his burning desire for a son to carry on the family name. As if a name matters!

We skirted the park and edged slowly down King Street. The city was bathed in sun and the gloom of yesterday had lifted. The footpaths were crowded with gaily clad women rushing to make their last-minute purchases for the week-end. A policeman in a sun-helmet was sorting out the traffic, waving the cars on briskly; trams were rumbling by with a thunderous roar that sounded as if every nut and bolt were about to fall apart; the whole town seemed to be on the move, caught up in a mad whirl of feverish activity.

Tony parked the car right outside the office and sprang out to help me alight. I thanked him for the lift and turned to walk up the big steps, when he put his hand on my arm and held me back.

"Gilly," he said abruptly, "who is Simon Ashton?"

If he'd asked me who Billy Hughes was, I couldn't have been more astonished.

"You know as much about him as I do." People were pushing past us as we stood blocking the middle of the pavement. "Why do you ask?"

He shrugged. "Clare hasn't been herself since that bloke arrived. I've got a feeling you don't like him either," he added with surprising insight. "What's wrong with him?"

It occurred to me that Clare could probably give him the answer. I certainly couldn't.

"He seems quite nice," I answered noncommittally.

Tony was looking thoughtful. "He's a bird of ill omen if you ask me. He no sooner sets foot in the place than a girl gets killed and the police start swarming round us like bees."

"You can hardly blame Simon for that."

"I suppose not." He gave me a deliciously confidential smile. "But between you and me, darling, he does give me rather a pain in the neck."

He let go my arm and turned towards the car. "Be seeing you."

I nodded and walked into the big *Sydney Daily Times* building, where the clock greeted me with the reminder that I'd have to hurry if my notes on the Welch party were to make the early afternoon edition.

As I climbed the stairs to my own little den I marvelled how easily things fell into Clare Welch's lap. She'd been born under a lucky star. She'd even managed to filch Tony Cambray from the grasp of a score of girls who would have given their eyeteeth to be wearing her big diamond engagement ring.

I've never been more popular than I was at the office that morning. Members of the staff who normally never bothered to say more than a good-natured or grumpy 'Lo, Gilly', according to their mood, suddenly discovered a yen for my company, and my room developed an attraction which was only rivalled by the pub round the corner. Alma, my assistant, treated me with a rather embarrassing deference.

The morning passed quickly and at one o'clock I packed up for the day and wandered into the street in search of lunch.

CHAPTER IX

I HAD no set intention of revisiting the café where I'd met Lisa, but when I found myself standing in front of it I suddenly decided to go in. Perhaps my subconscious urged me to try and form a reconstruction of the scene in the hope that I'd be able to pull forgotten details from the atmosphere. But if so, my subconscious was disappointed.

At the table by the window, where I'd sat yesterday, a middle-aged woman occupied Lisa's chair and munched unconcernedly, little knowing that she'd taken over the seat of the dead.

Nausea swamped me and I pushed my plate away hurriedly. It had been a mistake to come back again, and I'd gained nothing from it—not even a glimmer or flicker of what lay behind Lisa's odd little smile or her wild rush for the door. It would have been much more sensible to have gone home and opened a tin. And at home there might be news. Already McLean might have rounded up the murderer.

I was glad to get out of the café into the street, and now my one thought was to reach home quickly. But all the taxis appeared to be full and ignored my pleading gestures.

I stepped on to the road in mad defiance of the traffic swooping down on me, and raised my hand to a likely-looking cab, but before I could attract the driver's attention a voice called from the pavement.

"Gilly! What do you think you're doing? Committing suicide?"

I spun round. Clare and Finch were standing watching with evident enjoyment.

"I'm trying to get a taxi," I said with dignity.

Clare's laugh bubbled, and Finch was grinning broadly.

"Darling, you look so sweet and forlorn. We're just off to collect the car. Come on."

He walked between Clare and myself and told me I lacked

technique when it came to hailing cabs and what I needed was a good, strong whistle.

"I thought you were going swimming," I said to Clare, but she only smiled and replied that she'd changed her mind.

"Finch arrived after you'd left and he wanted to go shopping, so I decided to come too. It seemed a better idea than spending the morning with dear Miranda. We've had a heavenly time and bought masses of things we don't want. I always go on a buying spree when my morale's sinking. It's the perfect remedy."

One remedy for the rich and one for the poor. Clare was generous and impulsive but she only knew life as she lived it. She hadn't a clue how the rest of the world eked out an existence.

"Miranda was furious when Finch and I dashed off, because she wanted to embark on a long boring discussion about furniture and paint. Heaven alone knows why she wants to alter Coolibah. And Dad simply gives in to her at every turn, so long as she leaves his study as it is. He may be as wise as an owl in some ways, but where Miranda's concerned he's about as silly as a magpie."

Finch began to laugh.

Suddenly she laughed too, and so did I. "I'm sorry, Finch," she said. "I forgot you were to do the renovations to Coolibah. Don't think I'm underrating your talents. The trouble with me is that I say what I think, and then it lands me in a mess."

"Don't worry about my feelings." Finch was amused. "I've no intention of tackling a face-lift for the poor old house and I've told Miranda so, but she won't believe me. I've recommended her to get in touch with Miles Deering—it's more in his line than mine. But anyway, darling, you shouldn't criticize J.W., because you're rather like him, you know. You'll spoil Tony just the way he does Miranda."

He unlocked the car door and came round to the other side to help us in.

"Let me drive." Clare gazed at him pleadingly. "We'll get home much quicker that way."

She slid into the driver's seat and started up the car with a sudden, urgent desire to get away. I was in the middle with Finch's arm resting lightly on the back of the seat behind me. Clare threw me a glance of approval as she shoved in the clutch and I could tell she still had hopes of cementing my friendship with Finch into something more romantic.

"Gilly looks sweet, doesn't she?" she remarked.

I always dislike being spoken about as if I were invisible, so I listened in silence as they began a jolly patter about my better—and my worse—points. Finch's arm dropped from the seat to my shoulder and I felt it was time to put a stop to such nonsense, so I announced gaily that Tony would be pacing the floor wondering what had happened to Clare.

She lapsed into silence for a while and drove as if we were making a last-minute dash to catch a 'plane. It was really quite remarkable, I reflected, that Tony had managed to tame anyone as untamable as Clare. She was even beginning to learn the meaning of time.

"Tony's so madly punctual," she said, as if she knew what I'd been thinking.

"Don't worry about him." Finch was enjoying himself. "He and Simon can entertain each other until you arrive." He slid her a sly glance.

"Simon?" There was a faint catch to her voice. "I don't think he and Tony——" She broke off and paused. "I hope Tony waits for me. He's quite liable to drive back to his flat if he finds I'm not home."

And if so, she'd rush in and bring him, breathlessly apologetic, and Tony would growl a little to assert his authority, and soon they'd be enjoying a whale of a row, followed by a glorious reconciliation. It was the pattern Clare's affairs always followed—unless she'd altered more than I'd realized during the past few months. Her life had been made up of a series of enjoyable crises which assumed immense proportions in her own mind while they lasted.

"I can't believe last night was real," she said, quite out of the blue and catching me by surprise. I'd almost succeeded in forgetting about it for a moment. "Don't you feel the same, Gilly? Anyway, I've made up my mind not to think about it any more."

It was one crisis which offered no emotional pleasure. It was a steady black cloud without a silver lining.

"I approve of your philosophy," Finch said dryly, "but you won't find it easy to carry out. McLean will see to that."

"Oh no! You don't think he'll be worrying us again today? Why should he? We told him all we knew last night."

Finch shrugged and said nothing.

"I'm terribly sorry for the girl, but after all, we didn't know her. The shock of seeing her . . . like that . . . was simply ghastly, but I'd be a hypocrite if I sat down and wept for her. I guess Miranda's right. She sometimes is. Life has to go on just the same."

Finch stared at the road ahead. "Darling, can't you realize you're mixed up in it whether you like it or not?"

"What do you mean?"

"Only," he replied with the vestige of a sigh, "that McLean thinks one of us did it."

She concentrated on overtaking a Vauxhall. Her hair was flying in the breeze. She was like a streamlined gypsy—a gypsy who was running away from a pursuer who threatened to gain on her unless she went faster, faster. The speedo leaped alarmingly.

"You would say that, Finch. When I'd succeeded in forgetting it."

"I'm sorry, Clare."

We swept past the Mayfair Hotel. "It doesn't matter. I've got to face it some time, I suppose. But it's so horrible, so unbelievable, so untrue."

Finch opened his mouth and then shut it again as though he didn't want to be the one to shatter her illusions.

Then he smiled. "If you keep on driving like this, McLean will have a few more deaths to investigate."

She slowed down and laughed. "I love this car of yours. I never can resist treading on the juice."

It was a lovely car, I thought. And though for a fleeting second I wished I were riding in Barney's battered little M.G., I had to admit there was something about a Jaguar that appealed to every girl. Finch had chosen a low-slung sporty job painted cream. It was as conspicuous and as attractive as his small, smart cottage. It reflected his taste and his character.

"I'd like to drive and drive and never come back," Clare was saying.

Finch leaned across so that his cheek brushed mine. "Why run away, darling?" he asked her softly. "It doesn't do any good in the end."

"I don't know what you're talking about." There was the same hint of breathlessness—of fear—that I'd heard in her voice last night.

"I think you do, though." Finch's mouth curved slightly in a crooked smile. "You're frightened of yourself, aren't you? But running away wouldn't help and you'd regret it, bitterly. You've never been a coward. You're just a dope, darling, that's all. Somewhere in that scatterbrain you've got some good common sense, but you've never learnt to draw on it, and it's time you did. Don't try and finesse. Come out in the open."

It was the oddest speech I'd ever heard him make and I didn't understand a word of it. I don't think for a minute that I was meant to. He was talking straight at Clare and I saw her hand tighten round the steering wheel as she swung the car off the main road into Cottrill Street.

"Remember I'm a simple gal at heart and I can't fathom high-flown phrases."

"You're far from simple," Finch told her. "Wake up to yourself."

We fairly flew up the steep hill and stopped with a jerk outside my flat.

"I wonder why I like you, Finch, when you're so beastly to me." She pulled a face at him.

"It's my fatal fascination." His smile was gently mocking. "Gilly's the only female who can resist me, and she finds me intolerably dull. I don't even make her angry."

He opened the door and got out.

Clare leaned across the front seat. "Why don't you come straight over to Coolibah now? And then later we can all go swimming."

"I want to change," I told her truthfully, as Finch helped

me out of the car. "Besides, I've promised to collect Joey. I'll see you in an hour."

She blinked at me and I thought she was about to say something, but she changed her mind and started up the engine almost before Finch had time to climb in and slam the door.

He must be fond of Clare, I reflected, to allow her to drive his car. It was a comparatively new and very precious possession and the care and attention he lavished on it would have done credit to a Rolls. I'd never seen anyone else at the wheel but Finch himself—until today.

As I came through the swinging doors of the lobby, Joey bounded at me like an exuberant puppy and nearly knocked me over.

"I thought you were never coming home. Mum's broken the news to Dad about the bike and it's all right. I can really and truly have it. And Dad reckons there won't be much wrong with it that we can't get fixed. He knows a bloke at work who's a wizard mechanic and he's going to get him to give it the once-over. But I'll try it out this afternoon and see how she goes. I can still have it, can't I?"

I hastened to assure him that the whole matter was well in hand.

"Can we fetch it now? I'm ready."

"But I'm not. I want to change."

He studied me earnestly. "You look all right. Honest. What d'you need to change for? Gosh, you're as bad as Mum."

But even to satisfy Joey's impatience, I had no intention of swimming in my new shantung. And if this weather continued a swim would definitely be in the offing.

"I'll pick you up in half an hour."

Dawn strolled through the open doorway.

"He's been waiting hours for you to come back. This bike is driving us all mad, but at least it's made a nice change in the conversation after a couple of days of Test scores. . . . How're you feeling, darling? I adore your suit."

We nattered happily for a minute or two about the advantages and disadvantages of shantung while Joey stood on one foot and then on the other. At last he could bear it no longer, and rushed inside to tell Blue how impossible and unreasonable women were.

"By the way, Tony was here looking for Clare," Dawn said. "He's rather a dear. He was sweet to Joey and listened patiently to a long screed about cricket. You know what Joey's like. He thinks everyone ought to know about Harvey's wonderful catch, and about Miller's averages, and he really went to town on it, and Tony was an utter lamb and let him talk his head off."

I couldn't help smiling as I thought of Tony's fears that Joey might be a neurotic, sensitive child. I was glad he'd had the opportunity to find out for himself that a small thing like murder—nice and sensational while it lasted—had made no permanent impression on Joey's life. Not when there were such subjects as bikes and Tests to occupy his mind.

"If you're nervous, Gilly, come down and sit with us tonight," Dawn suggested. "I wonder if Mac's found out any more about your thief."

An icy trickle ran down my spine.

"I don't know."

"Oh well, I wouldn't worry. Mac says it's unlikely the fellow would come again. Burglars never do, you know. They cover new ground, not the old. But Mac's quite sure the whole incident ties up in some way with the murder last night. It's horrible, Gilly, isn't it? And I don't understand it."

I got into the lift hastily, because I didn't want to stay and discuss it—even with Dawn. I felt Clare's theory of running away had a lot to recommend it. As I passed the Simpsons' flat I wished wholeheartedly that its owners hadn't decided to visit their daughter in Brisbane. There is something rather eerie about empty, silent rooms that are normally filled with life.

I stood in my own lounge and listened, suddenly conscious of the silence below me, and I longed for the small sounds that told me Mrs. Simpson was running the tap in the kitchen or bullying her husband into mending the broken rocking-chair. The incessant tap-tap of the hammer would have been sweeter music to me, right then, that any Brahms lullaby.

E

I took off my shantung and put on a full-skirted sun-frock with a tiny matching bolero, and tried out a coral shade of lipstick. I tried to keep my mind away from the fact that Mac thought my burglary tied up with murder, but my thoughts for once were beyond my control and kept seeking a reason for an unknown hand to wait, with deadly intent, just inside my door. A hand which had touched mine.

My face in the mirror was suddenly too pale against my vivid mouth, and the eyes which stared at me were frightened. What had my burglar hoped to find? Something of Lisa's? Something that would point the finger irrevocably at her murderer?

Simon had announced quite openly that I'd picked up an object Lisa had left behind in her haste. But what did my unknown thief think it was? A letter? A document of some sort? Obviously he hadn't suspected the truth, because Lisa's little cross had been sitting on the mantel where anyone could find it at a glance. He'd expected something else, but before he could really get down to a thorough search I'd returned and interrupted him.

But none of the people at Coolibah would behave like that. And yet, my reason told me, they were the only beings in the whole wide world who knew that an article of Lisa's was in my possession. If McLean was right—if my intruder and a murderer were one and the same person—that meant he was not merely an acquaintance, but a friend. Unless it was Simon. And if I could have found any reasonable motive for him to murder Lisa, I would have pounced on Simon as my favourite suspect.

Surely, though, if he'd known her he would have spoken to her in the café. Or she would have spoken to him. Reluctantly I had to concede that he'd been telling the truth when he said they were strangers to each other. He could have no reason for wanting her out of the way. My unruly thoughts went round and round, monotonously, always ending with the query—What had my thief expected to find? It was unanswerable.

Later I learned that McLean had asked himself the same question, but, unlike me, he at least had found an answer—an answer so wild and fantastic that he doubted whether it would hold water. It was his first faint suspicion of the truth that lay behind Lisa's death, and, oddly enough, it was her little gold cross that gave him the lead to her murderer.

I pulled the curtains across the bedroom windows to keep the room cool and walked back into the lounge. I was still lingering on the possibilities of Simon being a criminal, when the door-bell gave a loud insistent peal that made me jump with fright.

Finch was standing on the threshold.

"I've been trying to see you on your own all day." He took my hand in his and closed the door behind us.

I remembered Mac's injunction not to be alone with anyone from Coolibah. But surely that didn't include Finch, who'd been in his own house when Lisa was killed.

Nevertheless I said, "Excuse me a second. I must ring Dawn and tell her I'll be down in a few moments. I promised to take Joey over to Coolibah to collect his bike some time today."

Finch gave the sort of smile that made me feel a heel and a fool as I picked up the 'phone and told Dawn that I'd been delayed but to expect me shortly, adding self-consciously, "Finch has just called."

She didn't sound at all surprised to hear from me, and I gathered Mac had already spoken a few words in her ear on the same lines that he'd delivered to me.

"I'm pleased you're using your head," was all she said, and hung up.

I turned to Finch. He was watching me with a small, hurt smile.

"You're wise, of course, not to trust anyone," he said evenly, "and it's rather clever of you to let Dawn know who's with you."

He was well aware that I could never think up a plan like that, because he said curiously, and just a little mockingly, "I wonder who suggested the idea. It's not your own, I'll bet."

I was flustered that he'd seen through my manœuvres so easily, and found myself apologizing.

"Don't be a goat, darling. You're perfectly right. Only

I'm shattered to think you don't trust me, of all people." He grinned wickedly. "I admit I do have a few ulterior motives where you're concerned, but they don't include murder—or theft. They're rather delicious but they need your co-operation and I don't think you'd give it. Oh well, it's nice to dream." He became serious. "I tried to see you this morning but Dawn was like a watchdog at the front door and I never even got as far as the stairs. She said you must have sleep and she wasn't going to allow a soul to disturb you! I'd been nearly frantic with worry about you, because I knew someone had broken in here last night and I was terrified the bloke might try again. Darling, you haven't any idea who it was? You didn't see his face or his coat or anything that migh⁺ help to identify him?"

I shook my head.

Did he relax, or did I only imagine it?

"Just a cat thief," he shrugged. "With all the odd bods milling around downstairs he'd have plenty of opportunity to slip up here unnoticed. But wasn't it strange he should pick on last night? There are 365 perfectly good evenings to choose from, yet he lands up bang on top of a murder. They say everything always happens at once. From now on I'll believe it. Anyway you're not hurt, darling, and that's all that matters."

But if I'd stepped inside the door, I probably wouldn't be sitting here now, I thought nervously. It wasn't a nice theory to dwell on, so I said quickly, "The Inspector thinks my robbery and the murder are tied up together some way."

"McLean said that?" His eyes were suddenly shrewd and sharp. "I wasn't going to mention it, but the same notion entered my sluggish brain. If only I knew what the fellow expected to find. Suppose you let me into the secret and tell me?"

He leaned back and gave me his most charming smile. It was a smile that told me he admired and liked me, that he wanted to help me. It somehow managed to turn our conversation into a cosy *tête-à-tête* between two people who were on the brink of falling in love.

Finch, I thought wryly, was rather good at conveying

128

impressions like that. He'd been leading women up the garden path all his life, probably from the very first moment when he discovered that his bony face and queer arched brows were the answer to a maiden's prayer. And he'd developed a formidable line to match them.

"How do I know what he wanted?" I felt unreasonably cross and didn't want to be badgered with questions I couldn't answer. "I don't want to talk about it."

He came and sat on the arm of my chair and looked down at me with a nice mixture of tenderness and concern.

"I know you don't, darling. That's what makes me think perhaps you're shielding someone. Try and get it into your addled little pate that loyalties cease to exist—even among friends—when there's a murderer on the loose. You know as well as I do that Lisa's murderer comes from Coolibah! Oh, I don't exclude myself. My front porch is only a stone's-throw from the driveway and I could have hopped across the lawn and said, 'Madam, will you come into Mr. Welch's sitting-room because I want to kill you?' I know the front door is always open in the daytime, because I've been in and out dozens of times. Unfortunately, I can't think up any motive for myself, and whoever killed the poor girl must have had a desperate reason for wanting her out of the way."

The sun slipped behind a cloud and the room became darker. I looked at Finch's face, all angles and shadows, and had the horrible feeling that I really knew very little about him.

"John's quite sure a stranger killed Lisa." There was an unmistakable note of fear in my voice. I wanted John to be right, yet I was afraid he was wrong.

"John's no fool. He knows perfectly well the finger of suspicion points straight to his own household. But he won't admit it, at least not openly. He's fighting to keep the inner circle intact, but it's a losing battle. We'll all be raked through the mud before this is through. Poor John. He'd sell his soul to save Miranda."

I gazed at him in quickening alarm.

"You're not suggesting Miranda . . ."

He didn't let me finish. "Where money's concerned Miranda would be capable of most things."

"But I thought you liked her. Everyone does."

"Darling, don't be naïve. Everyone likes a beautiful woman, and Miranda's one of the loveliest creatures God ever made. She's also a sweet shrew. She's made the only possible match—she's married for money. And nothing would prise her away from John's fortune, and God help any poor fool who tried."

"She didn't kill Lisa. She wouldn't have the strength."

He looked at me sadly and patiently. "Miranda's tougher than she looks. Ever seen her in the water or on the tennis court? The little brown mouse was tiny, remember, and it wouldn't take much strength to crack her with the poker and then give her a shove down the stairs. And that's what happened. Even Clare could have done it, and she's smaller than Miranda."

I stared at him with growing horror to hear him voicing suspicion of his friends so easily, so calmly. I'd always known there was a ruthless quality behind those thick-lashed eyes, but I'd never seen it in the open before. It was rather shocking.

"Clare couldn't hurt anyone intentionally." I was angry.

"But she's got a bloody awful temper." Suddenly he smiled as if he recalled a memory that amused him. "She never sits down and thinks. She drifts along on wild impulses and ends up in a muddle."

"She's scared of Simon. I'm sure she is." As soon as I'd spoken I wished I'd kept my thoughts to myself. I was doing exactly what Mac had warned me against—talking too much.

Finch grinned amiably. "Clare'll sort things out eventually. Right now she doesn't know where she is, but sooner or later she'll get one of her mad inspirations and she'll see the light. But darling, why on earth are we talking about the Welches? That's not why I came to see you. There's something I want to say——"

I never heard what it was because the 'phone cut right across his words and I crossed to the desk to lift it from its cradle. To my surprise it was Simon. Almost as if he'd sensed we'd been talking about him just a moment ago.

"Gilly? Clare asked me to ring you. Inspector McLean's here and he wants you to come over. I gather there's to be a round-up of suspects." His voice was calmly cheerful. "You wouldn't know where Finch is?"

I looked over at the chair where he was pulling a pipe out of his pocket and stuffing it with tobacco.

"He's here."

"Oh!" It was an expression of polite surprise which I interpreted as mild amusement that any male should voluntarily seek my company. "The Inspector's been trying to locate him. He's included in the round-up too, tell him. I'm sorry to break up your pleasant afternoon like this."

I replied coldly that Finch and I would leave at once. Then it dawned on me that Mac might have further news for us—perhaps good news—so I modified my voice to more friendly tones and asked Simon did he know why the Inspector wanted to see us. I waited anxiously for the reply, but it dashed my hopes.

"He's with John at the moment. He seems to be on the warpath and I imagine he's getting worried because he hasn't made an arrest yet. By the way, Clare told me you had a bad fright after I left you last night. I'm sorry about it. Perhaps you imagined more than actually happened. Let's hope so."

I heard three rings at my door, and I guessed Joey had arrived to hustle me on. I asked Finch to let him in, and turned my attention back to the 'phone. But Simon had nothing further to add to the conversation, so I hung up.

Joey was standing watching me with a pair of startlingly blue, impatient young eyes.

"You don't half take hours to get dressed."

Finch laughed with genuine enjoyment. "You'll get used to women in time."

Joey's shrug indicated that a purely masculine world would have been a much more sensible idea and it was annoying to find life cluttered by a lot of gibbering, stupid females.

However, he grinned at me sympathetically and rather patronizingly, to let me know that he realized I could do nothing about being born into the wrong sex. I'd just have to make the best of it.

Finch put his hand on my arm. "What did Simon want?"

"A message from Inspector McLean. We're to go to Coolibah."

I made it brief for Joey's sake, but I needn't have bothered, because he was walking towards the door with grim determination to brook no further delays.

"McLean can wait a while." Finch's fingers were tight on my arm. "I particularly wanted to speak to you, and I never seem to get the chance."

"Perhaps the Inspector can wait, but Joey can't."

I suddenly wished Finch would release his hold. "Anyway, I don't want to talk about last night."

He sighed and dropped his hand. "It's not last night I'm concerned about. It's the future."

I followed Joey on to the landing and Finch trailed reluctantly after us, looking sulky.

"I'm sorry if you find my presence a nuisance. I shouldn't have come. I should curb my emotions." His face was like an iceberg.

"Don't be silly," and I grabbed his hand and led him to the stairs, wondering what had got into him today. He seemed awfully touchy and it wasn't like him to take the huff easily.

He ignored me as we trundled past the Simpsons' flat down to the entrance hall, and engaged Joey in a conversation about the virtues of Jaguars.

Blue was leaning on the white gate outside, obviously waiting for us.

"I thought I'd better come along too," he said sheepishly. "Got to thank Mr. Welch and all that. It's darn decent of him. You don't think, Gilly, that I should offer to pay something? I don't like charity in any form."

I wanted to shake him. What did an old bike matter to John Welch? He could afford to give away a dozen if he wanted to.

"John's only being neighbourly," I explained gently, "and you mustn't dream of offering to pay. He'd be upset."

Blue gave a low growl and opened the gate for me.

The sunny morning had given way to a dull afternoon with banks of cloud piling across the sky, and the air was warm and sticky again, as if thunder was not far away. It would come later, I thought, and with it great heavy drops of rain crashing like crystal against the roof-tops and iron gutterings.

Joey led the way across the street and dominated the conversation with an analytical but distinctly biased account of Australia's batsmen. The Poms would never get them out, it appeared, and already that morning Miller had stunned the opposition by belting Bedser all over the ground. Finch and Blue agreed, smugly, that England might be capable of licking the South Africans but had Buckley's chance of beating the Australian eleven. In the face of such confidence I began to wish, rather treacherously, that the game would end in a spectacular victory for Hutton and Co. I also began to wish the pastime of cricket had never been invented.

Sport! I thought, wearily. Eternal sport! The most important side of life to the average Australian. Nothing, not even murder, could oust the all-absorbing interest in who would win the Test.

The talk flowed over my head and required no help from me, so I studied the big rambling house and let my mind drift to Clare and John and Miranda. It was incredible that this sprawling, peaceful home had been the scene of violent and horrible action. It was more incredible still to think that the occupants themselves could be mixed up in anything as sordid and primitive as murder.

As we drew nearer I saw that Clare was stretched out in a deck-chair, with Tony sitting on the edge of the verandah chewing, unhygienically, at a piece of grass.

They both got up when we tramped towards them and Clare said quickly, "Hi there! Hullo, Joey, come to inspect the ancient buggy? Simon wheeled it out for you and we find it's hanging together all right."

Blue began to say awkwardly, "It's jolly decent of you———"

She cut him off. "Forget it. Let's have a look at the old warrior."

Tony brushed the grass off his grey slacks. "Like me to show you how to ride? I was hot stuff on a bike in my early days. My brother used to double-dink me round the station until I got one of my own, and then I left him way behind. I could beat him no hands every time."

I laughed at the idea of Tony on a bike. Somehow one associated him with Bentleys and expensive yachts and thoroughbred horses—but not with bikes. He'd progressed a long way since his early days and all that remained of his harum-scarum youth was his wicked, charming grin. I hoped Joey would take him at his word and demand a demonstration, but he was much too interested in his new toy to be impressed by Tony's boasts.

It was leaning drunkenly against the front steps—a classy bright red model with the paint chipped off here and there.

Clare sidled over to where I stood watching Joey as he ran loving fingers over the handlebars and seat.

"Inspector McLean arrived after lunch, and he and Dad have been closeted in the study for ages. He wouldn't say a word about why he'd come. He said he wanted to wait till you and Finch arrived."

This morning she'd seemed her usual gay self, but now, as she glanced at me, I saw that her poise was outward only. There was fear—stark fear—in her round brown eyes.

I could only tell her that we must wait and see what was on the Inspector's mind. I couldn't read it any more than she could.

She turned away and joined in the lively comments surrounding Joey and his bike. Whatever her thoughts, she had them well under control, and when Joey swung his head round to look at her and say, "Gee, Clare. It's a beaut. Thanks a lot!" she answered him with a quick elfin smile, with not a hint of any emotion other than pleasure and amusement on her face.

The next few minutes were entirely Joey's.

"Betcha in two weeks I'll be riding no hands. I can already on Bill Hope's bike, but his is only a small affair," Joey said, with a touch of contempt for Bill's inferior job.

"No trick riding or you'll come a cropper. I came a beauty once, landed fair on my tail and it put me out of action for a whole week." Finch, I thought, must have been a formidable small boy. One of those rather beautiful children who look like delicate angels and have the constitution of an ox. I watched him as he gave Joey a leg-up on to the seat, and wondered whether his eyes had always been cynical and worldly-wise, even as a child.

Joey circled experimentally round the lawn, but his legs couldn't quite reach the pedals, so he abandoned all attempts at using the seat, and crouched over the handlebars with his sturdy bottom waving from side to side in rhythmic motion.

We roared with laughter. The bike was so big, and Joey so small, that his queer upright position made cycling look like hard work. His shirt had worked loose from his khaki shorts and flapped behind him like a sheet hanging out to dry. After the tension of the past few hours it was a refreshing sight and we enjoyed it to the full, finding it perhaps funnier than it really was. Joey was grinning from ear to ear and showing off a bit by waving one hand as he came up the drive towards the steps again.

Blue put out an arm and grabbed the bike, stopping it as effortlessly as if it were a toy train.

"Cut it out!" Joey was indignant. "I'm just getting the feel of it."

"Give us a go." Blue was like a big kid himself. "I haven't ridden one of these things for years."

Joey got off, reluctantly, and Blue heaved himself onto the seat.

The bike which had seemed too big for Joey was absurdly small beneath Blue's great frame, and we hooted and jeered at him. We were really letting our heads go. It was the first genuine laughter we'd had for hours.

And with Blue still perched, waiting to make a flying start, the smiles on our faces faded. Inspector McLean had stepped through the front door and was standing quietly watching us, and suddenly the scene was no longer funny but rather silly, and the whole gruesome reason for my presence at Coolibah came flying back to me. I wasn't here for lighthearted entertainment, I was here because an inspector of police wished to question all of us in connection with murder.

Joey and Blue were the only two who weren't affected by the sudden intrusion of the law, but even Blue got off the bike and stood with his hand resting on the handle, holding it upright.

"I hope I'm not interrupting," McLean grinned at Blue, their eyes meeting in mutual friendship and understanding that left the rest of us out in the cold. "No time for fun and games in my job."

Blue started to speak, and I'm sure he was about to ask Mac to drop in for a beer later, but then he left it unsaid, and turned to Joey instead.

"We'd better beat it."

"You'll stay and have tea? Or a drink?" Clare's face besought him not to go yet, as though she didn't want to face the unpleasant fact that the interlude of laughter was over.

"Thanks, Clare. But we'd better push, I think. Dawn'll have the kettle on by now. Joey can see Mr. Welch later and thank him for the bike."

"Oh, for God's sake! Don't bother about that." She walked up the big steps towards the front door and Tony leaped on to the verandah and put his arm through hers. But she barely seemed aware of him. She looked strangely tired, as if she'd just discovered life wasn't worth all the energy and emotion she put into it.

"Hang on, Blue. I want to speak to Joey for a second."

Even Clare stopped and stared at Mac.

"I know I asked you this morning whether you'd seen anyone hanging round here yesterday." He was speaking quietly, and had moved over to Joey's side, but we forgot our manners and listened intently, determined to catch every word. "I know you would have noticed a stranger. But did you see any of the tradesmen come in? Or the postman?"

Joey's eyes lit up with delight at being the centre of interest.

"No," he answered importantly. "And anyway, the postman comes much earlier. He'd been by the time I got here."

"Just one more thing. Mr. Martyn says he was watching the drive from his windows. Did you see him? Perhaps he called out to you—after all, it's only a few yards from this side of the lawn." He waved his hand towards Finch's front porch

—a blaze of yellow and dark blue blinds half hidden by trees. "Do you remember seeing Mr. Martyn?"

"You mean Finch?" Joey didn't believe in formality among friends. He only used surnames for those he disliked, or for those whose age demanded some show of respect. "No, I didn't see Finch yesterday. Not at all."

Finch threw him a friendly smile, but I noticed his eyes were wary. "You'll just have to take my word that I was there, Inspector. I actually did see Joey but he was intent on pushing the mower so I didn't disturb him. If I'd known, of course, that I'd shortly be in need of an alibi I would have cooked up a story for you." His words were airy and faintly mocking.

"Sometimes it's clever to have no alibi," Mac replied, hardly glancing at him, and leaning against the wide stone support in a relaxed position. "It's specially clever when no one else has an alibi either."

"I wasn't to know that," Finch said shrewdly. "If I'd been relying on it I might have slipped up badly."

Mac addressed Joey again, as if Finch hadn't spoken.

"You didn't see Mr. Martyn walk across to the house here?"

"Allow me to point out, Inspector, that I could easily have made my way across the lawn unnoticed. See those trees? They make a perfect cover from my door to the hedge and then I merely have to run the gauntlet to reach the verandah, but it's only a few strides, and I tackled much worse than that during the War."

He was going to a lot of trouble to show how he could have entered Coolibah.

"Thanks for the information." Mac was smiling at him now. "I'd thought it out for myself. But I'm always glad of help."

Finch was clever, I thought. He knew Mac had seen how it could be done. He hadn't told him a thing he didn't already know.

"I'll bet I would've seen you," Joey said confidently. "But I didn't see anyone, Mac, just like I told you. Only Clare and the Doc earlier and then that girl looking for Mr. Welch."

There was a horrible stillness.

"Looking for Mr. Welch?" Mac's face was studiously expressionless. "How do you know she wanted Mr. Welch?"

Joey had his hand on the bike, anxious to get away. " 'Cos she asked me if this was his house and I said yes."

I heard Clare draw her breath in sharply.

"Exactly what did she say, Joey?" McLean was holding himself in, showing neither surprise nor excessive interest. "You didn't tell me about this before."

"Didn't I? She just said she was looking for Mr. Welch and I said he lived here, then she buzzed up the path and I forgot about her. And then a bit later Gilly comes along and after that I scooted off."

I was glad Mac ended the conversation and wished Joey good riding and cheerio for now. I couldn't have said a word if I'd tried, and judging by Clare's face, she felt the same.

I watched Blue and Joey pushing the bike along between them and thought how extraordinary that all the time Joey had known more about Lisa's visit than any of us. He'd actually known whom she wanted to see. And we hadn't thought to ask him.

But it was preposterous that there could be any link between John and a pretty, uneducated English girl.

Tony was frowning. "Why, in God's name, would she want to find J.W.?"

Finch shrugged. "Perhaps she was looking for a job. Who knows?"

"Surely she wouldn't track him down to his private address."

Tony opened the door and we filed through into the hall. "We must wait and hear what Mr. Welch has to say." McLean turned to Clare and asked her whether she'd be good enough to find out if Mr. and Mrs. Welch and Mr. Ashton were available.

She hesitated. Her eyes were enormous and filled with a sort of sick dread.

"Yes, of course." She sped down the corridor.

We waited in the little lounge where McLean had questioned us last night. I sank into a chair, thankfully, and

138

watched Mac drape his long figure against the window-frame. Tony stood by the desk, but Finch came and sat beside me with a cheerful grin.

The grin was wiped off, however, when McLean focused his falsely dull eyes on Finch's face and asked, nonchalantly, "Did you see young Joey talking to that girl yesterday?"

"Afraid not. I saw her walk up the driveway but I lost interest in her before she met up with Joey. I happened to be busy. I don't spend all my day gazing at my neighbours—only when I've nothing better to do." He was trying to be flippant —and failing.

"A pity you can't prove you were in your own house all afternoon. It would simplify things. Oh well, I guess I can't scrub your name off the list just yet." Mac smiled disarmingly as if he were doing Finch a personal favour.

John and Miranda provided a diversion by walking into the room. Clare followed with Simon. By the time we'd all settled in chairs, the small lounge was uncomfortably full and airless.

"I'm a busy man, Inspector, and already this affair has taken up far too much of my time." John was irritable and the lines round his mouth and eyes had deepened in the past twenty-four hours. "Of course I'm anxious to help, but I've got a pile of work waiting to be done."

"Poor darling, it's too horrid for you." Miranda's voice was dove-like. She'd dressed for the part in an extravagantly simple white frock with enormous opal ear-rings. The effect, I had to admit, was chic. But her eyes were too sophisticated and knowing for virgin white. "I do hope, Inspector, that you can tell us you've solved the case. I'm sure none of us will sleep properly till we know the criminal's behind bars."

"Even if it turns out to be someone very close to you, Mrs. Welch?"

"Oh, Inspector—you don't still think—surely you realize it's not possible. . . ." Her lovely mouth drooped a little and there was an attractive break in the soft, husky voice.

"I'm afraid it's not only possible but highly probable."

"Oh no!" A small pulse was beating in her white throat. She closed her eyes briefly, yet I had the feeling she wasn't as shocked as she made out.

John put his hand on hers to give her strength. In view of what was coming, I thought it was John who needed strength, not Miranda. She might look fragile with that sleek fair hair and soft pretty skin, but she was tough enough to wander round in the black of night with an automatic in her purse. Then McLean was asking the question we'd been waiting for.

"Why should that girl want to see you yesterday, Mr. Welch?"

John's hand fell from Miranda's. "Me!" It was one short explosive word. "Do you mean she was looking for me? I'm certain, Inspector, I'd never seen her in my life, and I've got a pretty good memory for faces. So what would she want with me?"

"That's what I was hoping you'd tell us."

"I certainly would if I could. This is a complete surprise."

"It was Joey who told us. The girl stopped him and asked if you lived here." Clare was taut as a wire.

"Good God! I really don't know what to say. But does this throw any further light on the case? I can't really see what difference it makes."

Mac shrugged lazily. "Perhaps it doesn't make any difference. If she was looking for you, though, it does rather imply that she knew who you were, or had heard of you."

"A lot of people know me. And if she was carrying that confounded cutting around with her, of course she knew my name."

"But why bother to find out your address and come visiting you without an appointment? Her reason must have been urgent."

"Don't ask me. I get some odd types from time to time, wanting jobs or selling tickets for concerts and charity functions."

"I don't think she was the type to seek a job in an office. If she'd asked for Mrs. Welch, I might have thought she was applying for a household position. But not a business position. And remember she was a stranger here, so it's hardly likely she'd be selling tickets or anything else, for that matter. She was out of work when Miss Amery met her just a few hours before, and there's nothing to indicate she'd become a door-to-door canvasser in the meantime. She had no list of names and addresses. No letters. Not even her own name. The only bit of paper she carried was an article about you, Mr. Welch."

"Well, if you can make anything of that you're a better man than I am." John didn't seem worried, not the least bit put out. "Perhaps you know more about it than I do. After all, it's your job to find these things out, not mine. Perhaps you can tell me why she wanted to see me."

"There's one obvious theory. Blackmail."

John threw back his head and laughed. "Luckily my conscience is clear. No one has ever tried to blackmail me in my life."

"There's always a first time."

I couldn't stand it any longer, and I began my parrot cry that Lisa hadn't been the nasty, slimy specimen they kept trying to make her. I wondered how long I'd have to go on repeating it before it sank in.

I wasn't prepared for McLean to turn on me fiercely.

There was a chilly gleam in his eye. "Miss Amery, will you please keep out of this?"

I subsided before I'd finished having my say.

Oddly enough, John agreed with the Inspector. "He's quite right, Gilly dear. Leave things alone. Let him find out the truth for himself."

I retreated in front of the battery, but I did think it strange that John, too, should turn against me.

Then it struck me! John actually welcomed suspicion. He knew that McLean was concentrating on the family circle, and if the spotlight fell on him, at least it kept its beam away from Miranda. The old fool, I thought! The chivalrous, darling old fool! Nutty about a blonde siren half his own age. But I kept quiet after that.

In any case, I didn't have a chance to speak, because McLean was holding the floor and what he was saying made my ears flap. Having warned me about the dangers of talking too much, he was now proceeding to go into lengthy details about my burglary last night! They all listened politely as if they were hearing the story for the first time.

I studied the faces in the room and thought how absurd it was to suspect any of them of murder. They were nice, ordinary faces belonging to nice, ordinary people. Tony with his boyish grin; Clare with her quick movements and restless hands; John, calm and confident; Finch with his easy, effortless charm; even Simon looked an average young Englishman in well-cut slacks and sports jacket, and I reminded myself that his long silent stretches were merely the reserve for which the English are so famous, while his uncannily pale eyes probably indicated nothing more sinister than that he needed glasses. As for Miranda—I was certain the secrets behind her heavy-lidded eyes were connected solely with money and the desire to hang on to it. She was no different, and certainly no worse, than dozens of girls I knew who had a natural preference for diamonds and mink, and who could blame them?

If I'd been asked to spot a murderer in that small lounge-room, I would have jumped on Inspector McLean. He had the poker face of a gambler and could hop with the agility of a kangaroo from solemnity to smiles. Just now he was giving us a sample of an earnest detective being perfectly frank with his seven chosen suspects.

"I feel it's only fair to tell you as much as I know myself about Miss Amery's unknown thief. In the first place, I'm convinced he really did exist, although I know," a quick, humorous glance at me, "that Miss Amery has the gift of imagination. But the lift which should have been upstairs was on the ground floor and the telephone was off the hook. I'm sure Miss Amery wouldn't leave it like that. Blue replaced it when he went to search her flat, but he thought it wisest not to mention the matter except to me."

The sly fox!

"The occupants of the first floor are away, which made it nice and easy for Miss Amery's burglar to wait on the dark landing until he saw the coast was clear. A wonderful vantage place. He could see anyone who came up or went down from above. And when Miss Amery passed him in the lift, he probably had the idea she was on her way to join Blue's party, and it gave him the opportunity he'd been waiting for. He nipped up the stairs, found the door open to make things even easier for him, and the light on—a natural precaution for a girl who was unduly nervous after a rather harrowing experience earlier in the night. The open door must have made him realize she didn't intend to stay long at Blue's, so he set to work quickly, taking the 'phone off first so that there would be no interruptions. But before he'd really got down to his job, he heard the lift. He didn't know who it might be. Perhaps it was a stranger who'd call out to Miss Amery and go away when she didn't answer. So he switched out the light and waited just inside the door. The rest you know. If Miss Amery hadn't left the flat and given him the chance he wanted, I think he'd have waited till he thought she was asleep and then would have forced an entry."

"My lock's a Yale," I stated. I had faith in Yale locks.

Mac threw me a glance of sheer pity. "Give me two minutes with any Yale!"

It confirmed my belief that he was more the criminal type than anyone else in the room. The average man doesn't include picking locks in his list of accomplishments.

"The reason for burglary really baffled me," he went on, with nice honesty, "until I saw Miss Amery this morning and she produced the information, known to all of you, that she possessed an article belonging to the dead girl."

"I didn't know." Finch looked at me accusingly as though I had no right to keep secrets from him. I remembered he hadn't been at Coolibah when I'd mentioned Lisa's flight from the café.

"Someone could have told you about it," Mac remarked, drawing Finch neatly back into the group of suspects. "Anyway, when Miss Amery finally got around to telling me about this article, I began to see a bit of light."

"What was it?" Tony asked bluntly.

In the pause that followed I could swear the atmosphere tightened in some queer way, and I could feel a wave of fear sweep through the room, as tangible and real as a quick gust of wind.

Someone was desperately frightened.

Slowly the Inspector drew his hand from his pocket and every eye followed the movement. He savoured the moment, prolonging it unnecessarily while he smiled encouragingly at the watchful faces. They told him nothing. They wore expressions of curiosity and polite interest. Nothing more. Silently he dangled Lisa's cross in the air. It swung innocently from his fingers—a small fragile object at the end of a broken gold chain. The wave of fear receded, and the room became friendly and relaxed.

Finch began to laugh. "Do you think a thief went to so much trouble merely to find a thing like that?"

Miranda was staring at it as if it were a new type of ornament which she found in rather bad taste.

"I don't think for a minute that this is what Miss Amery's visitor expected to find. If she'd mentioned what it was the girl dropped in the café, she would've saved herself that nasty ordeal last night. But she didn't. She simply said it was nothing valuable—which might have meant nothing valuable by Miss Amery's standards but infinitely dangerous to a murderer. So dangerous that he determined to find it, because he thought he knew exactly what it was, and if he were right, that object had to be found at all costs before Miss Amery handed it over to me. He didn't know he was looking for something that wasn't there." He grinned suddenly. "That's about all I've got to tell you. We've made some progress though. You can see that."

"You might see it, but I can't." Clare sounded sceptical. "All we know is that Gilly had a visitor who was looking for what didn't exist. If you know what I mean."

Finch winked at her and said, "Darling, you always put things so clearly."

McLean heaved himself out of his chair with great physical effort. He reminded me of a snake uncoiling lazily in the sun after a full meal.

"I needn't keep you much longer. If you'll write your names on this paper for me, I'll take myself off and let you enjoy the day in peace."

He offered no explanation for the strange request. It was greeted by a sharp, puzzled silence.

"Good lord, whatever for?" Clare exploded. "Surely you know our names by now."

He handed her a pen and the sheet of paper with a winning smile. "I'm sure you won't mind humouring me for once. We police have our odd whims."

She shrugged and scrawled 'Clare Bentley Welch' across the top of the page. 'Bentley' had been her mother's maiden name. She passed it over to John, who signed as he always did 'J. A. Welch'.

McLean said apologetically, "Your full names, please, Mr. Welch."

John raised his eyebrows, but did as he was asked. 'John Arthur Welch.'

I couldn't help a smile of pure pleasure when I saw Miranda reluctantly adding 'Agnes' to her signature. I'm sure she wrote it with an involuntary shudder.

My writing was all angles and strokes after her fat firm backhand.

"What's the meaning of this little game?" Finch was idly amused. "I like to think you're a handwriting expert. The Press would be interested to know that a leading member of the C.I.D. solves his most difficult cases by the novel method of graphology. Graphology is the correct term, isn't it?"

But the Inspector was unmoved by Finch's gibes. He was busy watching Simon's neat, legible 'Simon Marcus Ashton'.

"Don't you think, Inspector, that we're entitled to know why you want specimens of our writing?" Miranda implored, pitching her voice attractively low. "You've told us so very little about the case. You haven't even told us why Gilly's flat was robbed."

Mac shrugged indolently. "I've told you as much as I know. You can guess, just as I can, what Miss Amery was supposed to have picked up in the café."

"Jewellery, I suppose." Miranda's gaze was almost reverent as she followed a new, exciting chain of thought. "She must have possessed a fabulous ring or necklace, probably handed down to her from her mother and her mother's mother. . . ."

"No." John shook his head. "Not a girl like that. More probably it was a letter of some sort. And that accounts for the Inspector's interest in our writing."

"If there was a letter I didn't find it." McLean squashed the theory.

Finch took the piece of paper from Tony and studied our signatures carefully. He seemed to be in no hurry to sign.

"Your writing is quite unexpected for a doctor," he told Tony, with a broad grin. " 'Anthony Jonathan Cambray.' Usually when a doctor signs a prescription it looks like a map of Australia, and God knows how the poor chemists ever decipher it."

McLean was standing over him, waiting. But Finch was determined to dawdle.

"I have a natural reluctance to put my name to paper unless I know what it's for. I'm rather cautious—I've been caught once or twice in my youth and I learned the hard way that a signature carelessly given seldom profits the one who signs."

He produced his own pen, however, and began writing 'Finchley Martyn' in bold, firm letters.

"What sporting parents you people have." He held the paper with his name at the bottom of the list, and surveyed it as if it were a painting. "My poor old folks ran out of imagination. They could only think up one name for me. I always think it's a pity not to give children a wide choice to select from when they grow older."

He handed the paper to McLean with a flourish. McLean didn't even look at it. He was staring at Finch, and for a second he put me in mind of a lean, hungry crow about to descend on a carcase. Then he smiled in a rather fatherly fashion and handed the paper back to Finch.

"I'd be glad, Mr. Martyn, if you'd write your real name."

We were all watching Finch now, with eager, puzzled eyes.

"What on earth do you mean?" Clare cried resentfully. "Of course his name is Finch Martyn. We all know that."

McLean took no notice of her.

"Have you any objection, Mr. Martyn?" He was very polite, very smooth.

"I assure you I've written my name." Finch met his gaze squarely.

146

"Then I must ask you to put down the name you were born with."

Suddenly Finch shrugged. "Very well, Inspector. If you must delve into my past history."

We craned our necks with unmannerly curiosity as he wrote the unexpected words 'Bill Brown'.

I was filled with a wild desire to laugh, and only the thought of hurting his feelings stopped me. 'Bill Brown' conjured up a good hearty type with simple tastes. No doubt it could have suited thousands of men, but Finch wasn't one of them.

"Darling, it's a sweet name. Why ever are you ashamed of it?" Clare moved beside him and perched on the arm of his chair, tucking her hand in his.

He glanced up at her quickly, and I knew he was touched by her words. Suddenly he laughed with genuine amusement.

"It's not a question of being ashamed. It simply seemed the wrong name for an interior decorator. Mrs. Willys-Fyffe and Mrs. Hamilton are far more impressed with a fancy name like Finchley Martyn than by plain Bill Brown. Bill, they think, will give them suburban furniture and good solid oak, but Finchley is likely to dream up something as ornamental as his name. You know what women are! It simply amounts to the difference between Bill Brown designing the commonplace and Finchley Martyn designing the extraordinary. So now they get Bill's ideas wrapped up in a fancy name and they love it. Houses have always been my passion and even when I was quite young I used to see badly arranged rooms, and my fingers would itch to start pulling the furniture around, and instead of listening to the conversation I'd find I was planning larger windows and tinted walls to make the place seem brighter. I knew then exactly how I wanted to spend my life, and as I grew older I realized my field lay among women with plenty of money and no taste. And they're the types who distrust a good plain name because it reminds them too clearly of their own stock and background. So I took my mother's name—by deed poll—and began to hack out a career as Finchley Martyn."

John smiled at him, shaking his head. "If a man's good in

his own profession nothing'll hold him back. Certainly not a name." He was vaguely disapproving.

"But you don't deal with women," Finch explained, "and the name of Welch had quite a legend behind it before you came on the scene. It was well established. And you don't know how stupid my best clients are—they've got to be or they'd have no use for me. A woman with money and taste doesn't need my services because she's got plenty of ideas of her own, and I'm not interested in carrying out other people's schemes. I like a free hand. And the poor dears who consult me have enough money to pay through the nose for what they haven't got—taste. A man can make his pile and buy the little woman sables and rubies, but she'll never hit the top unless she forgets she once came from a four-roomed house in a working-class suburb. I give her the right setting, and she has the satisfaction of hearing her home labelled as 'artistic' and 'elegant' and soon she finds her parties are acceptable to the right people and everyone's forgotten she was once poor little Mollie Jones with not a brain in her head. She's arrived. All she has to do from now on is to keep her friends in food and drink and hide her husband away in case he picks his nose in public or forgets his grammar. And even if he's bewildered by it all, he soon learns to restrict his conversation to a few well-chosen swear words which will earn him a reputation for wit. Have you ever noticed how many silent husbands there are in any social circle? Silence is golden compared with a dropped 'h'."

John looked shocked, but Clare and I both began to laugh with sheer delight.

"Is Australia really like that?" Simon was amused, but puzzled.

"Only Sydney," Finch told him slyly, having originally hailed from Melbourne.

"I still can't see what's wrong with 'Brown'," Tony said stolidly.

Finch sighed. "You weren't born with it. Besides, it wouldn't matter in your profession. It would merely inspire confidence."

"There've been a lot of famous men with common

148

names." Tony seemed awfully dense and humourless. "There's Freddie Brown . . ."

Finch blinked and then said, "Oh! You mean the cricketer. Your sporting instincts are more highly developed than your artistic ones, Tony. Anyway . . . what the hell?"

I'd been enjoying myself listening to Finch. I'd even forgotten Inspector McLean was with us until he said, "Let's get back to the name of Brown. It's a fairly common name. But it's strange that the girl who was murdered here last night was called Elizabeth Brown."

Our laughter and smiles stopped with horrified abruptness. It wasn't funny any more that Finch had been born Bill Brown. It was rather terrible. It had implications. No one spoke. Then Clare gave a queer, high-pitched laugh which sounded very loud in the small quiet room. It broke off as abruptly as it began.

"I'm sorry. But it's so silly. Such an anticlimax. She should have turned out to be a Russian or a Pole or a disinherited member of aristocracy. But not Elizabeth Brown."

Miranda lifted her thick black lashes and fixed her eyes reproachfully on Finch. He looked at her, then looked away.

"You never told us your real name," she said.

"Why should I?" He shrugged.

McLean leaned against the little table and held the list of names in front of him. "You're quite sure, Mr. Martyn, that you'd never met the girl?"

"To the best of my knowledge, never."

"She wasn't, by any chance, a relative of yours? Even a long-distant one?"

"No. All Browns aren't related, you know. We're a common herd. Not like the McLeods and the exclusive Scottish clans." He didn't sound worried. Merely amused.

"Quite! A coincidence, I suppose. But quite extraordinary you should both bear the same surname. And just another coincidence that Miss Amery should call the girl by a derivative of her correct name. 'Elizabeth' often becomes 'Lisa', I understand."

His eyes were friendly enough, but they had a fixed

intensity that made me nervous. "How did you know she was Elizabeth? Did she tell you?"

"No," I replied honestly. "To me she was simply Lisa. And I don't think you can say it's an ordinary name. 'Elizabeth' usually becomes 'Liz' or 'Beth'."

McLean was still gazing at me speculatively when Miranda said in her sweet low voice, "How clever of you, Inspector, to find out such a lot about the girl. How did you manage it?"

I could have told her she was wasting her time trying to wheedle information out of him. He'd tell us as much as he wanted us to know—and no more.

"People are always willing to come out with a few items about a girl who's been murdered. Provided, of course, they themselves were miles from the scene and can prove their alibi."

"So her name was Brown and she was looking for me." John appeared to come out of a trance. "Well, I don't know that you've advanced much, unless you've discovered more than you're telling us."

Mac folded his list of names and put it away in his pocket.

"We found out where she was staying—in a boarding-house just off the Cross—and we went through her things. Her passport was made out in the name of Elizabeth Brown and she was born in Croydon. She came out as a passenger on the *Stratheden* and arrived in Australia three months ago. Judging by a photo she carried, her parents were working folk and they had a dog called Toby. She'd written across the back of the snap 'Mum and Dad and Toby'."

I could recall the images of her parents easily. I remembered Lisa handing me that very photo over the check-topped table in the café.

"I wouldn't say we've made no progress, Mr. Welch," the Inspector went on. "At least I know who she was looking for. You!"

"Stop talking about it." Clare was fluttery as a mother hen. "I think you're beastly. First you try and make out she was blackmailing Dad, and then you attack Finch just because his name once happened to be Brown, and next you'll be telling me she was my Siamese twin."

"Pipe down, darling. You only make things worse." There was irritation in Tony's voice.

She turned on him. "Wait till the Inspector starts on you."

He laughed. "You'll fly to my defence just as you do to J.W.'s and to Finch's."

He knew her rather well, I thought. She was a champion of the underdog, of the falsely accused. Her instinct for justice was strong, but occasionally it misfired.

Simon was watching her like a cat with a mouse, and she caught his glance and looked hurriedly away. He was so quiet I'd forgotten his presence. But Clare hadn't. She was painfully aware of him. She patted Finch on the arm, absentmindedly, and rose and walked to a chair at the far end of the room, out of the range of Simon's gaze. She began talking very fast, and I knew she was nervous—and scared.

"Why don't we go for a swim? It's stinking hot and I've been longing to get to the beach all day. We could stay till it's dark and then eat Chinese. Lee Sam makes the most wonderful chicken and almond dish and his Bor Lor Guy is something to dream about. I went there the other day with Mamie Loring and she said——"

I never discovered what pearls of wisdom poured from Mamie's ruby lips, because Clare stopped talking and stared at the window and the expression on her face changed to stark, naked terror as she jerked herself to her feet. Her hands clutched at her skirt convulsively and her mouth was a twisted, scarlet gash. Her huge eyes were glued to the window —to the garden outside.

I stared at her. She moistened her lips as if she were trying to speak. She screamed. It was a shocking sound that filled the room with dread.

Tony was by her side, holding her, pulling her back as she began to run towards the open french windows.

I looked out, terrified to see what Clare had seen, yet unable to stop my eyes from searching. . . . Blue was standing on the verandah with his shirt covered in great red smears and blood dripping from a long scratch across his cheek. His hair was on end and below his torn khaki shorts his legs were spattered with dirt.

"Blue." I thought I was screaming too, but my voice came out in a whisper.

He strode into the room, sweeping us all with a single glance and finding McLean. Miranda clutched at her throat and drew back as though she feared he might touch her and stain her white dress with blood.

"Good God! You're hurt," John said inadequately.

Tony made a move, but Blue's hand brushed him aside brusquely. I saw then why Miranda was terrified. It wasn't the sight of blood that frightened her. It was the deadly, murderous gleam in Blue's eyes.

And I knew only an accident to Dawn or Joey could make him look like that, and I began to babble, "What's happened? It's not Dawn—or Joey—is it?"

He cut right across my words as if they hadn't been spoken.

"Some bastard tried to murder Joey."

CHAPTER X

CLARE screamed again.

The sound seemed to filter through to Blue as he gazed at the faces around him, one by one, as though he were slowly waking from a dream and finding that he and McLean weren't alone.

"I don't care which of you did it," he said slowly, "I intend to get the bastard."

Every word was an icy drip of water down my spine.

"Leave that stuff to me." Mac put his hand on Blue's shoulder. His eyes had that hard, diamond glitter again. "Where is Joey? Is he badly hurt?"

Blue shook himself free. "You'd better come right away. I've left him with Dawn. They're alone. I didn't want to leave them, but I had to find you."

He strode to the window and Mac followed him without a word, without a backward glance.

"God Almighty! Can't you do something? You're a doctor, you might be needed. Don't stand there. Do something!" Clare plucked at Tony's sleeve with nervous, jerky little motions.

"I'd be glad to. . . ." Tony paused. He had greater insight, greater intuition for once, than Clare. He knew damn well Blue wouldn't allow one of us within a stone's throw of Joey.

Mac was on the verandah, but he heard Clare's voice rising shrilly, hysterically, and he looked over his shoulder at her.

"I'll call Dr. Cambray if necessary," he said quietly.

He hurried swiftly across the lawn. I wanted to run after them, but I knew it was no use. All I could do was sit and wait, with my heart beating in my ears and a strangled feeling in my throat.

Not Joey! I said to myself, over and over again. Oh, God, don't let anything have happened to him. I think I prayed with my whole soul in those few seconds. Every incident of the past—even Lisa's murder—faded into nothingness compared with the ghastly, hideous knowledge that Joey was ill—perhaps dying.

I thought of his freckled nose and tousled hair and his wild enthusiasms, and I vowed that if only he lived, never again would I complain when he dropped tarantulas on my hair and planted frogs in my lounge.

I realized Miranda was speaking.

"What an extraordinary way to behave—as though one of us had attacked his child. He's Joey's father I suppose? I can understand, of course, that he's desperately worried, but it's a bit thick to come bursting in here accusing us."

Underneath she was frightened. She was hanging on to her poise grimly, but it was wearing thin at the edges. As she spoke, my eyes strayed to her throat, fascinated by that steady, throbbing pulse over which she had no control.

"I think he's unbalanced," she continued. "Joey's probably sick and it's unhinged his mind. How could one of us try to murder Joey when we've all been together in this room? Thank heaven the Inspector can prove that. I only hope he puts a bit of sense into the man's head. I don't like being accused of murdering small boys."

Simon walked to the window and gazed at the dry, brittle lawn. "He's not the type of man, I'd say, to make wild statements. He must have some proof to go on. I don't know what's happened, but I can make a guess."

"The less we start guessing the better. I suggest we keep calm until we hear what McLean has to say." Finch squeezed my hand. "Don't worry, darling. Joey's too much of a young devil to die yet. Blue wouldn't have come over here if he thought Joey was in immediate danger—he'd be hanging over the bedside. And believe me, he wasn't overcome with grief. He was overcome with rage. He was in a helluva temper, and if what he says is true, I don't blame him."

It was wonderful how Finch knew the right words to comfort me, and I felt a sudden surge of affection for him. He could be malicious and inquisitive, but he could also be rather sweet.

What he said made sense, too, I persuaded myself. Blue had been sweating with rage.

My spirits rose a little, but I wished I knew what the whole ghastly business meant. Blue had made it quite clear that someone in this very room had attacked Joey. It sounded not only improbable, but quite impossible. As Miranda had pointed out, we'd been together for the past half-hour. We'd been signing our names to satisfy a whim of Inspector McLean.

Nothing, I decided, made sense any more. Lisa's death—this news about Joey—my burglary—were steeped in nightmare fantasy.

And in the midst of the fantasy, Miranda said calmly, "We'll have tea in the sun-room."

I wanted to scream. I wished she wouldn't try so hard to be calm and civilized.

John walked to the door and stood with his hand resting on the knob. Some of the old buoyancy and confidence had dropped and he was showing his age. "If you'll excuse me, I want to get on with some work. I'll be in the study." His worried eyes rested on me. "Gilly, try and find out what you can. Blue trusts you. He'll talk to you. You needn't say I told you, but if there's anything we can do, no matter what it is, let me know. I'd like to help. I'm fond of Joey."

He disappeared down the corridor.

Miranda sighed. "Of course we'll do anything we can. You know that, Gilly. But in the meantime, surely it'd be more sensible to have tea than to sit about wondering and waiting."

It was a relief when she went out. I couldn't live up to her code which demanded that we carry on as if this was a normal afternoon.

But I admired her. It took courage to keep up a front when below her calm façade she was just as scarey and frightened as I was. I'd seen the terror in her long green eyes when she looked at Blue. She might be determined to ignore what was sordid and ugly and horrible, but the long tentacles of fear were reaching out and touching her, against her will. And all John's care and solicitude couldn't save her from contamination.

Clare said in a thin wail, "If only we knew. . . ."

Tony put his arm round her and said briskly, "Cheer up. There's nothing we can do about it."

I hurried to the door. I didn't even bother to say goodbye. I felt the same urgency that I'd felt last night, to shake the dust of Coolibah from my feet. And now I had an even more pressing reason for wanting to run back to my own flat. I wanted desperately to see Dawn—and Joey.

Clare was clinging to Tony like a barnacle to a ship, and I wished Barney were here, so that I could do a little clinging of my own.

Today Simon made no move to accompany me, and I was glad. He stood by the window looking out on to the lawn. He melted into the scene like the blackcloth to a stage. He was always on the spot, saying little, noticing everything with those queer, shallow eyes.

Finch sprang up when he saw I was leaving and came out into the hall, clutching me by the arm with his long thin fingers.

"Don't go, darling. Stay here until McLean comes back. He will, you know, as soon as he finds out what it's all about."

I walked straight out on to the verandah. "You don't understand. I must see Dawn."

"Of course I understand. But you'd only be in the way over there. Look, there's something I want to tell you. I tried earlier this afternoon and you wouldn't listen to me."

He swung me round roughly to face him.

"I'm going away!"

I was startled into stillness.

"Away? But you can't. Not yet. Not till this business is cleared up."

"As soon as McLean will let me, I'm off. I haven't told a soul except you. I'll try England, the Continent, anywhere, but I'm getting out of Sydney."

Sydney without Finch! He knew everyone, went everywhere. He'd built himself a lucrative living. He was pampered and spoilt and fussed over. And he was throwing it all away just when he'd made a firm foothold towards success and wealth.

"But you can't," I told him.

"Why not? I'm good at my work. I'll always get on all right."

How true! There'd always be women to fall on his neck and get good-looking, attractive Finch Martyn to renovate their homes. The female species in England would be no different from here.

And then I thought of Joey, and I tried to pull away, but he held me fast.

"I want you to come with me."

The words didn't make sense. He was gazing at me with a crooked little smile twisting his mouth, and his eyes were searching my face trying to find an emotion that wasn't there.

"I want you to marry me, Gilly."

If it had been any other time and any other place I would have known he was joking. But Finch wouldn't be heartless enough to spring a mock proposal when I was nearly out of my wits with worry.

"I've never been more serious in my life," he said earnestly. "I want to know we'll be together after this mess is cleaned up. I understand you much better than you think—much better than Barney does. I know how to make you happy."

He put his arms round me and I rested my head against him because I realized I was terribly fond of him, but not nearly fond enough to marry him. I had a crazy desire to cry because his proposal was rather touching and I felt honoured and almost wished I were in love with him, but then a vision of Barney floated into my brain and I knew that whoever I married, it would never, never be Finch Martyn.

"I'm sorry, Finch. I can't. But . . . thanks."

Nevertheless I wallowed on his shoulder for a moment and he stroked my hair gently before I pulled myself away.

"There's something else I should tell you, too, Gilly, because it's only fair you should know."

I don't know why he turned round. I hadn't heard a sound and I doubt if he had either, but an instinct must have warned him we were no longer alone. I looked quickly past him. Miranda was standing holding the wire door open, with one foot on the verandah and the other in the hall, like a sprinter about to take off. There was an odd stillness about her. She

F

might have been a statue carved in pale marble, but for those angry hostile eyes burning into mine. I knew, with every instinct in my body, that she'd been standing there for some time listening.

"I hate to interrupt, but I'd like to talk to Finch. I'm sure you won't mind, Gilly." Her voice swept over me like a chilly, winter wind. "It's nice you're able to treat this horrible business so cheerfully. I thought Joey's parents were friends of yours, but you hardly seem to be worrying about them. I quite imagined you'd be rushing over to see what was wrong. I certainly didn't imagine you'd be indulging in a love scene on the front doorstep."

I felt the blood rush to my face in a sickening wave of fury. "I was on my way——"

"Don't apologize!" Finch's voice was dangerous. He faced Miranda. "Why don't you mind your own business?"

"I think it is my business—how people behave in my house."

She didn't look at Finch. She looked at me, and the smouldering dislike in her eyes suddenly burst into a bitter flame of hatred.

I turned away, blindly. A cold hand seemed to tighten round my throat, so that I couldn't speak.

Perhaps she knew her eyes had betrayed her. I heard her voice behind me, soft and sweet and pleading. "I didn't mean to be rude, Gilly. I guess my nerves are on edge, that's all."

Her nerves, I thought, were sheathed in iron. There was more to it than that. But I didn't stop to analyse her likes and dislikes, but fled down the lawn to the big gates. Finch must have started after me, because I heard her voice calling him back.

I pounded on across the street and up the steps into the lobby of the flats. Miranda's behaviour meant nothing in my young life, I told myself, and if she wanted to hate me she was welcome. Our beautiful friendship had been phoney right from the start, and I'd never been comfortable in her presence. From now on she could do without me.

All that mattered was Joey. I had to know that he was all right.

McLean was coming out of the Baileys' door just as I was about to knock. He caught me by the arm and led me out into the tiny garden again, and I noticed, as I glanced at the french windows to Dawn's lounge, that the curtains were drawn. My heart sank. I'd never seen those curtains drawn across in the daytime before.

There wasn't a sound from the flat. I was terrified to ask the question uppermost in my mind and I tried to read the answer in McLean's face. It was like a piece of granite. I remembered then that Joey was his godchild.

"Joey?" I couldn't say more.

He patted me on the arm. "He'll be okay—I hope. Dawn and Blue have taken him away. I'd leave them alone for a while if I were you. Dawn's pretty upset and Blue's reached boiling point. There's nothing you can do. Later Dawn'll probably be glad to see you."

We walked down the path and he leaned against the gate in sudden weariness.

"How could I have known Joey was in danger? If only he'd told me earlier that he'd spoken to the Brown girl ... It was you I was anxious about. I never dreamed that Joey ..."

He was talking to himself more than to me, and I felt a surge of pity for him. How, indeed, could a mere policeman foresee what was going to happen?

"Whatever happened to Joey, I'm sure it wasn't your fault. You mustn't blame yourself." I couldn't help trying to comfort him, because he looked depressed and angry with himself. It was the only time I ever saw his feelings get the better of him and it was rather pathetic to see his poker face registering genuine emotion.

I was aching to know how and why Joey had been in danger.

McLean looked down at me. His face was expressionless again. "Someone at Coolibah tried to murder the kid. I might as well tell you now, because you'll certainly hear about it later."

I seemed to be having difficulty with my breathing and my voice refused to function properly.

"But he was all right—Joey I mean—when he left with

Blue. I watched them go. You were there yourself. You saw them. And no one left the house after that because we were with you."

"No one needed to leave the house. The bike Joey was so thrilled about had already been fixed. The brakes were cut almost through—quite a neat job."

He opened the gate and stepped on to the pavement outside. I couldn't move. I was petrified. He waved his hand towards the steep decline which led to the main road. I could see the stream of cars in the distance down there, tearing past on their way to the city.

"Cottrill Street leads in only one direction—to the main road. And it's a pretty sharp hill. If you were on a bike, you'd need to apply the brakes hard before you came to the intersection. That's exactly what a murderer banked on. He knew Joey would have to cross the main road or else turn into it, because there's nowhere else you can go from here unless you're going to ride to the dead end of Cottrill Street beyond the Welch house and then come back here. And that's a tame route. Not much scope there for a boy who wants to try out his new bike. He'd choose the hill—and come to a stop at the bottom if his brakes were working. And if they weren't he'd probably know it on the way down and try and stop himself before he reached the traffic. But if the brake cable was nearly cut through, so that one strand held until a little extra pressure snapped it apart, the rider wouldn't have much chance to do anything about it. Especially when the bike was too big for him and it was quite a job to reach the ground with his foot. Whoever tampered with Joey's bike knew exactly what he was doing."

I don't know a thing about mechanics but I understood the Inspector perfectly. I could see it all happening right in front of my eyes—Joey on the bike, the traffic ahead. . . .

My hands were shaking and I couldn't control them.

"But no one at Coolibah would do a thing like that. It's too monstrous. A small boy like Joey. Who would want to hurt him?"

McLean was still looking down the street at the never-ending flow of swiftly moving cars.

"Someone was very anxious that Joey should be out of action—perhaps permanently—before he could tell a tale." He looked at me suddenly. "Don't keep saying it couldn't be anyone from Coolibah." He was impatient and angry and tired all at the same time. "The person who killed Elizabeth Brown tried to murder Joey and damn nearly succeeded."

"Where is he? Joey?" My heart was in my boots.

"He's out of reach where he'll be well looked after."

"In hospital?" I had to find out where, so that I could send him anything and everything that might help to make him happy.

McLean said queerly, "I don't intend to tell you or anyone else where he is. So stop asking me. It's only a fluke the kid's alive now, and by God he's going to stay that way. You'd better get it right into your head, in case you've still got doubts, that one of your friends is a murderer. After he'd finished off that poor girl, he found, to his horror, that you'd not only met her and spoken to her but had actually picked up something she'd dropped in the café. And he couldn't be sure what it was. He was so worried about it he decided to investigate and find out how much you knew. That's why I told them exactly what it was you found in the café. A harmless little cross. I thought you'd be safer if a murderer knew you had nothing incriminating in your possession. I was so worried about you that I overlooked Joey. I'd questioned him and he didn't seem to know anything of importance. He told me he'd seen the girl, but I was too dumb to realize he'd actually spoken to her. And anyone who came into contact with Elizabeth Brown is in danger—great danger."

I was quivering like an aspen leaf, but I was also hanging on to every word he said.

"Either the murderer knew Joey had spoken to your Lisa or he knew Joey had seen something terribly important. So important that Joey became a menace in case he mentioned a trivial fact that meant nothing unless it was linked up with murder. But the danger was that I'd do just that—I'd see the whole point. And murderers, Miss Amery, are very sensitive about their own safety. They'd sooner kill than be hanged themselves. Even if it means killing a small boy. Right now someone's getting jumpy, because he's wondering how much I know, or how much I've guessed."

"Simon, John, Tony . . . Finch." I barely knew I'd spoken. I was thinking my thoughts aloud. They sounded even more terrible when put into words.

"Why exclude Miranda and Clare Welch?" McLean was watching me.

"They wouldn't know a thing about bikes. Can you imagine Miranda knowing how to put brakes out of action?"

"Miranda Welch may not know. But Miranda Grey certainly did. She was the eldest of three children and her father was a grocer. He was an Englishman, and just before the War he decided to retire and take his family back to the old country with him. But Miranda didn't like settling down to suburban chores on the outskirts of London and she decided to cut adrift. She got a job as a mannequin."

I thought of her graceful walk. It was the result of training, of course, but I'd never realized it before.

"Once she'd dropped her family and her old friends she started to go places. And then she got the chance of a job in Melbourne and she jumped at it. She became the buyer for one of the big stores and it brought her into contact with some wealthy clients. One of them was an elderly man who fell for her hook, line and sinker, and when he died a year or so later he left her enough to live on without working. But she was much too ambitious to be content with merely a small income, so she drifted to Sydney and set about mixing with the right people. If she hadn't met John Welch she would have met some other elderly bloke ready to fall for her."

I was open-mouthed at the amount of information he'd dug up about her in a matter of hours. More than I'd ever known.

"She's far more capable than she looks," he added slowly, "and so is Clare Welch. I know she's your old school chum and all that nonsense, but how much do you really know about her? You haven't seen much of her in the past two years, have you?" He gave a sudden grin. "I could tell you quite a bit about yourself too, but I won't. I'm going over to Coolibah before Dr. Cambray decides he's got a pressing engagement in town, or before Finch Martyn discovers an urge to visit the country. I want them all together and you can thank your lucky stars you won't be there, because I'm going to tear them apart one by one."

He took his elbow off the gate and turned towards Coolibah, then stopped and faced me again.

"I wonder if there's anything you haven't told me, Miss Amery. You'd be rather foolish to keep back any secrets at this stage."

I didn't like the way he was looking at me. There was a touch of the dingo about him. Lean and brown and cunning.

"I can't think of anything," I told him truthfully. And then I remembered one small incident I'd kept to myself. The conversation between Simon and Clare on Coolibah's verandah last night. I hesitated, then repeated it to him, expecting at least some reaction. But he barely seemed interested, and I told myself I'd been wasting his time.

"Don't worry about Clare Welch!" was all he said. "She'll sort out her own problems and she won't thank you to interfere. Leave well alone. My God! Women!" And he loped off down the street.

I watched him turn into the driveway and then I retraced my steps into the lobby where I'd met him. There was no sound or sign of life from the Baileys' flat and I wondered whether they were with Joey in hospital. If only I knew where he was!

I couldn't believe any human being could plan, in cold blood, to wreck the life of a small, cheerful boy. The very thought brought me out in a cold sweat of fury and loathing for a mind capable of such infinite wickedness and evil.

I walked up the stairs trying to remember who it was who had first suggested giving the bike to Joey. I was certain it had been John. But I myself had led the way to it by announcing that Joey was saving for a bike. And John had offered to give him the gardener's. Yes, that was how it came up. But the whole conversation had been easy and natural and I could swear there was no dark and horrible motive behind John's good-natured offer. I couldn't imagine John Welch hurting any child. That seemed to rule him out.

Simon and Tony both knew Joey would be collecting the bike today—but neither of them had shown much interest. Tony had been anxious about the effect of murder on Joey's mental outlook, and it was hardly likely he'd be worrying about his mental state and planning to wreck him physically all in the one breath. Besides, Tony dealt in life, not in death.

As for Simon—I had to admit I knew little about him. He could be pleasant enough, but there were reserves of energy and will lurking behind his impassive face and expressionless voice. If the motive were strong enough, I imagined Simon could accomplish most things he set his heart on.

And then I remembered it was Simon who'd wheeled the bike out of the garage in readiness for Joey. Clare had told us that. But Simon was a stranger to the district. How could he know, as the rest of us certainly did, that Cottrill Street came to a dead end at the top of the hill past Coolibah? He'd only arrived yesterday, and he certainly hadn't had time to explore the street and discover that the only exit was right down that steep, deadly hill. Simon was far and away my best suspect, yet the very fact that he was a stranger seemed to prove his innocence.

I was so engrossed in my own thoughts that I walked right past the empty flat on the first floor without giving it a glance. There is nothing like a good honest rage to make you forget your own troubles, and I was so shaken by Joey's accident that my personal fears receded.

And yet, I couldn't find a specific person to blame. There was no one I could vent my anger on—no focusing point—because my imagination baulked at the idea of any of the people I knew planning a maniacal, diabolical attempt on a child's life.

Perhaps I was prejudiced in Finch's favour, because I barely considered him. No girl likes to think that a man who has just proposed to her is a monster. But there was more to it than that. Finch hadn't been at Coolibah when John had made his offer of the bike. He hadn't known that Joey was about to become the proud possessor of an ancient two-wheeler. Admittedly, Clare could have told him about it, but she was eaten up with her own worries and I doubted whether it would have occurred to her to mention a trivial matter like an old bike.

I let myself into the flat and flung myself into a chair to brood.

McLean might be certain that Clare or Miranda knew enough about bikes to stage an accident, but I was equally certain they wouldn't know, any more than I did, where to begin looking for brakes. Much less how to tamper with them successfully and put them out of working order.

And there the case, Gillian Amery *versus* Coolibah, came to an end. It simply wasn't possible that one of the Welches or Simon or Tony or Finch could have killed Lisa, paid me a midnight visit and rounded off the jolly series of events with a vicious attack on Joey.

I wished I knew where Joey was and how badly he'd been injured.

I couldn't bear to think of it, so I went into the bathroom and took a cold shower and changed into another dress.

The afternoon wore on at a snail's pace and I almost wished I hadn't left Coolibah. Solitude can be pleasant, but not when one is waiting and longing for news. However, when the sharp ring of the 'phone brought me hastily to my feet I was filled with dread. I grabbed it and tried to say "Hullo" in my usual voice.

Clare answered me and I sat down with a feeling of disappointment—and yet of relief too—that it wasn't Dawn. No news is good news, I told myself tritely.

"You've heard about Joey," Clare said, and didn't wait for my reply. "Isn't it awful, darling? We're nearly frantic with worry and we wanted to find out what hospital he's in—Joey I mean—and the Inspector wouldn't tell us and we thought you might know, so I said I'd ring you, and Dad's ordered lashings of books and sweets to send him, but it's hopeless when we haven't got the address. And Tony wanted to visit Joey and see for himself just how bad he was, but Inspector McLean was simply horrid and wouldn't hear of it. Dad's terribly upset and Miranda's in a mood." She stopped only because she'd run out of breath. I heard her give a little gasp and run on again, like a record with a crack in the middle. "Who'd want to do a thing like that to Joey? I don't understand. Gilly, it's not one of us."

I'd been thinking the same thing.

"It's the awfulness of not knowing that gets me. I can't stand it. I'm a coward, I suppose, but I wanted to get married right away and dash off somewhere with Tony, but he's got some old-school-tie notion that we mustn't think of ourselves. He says we've got to stick together with the others through this mess, and try and carry on normally. And anyway, the Inspector won't let any of us leave. He looks at us, darling, as if we're criminals. I'm frightened."

I knew she was. I could hear it in her voice.

"Do tell me where Joey is. I'll do anything to help him. The Inspector said it was a miracle he wasn't killed and Dad went as white as a sheet. I've never seen him really shattered before—you know how calm and practical he is. He said to tell you money doesn't matter where Joey's concerned, and he must have the very best specialists and the Baileys can take him to our cottage at Palm Beach as soon as he's well enough to leave hospital. But have you heard any news of him, darling?"

I told her I knew as little as she did and I couldn't supply the address of the hospital because I didn't know it.

"You will let me know if you hear anything, won't you?" she asked anxiously.

I promised her I would, and hung up hastily. I didn't want the 'phone to be engaged in case Dawn rang.

It was starting to get dark when I heard the sound of the front gate. I rushed to the window and peered out. I thought I saw Dawn's skirt disappearing up the steps, so I scuttled downstairs as fast as I could.

CHAPTER XI

THE Baileys' front door was shut but I could hear sounds behind it and I lifted my hand, hesitantly, to knock.

But just as my fingers touched the wooden panel I caught the faint murmur of a noise so queer, so unexpected, that my hand froze in mid air and I stood motionless with amazement.

Inside the flat I heard Dawn laugh. Admittedly it wasn't a very joyful or amused laugh. It was a laugh nevertheless, even though it did sound somewhat forced. The idea of Dawn even being able to smile, with Joey lying in hospital, was beyond the bounds of possibility. The Baileys' whole existence centred round the apple of their eye, no matter how much they joked about him and swore he was the original limb of Satan.

I listened. I could hear Blue's voice and then the radio was switched on and the drone of the commentator from Melbourne describing an in-swinger of Bedser's drowned all other sounds.

Dawn could find something to laugh at, and Blue could settle down calmly to a session of cricket! I was thunderstruck! Something, I told myself, was rotten in the state of Denmark. A gay smile and light entertainment while Joey lay at death's door! I felt my spirits soaring because I knew Joey was out of danger.

I rapped sharply on the door and the radio was tuned down and Dawn's quick steps sounded across the room as she came to answer my knock.

"Gilly! Come in."

I searched her face anxiously for confirmation of my hopes. She was pale but she seemed quite calm and her grey eyes were steadfast and friendly.

"I was coming up to see you later, but I didn't know whether you were home."

Blue heaved himself out of a chair and perched on

the edge of the table with a grin. There was a piece of sticking-plaster down the side of his face and his carroty hair was still on end. But he'd lost the grim look. He was himself again.

I knew then that I needn't worry about Joey and the relief was so great that I flopped into the chair Blue had vacated and fought to keep back the tears. There was a lump in my throat the size of an emu's egg and it interfered with my speech.

"Joey's all right?" The words were disjointed.

Dawn sat beside me.

"Poor Gilly! Yes, he's quite safe. You must believe me, darling, because it's true."

Like a fool, I burst into tears. I'd come down expecting to comfort Dawn and Blue, but the tables were turned. Blue handed me a large-sized hanky and strolled into the kitchen and put the kettle on. I could hear him banging around with cups and I knew he was about to apply the universal panacea for weeping women—the inevitable cup of tea.

"I've been nearly out of my mind," I sniffled to Dawn, "because you see the whole business was really my fault. I was the one who told John that Joey wanted a bike, and if I hadn't mentioned it, this would never have happened."

Dawn said calmly, "It might have been worse. As it is, things haven't turned out too badly. And I rather think Mac's got the lead he's been looking for."

There was no one in the world, I thought, quite as nice as Dawn.

Blue came in with a tray in one hand, and I saw his eyes meet Dawn's as he began setting the teapot and cups on the table.

Dawn walked over to him and poured the tea. It slopped a little because her hand was shaking. She wasn't as calm as she pretended.

"I'm going to tell Gilly."

Blue shrugged. "If you do, you'll have Mac to deal with."

Dawn handed me a cup and began to stir her own tea thoughtfully. I knew she was making up her mind and coming

168

to a decision—a big decision. I didn't speak. Nor did Blue. He handed us cigarettes and lit them, and retrieved his damp hanky.

"I know Mac'll be wild with me for telling you, Gilly, but I honestly think it won't matter, because I know you won't breathe a word to a soul."

She looked at me so trustingly that I swore to myself her confidence wouldn't be misplaced, and I mentally crossed my heart and vowed that torture wouldn't drag a word from my lips.

Being Dawn, she didn't ask for any promises. She simply assumed them.

"Joey didn't have an accident at all."

My mouth fell open and I nearly dropped my cup.

"But—the Inspector said it was only a fluke he wasn't killed."

"So it was. Because, you see, it was Blue who was having first ride. Not Joey. But it easily could have been Joey."

I gazed at the sticking-plaster on Blue's cheek and the whole scene became as clear as daylight. He was grinning at me rather sheepishly.

A raucous burst of laughter filled the room—laughter that bordered on hysteria, wild and uncontrolled. It was coming from me. I tried to stop it, but found I couldn't. Not that there was anything funny about Blue being scratched and bruised with a strip of white plaster across his face. That laughter was simply an outpouring of relief, a sheer wild cry of delight because Joey was safe. Dawn was smiling, and then Blue's voice joined mine in a great hoot of mirth.

And when eventually I subsided, I realized Miranda was right. I was the hysterical type, after all.

"I'm sorry, Blue. It's not really funny. I don't know why I laughed."

He was still grinning. Our laughter had broken the tension. I felt as if a weight I'd been carrying had suddenly been removed and I was able to breathe freely again. The joy of it left me lightheaded. Dawn sagged in her chair as though she'd been holding herself straight and now found she remembered how to relax. Blue heaved himself on to the table and sat swinging his legs.

"I bloody nearly turned turtle on that damn bike. I knew it had let me down. Then I came a beaut. And when I picked myself up I had a good look at it and I found the brakes had broken clean through. So I shoved the bike back up the hill where the kid was waiting for me. He'd seen the lot and thought it a helluva joke that his old man was such a mug rider. He had the nerve to tell me that I might be a crack surfer but I didn't know how to sit a bike. I didn't let on to him. But I wouldn't let him ride it and I had to get him out of the way, so I sent him off on a phoney message while I examined the brakes. And when I did I knew exactly what'd happened. The cut was too clean and too new for an old bike, and I didn't have to be a master mind to guess what was going on. Someone had put the thing out of action. Of course I did my act good and proper—you saw that—because it was plain that one of the Coolibah push was out to get Joey. It wasn't hard to work it out. Joey must have seen more than he was meant to see yesterday, when that girl was murdered. I can tell you, I sweated blood when I thought of it, and if I could've got my hands on the bastard . . ."

He looked as if he were about to sweat blood all over again, then he grinned. "So you see, I'm the only casualty. And my loving wife isn't at all worried about me. Oh no! She reckons I'm big enough and ugly enough to look after myself."

"You are!" Dawn said heartlessly. "But it's all so horrible, it frightens me. Thank God, Joey's out of it—Mac always did think the murderer could be pinned down to one of a small group of people, but I hoped he was wrong. Now he's quite certain he was on the right track all the time, and I'm afraid he is, too. He doesn't want the truth about Joey to leak out, and that's why it's terribly important for you to keep it under your hat. I can't tell you where he is. We've taken him away, but I won't give the address to you or to anyone else, darling, and you understand why. It's not that I don't trust you. But the fewer people who know the less chance there is of—a murderer—finding out. Mac says Joey's only safe if he stays in obscurity till the show's over."

Her cup clanked against the saucer. She couldn't keep her hand steady.

I was glad she didn't tell me where Joey was because I didn't want to know. It was quite enough to learn that he was safe and sound—and still Joey.

I asked her if she'd deliver some books and comics from me as a sort of thanksgiving present, and she promised she would.

"We'll probably see him tomorrow, though I hate the idea of going off and leaving you alone in this building. If only the Simpsons would come back!"

I assured her with false bravery that I'd be perfectly safe.

"That's what Mac keeps saying every time I mention your name. He's quite determined no one else is going to be hurt, and he's watching the place like a hawk. He thought all along that you might be in danger because you knew more than you realized about that girl."

"I don't know a thing I haven't told him."

"Every time I've spoken to you since yesterday you've been in too much of a flap to tell me anything." Dawn's eyes were curious. "I didn't like to question you. But there's such a lot I want to know."

I suspected Mac had told them quite a bit of the story, but I began at the beginning, from the fateful moment when I'd stepped into the café and found Lisa.

They listened to every word, and in the background the forgotten radio murmured insistently that the day's play was over, but that's all I heard because I was carried away with my own voice, with my stumbling reconstruction of every incident from the time when Lisa had crossed my life and then vanished, leaving a trail of memories behind her—memories of her Cockney accent, her mouse-brown hair, her sweet far-away smile.

Blue made no attempt to turn the radio up and hear the final scores. If I'd thought about it, I would have realized it was the only occasion when he'd found my conversation more interesting than a sporting commentary. It was a sure indication that he was far more worried than he let on.

Every time I hesitated, one of them prompted me with a question, demanding that I pick up the threads again. I'd never had more attentive listeners.

Outside darkness was drawing in and the air was very still. A few big drops of rain splashed the path and then stopped, as if the effort of falling was too great for them. We sat on in the gloom, too absorbed to notice that we could barely see each other.

At last I finished and Blue seemed to realize, for the first time, that it was almost dark, and he switched on the reading lamp.

By its glow I could see Dawn's face, her chin resting in her hand. Her bare brown legs were curled round each other—a position she always assumed when she was deep in thought.

"Mac's quite right," she said slowly. "You do know an awful lot about Lisa and I can understand now why he's worried about you."

I stretched lazily. Oddly enough, I was more relaxed and comfortable than I'd been for hours.

"What do I know? I wish someone would tell me."

Dawn began enumerating on her fingers. "A little of her history and her home—her parents and Toby and Jock. You know she was blitzed and terribly ill and saved by the nuns at the Convent. You found her little cross and that tells its own story. And you saw the way she fled from the café."

"And that's all. It doesn't sound much to me."

We gazed at each other.

"It must add up," Dawn said thoughtfully, "but I'm darned if I can see how. If only we knew what startled her in the café. It's not natural for a girl to run off like that. Perhaps there's some link between her and this Simon Ashton, something we don't know about. And wasn't it queer, darling, that Miranda Welch should come popping over to see you straight after the murder?—and with her little gun tucked in her no-doubt costly bag. You know, I always think that woman's too beautiful to be true."

"Jealousy," Blue remarked slyly.

"But of course it is, darling. No girl's got any right to be as good-looking as she is with all that straight fair hair and those lovely eyes. And doesn't she know it!"

Blue began to grin in the superior attitude males adopt when they listen in on a cat session, so we ignored him and told each other that John Welch was a dear but notoriously dim about women, Tony was nice but uninspiring, Clare a trifle neurotic, and Miranda beautiful but vain.

We couldn't come to any definite decision about Simon because Dawn had never met him, but she admired his well-cut clothes and thought he looked attractive if he'd only let his hair down and relax. I supposed Simon did have something—a strong face, a silent manner and a pair of emotionless blue eyes. Not a combination that appealed to me.

"I wonder why Clare's scared of him?" I asked.

Dawn shrugged. "Who knows? Perhaps you're only imagining it, darling. I wouldn't worry about Clare if I were you. Start worrying about yourself."

Till then I'd almost succeeded in forgetting the horrible chain of events which had led up to this cosy gossip, but now the fear of lurking danger came rushing back.

I stood up. I couldn't stay at the Baileys' for ever, drawing security and comfort from Blue's strength and from Dawn's common sense. Sooner or later I had to face the solitude of my own flat, and the longer I put it off, the harder it became to tear myself away from the friendly shelter down here.

I left, refusing Dawn's invitation to stay and eat, but relieved when Blue insisted on accompanying me up in the lift.

I gave him the key and he went in first, peering round the rooms and poking behind doors and in cupboards. When he was satisfied no strangers were hiding on the premises, he stood at the front door with a cheerful grin spreading over his face.

"It's time Barney came back to Sydney to keep an eye on you. In the meantime, I guess I can cope with you and Dawn both—now that Joey's off my mind."

"God knows what I'd do without you and Dawn." It was an utterance from the depths of my heart.

He looked embarrassed. "Don't talk bosh."

The door slammed and he ran downstairs. I sighed. I'd never met anyone less receptive to thanks than Blue.

I leaned out of the window. In the distance the lights were gradually coming on, one by one, piercing the darkness. They winked and blinked at me like a thousand watchful eyes.

And somewhere, in the fairyland out there, a murderer mingled with his fellows and joined his voice with theirs. An ordinary nice man. But a man without a conscience.

The 'phone interrupted my session of gloom. It was Finch. He sounded surprisingly unworried in view of all that had gone before him today.

"I tried to get you earlier but you weren't in. How about having dinner with me?"

I began to refuse hastily, because I didn't want to see Finch or anyone else. I wanted to be alone.

"John and Miranda are coming too, so you'll be well chaperoned," he said dryly. "I knew you wouldn't enjoy my undiluted company and John needs cheering up, so it seemed a good idea to get together and try and forget about murder."

I remembered Barney was due to ring me tonight, so I told Finch the truth. I was expecting a call and didn't want to miss it.

"A call from Melbourne, I suppose." He was peevish. "Oh well, I can't persuade you against your will. I've never been able to yet, have I? But you mustn't go into hibernation. You weren't built for it. You'll work yourself into a panic if you stay home and brood all the time. Thank God you'd gone before McLean started putting us through the hoop today. He really got going on us. It even shook Miranda, and poor old J.W. aged about fifty years and Simon just stood and took it all without uttering a word, and that left Tony and myself to bear the brunt with Clare throwing in the odd phrase that only stoked the fire more than ever. Have you heard how Joey is?"

I told him quickly that I'd heard nothing.

Perhaps I spoke too hastily, because he said with unmistakable suspicion, "I thought you would've seen Dawn by now. Anyway, don't go eating your heart out with worry about young Joey. He'll live to don khaki for the atom war—unless it breaks before then."

He was singularly unperturbed about Joey's health and I couldn't help saying so.

"Inspector McLean and Blue may pull the wool over your eyes, darling, but they can't over mine. Believe me, I wouldn't be so cheerful if I thought anything had really happened to the young devil, but my sense, or perhaps I should say my psychic, tells me the whole affair stinks. That's just my private opinion, not to be bruited abroad. I'm only telling you because it may cheer you up a bit. I honestly believe he's okay, though I won't deny someone tried to murder him. But all's well that ends well, and even if Joey's got a few scratches he's not on his deathbed yet. Some day we'll know the true story and you'll find I'm right."

"Why are you so certain?"

"Because I've met men like Blue before and I know how they react. McLean's working a swiftie on us and I'm happy to play along if it's going to sort out this wretched tangle. At the moment I seem to be rather in the limelight myself. And all because I was blessed with the uninteresting name of Brown. What's in a name? You're sure you won't change your mind? Don't let Miranda's presence put you off. She was pretty beastly to you this afternoon, but she can't help herself. She's probably got over the sulks by now."

To call that flaming burst of hatred by the term 'sulks' was the sort of gross understatement males indulge in.

"You're sure I can't lure you with the mention of roast duck or Hawaiian salad or lobster mayonnaise? My other offer still stands too, the one I made today. Or have you forgotten about it already?"

He paused and I had to say something.

"It's no use. . . ."

"I'm the stubborn type. I never give up hope."

If only I didn't like him so much, I thought sadly.

"What were you going to tell me when Miranda interrupted?" I was suddenly curious to know.

But his answer was disappointing. "Oh, nothing very

175

much I guess. Probably how much I loved your silly little nose and your big grey eyes."

He was lying in his teeth. Whatever had been on his mind, it certainly wasn't my facial features. But I didn't press the point. Instead I asked him whether he'd seen Clare and how she was.

"Women in love have inner resources, darling. You should know that," he said. "Clare's got a couple of stalwarts by her side to see her through. Simon's like a tracker on the scent, always at hand, and I think it's driving Tony nuts, poor bloke. The three of them have gone off somewhere to drown their sorrows. Poor Clare!"

Funny how he wasted so much sympathy on a girl who had everything—even including the man of her choice.

"Lock your door tonight, Gilly. And don't answer if anyone knocks, until you find out who's there. If it turns out to be one of McLean's chosen herd, keep your door locked! Firmly locked."

I was terribly alone after he rang off and the flat seemed bare and empty. I didn't like his last words. They reminded me far too plainly that danger hovered about our heads and would continue to hover, until the law caught up with a murderer.

I didn't like the idea that Simon was hanging around Clare either. I hoped the Inspector would worm the truth out of her and send him packing. If only Mac would realize that Lisa had been no blackmailer, and if only he'd start concentrating on Simon instead, he'd be far nearer the truth. Dawn had said that Mac had found a lead. A lead indeed! What we wanted was an arrest, not a vague hunch that had no foundation of fact.

I was sick of sitting still. What I needed was the sound of friendly human beings around me, the noise of laughter, the reminder that life could be gay and happy for others, even though for me it had turned into a dark and sinister road. I wanted to see normal smiling faces. I wanted, for a brief space of time at least, to be part and parcel of the crowd that pours into the open on a hot summer evening.

I rang for a taxi, made up my face and put on high-heeled sandals.

I didn't move from the flat until I heard the honk of a car horn down below, and then I shut my door tightly and rang for the lift, eyeing the shadows on the landing nervously, as I waited for the cage to come groaning upstairs.

The black-and-silver cab I'd ordered was standing at the front gate and the driver was at the lobby doors searching the name plates on the wall. I jumped into the car, then realized I hadn't the vaguest notion where I wanted to go. The driver waited while I tried to decide on a favourite café.

"The Cross," I told him. That was a safe opening. There were many eating places around there, and the streets would be packed with people on a Saturday night. I'd buy Joey the biggest stack of comics I could find, and then I'd have an omelette or perhaps a toasted sandwich, and after that I'd join the window-shoppers until I was too tired to think of anything other than sleep. I'd be home by nine, in time for Barney's call, and I'd tell him every single ghastly incident of the past twenty-four hours. Then I'd fall into bed and sleep.

We neared the Cross intersection and the driver half turned his head expectantly, awaiting my further instructions. As we appeared to be blocking the traffic, I decided to pay off the cab and walk until I found a likely eating house.

The Cross was jammed with cars and people. I ambled along, staring into brilliantly lit windows, singling out a pair of ear-rings and a hat which would definitely bear investigation later in the week—after pay-day. I went into a book-shop and bought a pile of comics and a couple of cowboy stories of no educational value, but which, the attendant assured me, would go right to the heart of any small boy.

A small dark man was gazing in at the shop window. I noticed him as I stood, hesitantly, wondering which way to go. Further on the street became darker and I didn't want to wander through any poorly lit areas, so I retraced my steps back to the big intersection. Perhaps he had the same thought, because I saw him in the swarm of faces behind me as I paused to cross the road.

Ahead of me I had caught sight of a sign which promised authentic continental cooking if one followed the stairs to the basement below. Le Coq d'Or. It was a new café and someone —I couldn't remember who—had told me about it in glowing terms. On the spur of the moment I decided to sample a French omelette.

A commissionaire bowed me down the steps, which were gaily carpeted in red, and at the big glass doors of the café itself a blonde hostess asked me, in super-refined tones, whether I wanted a table for one.

It was a quaint little place with murals round the walls and small tables decked with candles whose beams threw a soft, kind light on women's faces, yet brought out the dazzling sparkle of every jewel. I followed the waiter across the room, wishing I'd worn a slightly more dashing outfit than a simple frock and linen coat.

In one corner a violinist was hashing out a romantic gypsy melody designed to stimulate the desire for good food and good wine. He strolled in among the diners, swaying to the rhythm of his own music. But always his eyes flickered back to one table as though the woman sitting there was no less a person than the Gypsy Queen herself.

I looked at her. And my heart sank. If it had been possible I would have turned and sneaked out. There was no trace of gypsy about her soft yellow hair and smooth petal-like skin, but she was infinitely lovely.

She suddenly looked past the entranced violinist and saw me. It was too late to retreat. John was standing up, trying to attract my attention, and Finch was pushing back his chair and striding over to me. He reached me before I'd had time to sit down.

"Rotten luck, darling, to pick the one café you wanted to avoid. Life's like that, isn't it?" he said with a sarcastic grin. "But now you're here you'll just have to make the best of it. God knows I need a bit of help, what with Miranda showing her claws and John in one of his strong silent moods. Come along. Come and join the happy party."

There was nothing else I could do.

As we wended our way through the tables, I noticed the small dark man I'd seen earlier, settling himself in for an evening meal.

"I thought you were determined not to budge till you'd got your 'phone call?" Finch said slyly.

I began to babble apologetically that I hadn't realized Barney wouldn't 'phone till about nine. Finch merely grinned and said nothing, and I was glad we reached his table at that moment and I was saved further explanations.

John was standing waiting for me, smiling.

"Gilly dear, what a pleasant surprise." He honestly seemed pleased to see me, and held out a chair before the waiter could reach it.

Miranda was smiling, too.

"How clever of you, darling, to know we were coming here. What a happy thought to follow us. We're delighted to see you."

Her voice was warm and soft and I thought I'd never met any woman more charmingly catty than Miranda. Her claws were so carefully, so cunningly, sheathed.

"I had no idea you were here. It was just chance."

"And good judgment, darling." She lowered her long lashes and picked up her knife and fork again and began prodding at a piece of chicken. "It's quite a charming place, isn't it?"

The waiter held a menu in front of me, a great long screed of fancy names that required earnest study and concentration. I waved it aside and ordered a salad.

My evening was spoilt. All I wanted was to make a pretence of eating and then to rush back to my flat. I certainly didn't intend to sit about trying to make small-talk.

"Have you heard how Joey is?" John's eyes were anxious. "He's been on my mind all afternoon. I can't understand McLean's attitude, keeping the whole thing secret. Does he imagine we'll send poisoned sweets to the hospital? If anything's happened to that boy, I'll never forgive myself. Why did I ever suggest he should have the bike? Damn it all, how was I to know?"

He fixed his eyes on me, waiting. I didn't look at him as I replied that, as yet, I hadn't an idea where Joey was. At least that was the truth. But I didn't dare look up. I didn't want him to guess I knew more than I was telling.

He pushed his plate to one side as if the thought of food was nauseating. "We'll have to wait until the Inspector sees fit to release some information, I suppose."

Finch turned the subject adroitly to lighter topics, and while I nibbled at a lettuce leaf he worked hard on tales of various homes he'd visited—how he'd been mistaken for the laundryman and had a pile of dirty clothes pushed on to him, and once, how a shortsighted client had offered him a drink of turps.

John listened politely, but I doubt if he heard a word of it. He waited till Miranda's laughter had died down.

"I'm afraid I'm dull company tonight. I've got a lot on my mind. I'm not referring only to this dreadful affair we've been dragged into, but that's hastened my decision. I've been thinking for some time now that I should sit back and let a younger man carry the reins. Now I know I'm right. No matter what the outcome of McLean's case, there'll be loose talk flying about, and for the sake of the firm, I'm cutting adrift. The name of Welch," he added bitterly, "may not have the standing in the future that it's had in the past. I never thought the day would come when it would be mixed up in an unsavoury court case. But it looks as though we can't escape."

Alarm sprang into Miranda's eyes. "What do you mean?"

He put his hand on hers. "Simply, my dear, that I'm handing in my resignation. Work's taken up far too much of my life since we've been married and you've been wonderful about it. Never a complaint. But in the future it'll be different. We'll spend our time together."

I was glad he was looking at her long slim fingers resting in his. I was glad, so very glad, that he didn't see the sudden fear and horror that flooded her face.

"But, John . . . you can't——"

"Why not? The firm won't collapse without me, you know I'm not as infallible as you think I am, bless you."

She gave a hollow laugh. "But you'll be lost without your work."

It was a desperate attempt to stave off disaster. Nothing,

not even murder, had touched her to such depths as John's decision to devote the rest of his life to her. She was appalled at the very thought of a lifetime alone with her husband, with no regular work to send him to the office each day. John for ever at her heels—a long, boring prospect!

Finch's smile was malicious. "How wise you are, John."

John flashed him a quick look. "A man's place is by his wife's side," he said with old-fashioned sweetness.

"I agree. If one's lucky enough to find the right woman. I'd like to try your recipe—with Gilly. But she won't agree. I haven't given up hope of persuading her." He was smooth as butter.

I abandoned all attempt at eating. This conversation was worse than talking about—murder. I put down my knife and fork.

John looked startled. "You and Gilly! . . ." He couldn't hide his disapproval.

Finch produced cigarettes calmly. "I can't offer her the lap of luxury but whatever I have is hers, including my heart." He made me a small theatrical bow and I could have slapped him.

Why did he have to behave like this? We'd covered the ground before, and he knew my answer. Why bring it up now —and in front of John and Miranda?

I looked at his attractive face, and in that instant I knew the truth about Finch—a truth I'd never faced before. He wanted me because he couldn't have me. He wasn't interested in the dozens of women ready to swoon at his feet, he was only interested in the unattainable. Once I'd joined the swooners I'd be tossed aside as carelessly as an old shoe, and his eyes would roam the crowd for another victim. He could no more help himself than Miranda could help loving emeralds and diamonds. It was simply the way he was made.

Miranda was trying to give her usual trilling laugh, but it came out oddly high-pitched and shrill. "You and Gilly! You do get the most extraordinary ideas, Finch."

Something in her tone brought my eyes sharply to her face, and then I wished I hadn't looked at her. In that swift second I realized more than I wanted to know about Miranda. I saw her composure ripped apart, revealing naked, blind hatred. And even more dreadful was the burning jealousy in her green eyes—a passionate, blazing emotion that centred its fire around me.

I glanced down at my plate quickly. I was filled with an overwhelming pity for her, because, for the first time, I knew what lay behind those lovely, heavy-lidded eyes, and I marvelled that I'd never realized before that she was madly in love with Finch. She wanted John's money, but she wanted Finch too. She wanted to have her cake and eat it.

Pictures suddenly floated through my brain with horrible clarity—Miranda rushing over to see me in the dead of night —Miranda trying to stifle any mention that might connect her, dangerously, with the Oceana Hotel. Miranda standing on the verandah at Coolibah watching me weep on Finch's shoulder, trying to stem the hatred that boiled up inside her.

I suddenly thought of John. He mustn't know. He must never find out. Oh God, don't let him realize.

I looked up. Miranda was her smiling self again, cool and composed and lovely.

I forced my eyes to John's face. I had to find out whether he suspected.

He was smiling fondly at Miranda. "You'd like everyone to be as happy as we are, wouldn't you, darling? But you must stop worrying about other folk and think of yourself for a change."

I felt sick in the pit of my stomach—sick with utter relief that he was incapable of seeing Miranda as she really was. He'd built up an image of kindness and goodness to match her beauty and nothing would ever shake his faith in her.

I stood up dizzily. I couldn't stay a moment longer. I couldn't stay and watch Finch, with his knowing, amused eyes, John with his pathetic devotion, and Miranda with her sweet, angelic smile. I had to get away.

"What's the matter, Gilly? You're not running off? You haven't had coffee. Besides, we'll be going shortly—and the car's outside."

I managed to look John squarely in the eye. "I'm afraid my taxi will be waiting. I ordered it."

Finch was on his feet. "I'll see you home."

"No. Please."

He took my arm firmly. "I'll see you into a taxi anyway."

I heard John's voice call after me, "Try and find out about Joey. . . ."

I knew he and Miranda were both watching me, so I walked slowly, sedately, restraining the impulse to burst into a run. I wanted to shake off Finch's possessive hand, but I knew I daren't make a scene.

We walked to the door together.

"Don't come any further."

He stopped, but his hand tightened as if he were scared I'd dash off and leave him before he had a chance to speak.

"Listen, darling, I know what you're thinking, but you're wrong. There's nothing between Miranda and me, absolutely nothing. And there never——"

He paused.

"Never has been?" I asked coldly.

"I wanted to tell you about it, but you wouldn't let me. And there was nothing in it, darling. Not really. It's over long ago. It's all washed up."

It might have been for him. But not for Miranda.

"I happen to be in love with you, Gilly. What do you want me to do to convince you? Go down on one knee?"

"I suppose you said the same words to Miranda—when you persuaded her to stay with you at the Oceana." I was angry.

He laughed softly. "Oh my God! Miranda isn't as—difficult, shall we say?—as you are."

A thought struck me, and I put it into words before I could hold them back. "You and Miranda had both seen Lisa before she ever set foot in Coolibah."

His hand dropped and he took a step away from me. "The Inspector, my dear Gilly, knows all about it. I gave him the information he needed when I signed my real name this afternoon." He gave a queer, crooked smile. "Hotels have registers, you know, and I bet the police have been buzzing round that horrid little pub like bees."

"Finch, how could you?" I said in disgust. "I'll never forgive you, never, for hurting John."

He actually laughed. "My dear girl, John wouldn't believe it if you told him. Gilly, don't be this way. You're not going to hold a small thing against me?" Not one word of contrition. Not one word of remorse.

I walked off and left him. As far as I was concerned, I was walking out of his life—for ever.

I hurried into the street in search of a taxi. As we drove along, leaving the more brilliantly lit area behind us, I reflected on the queer chance that had taken me to Le Coq d'Or. If I hadn't gone there I wouldn't have found out about Finch—and Miranda. Life, I thought, is like that—full of strange turnings that lead to unexpected discoveries, sometimes pleasant, sometimes, like tonight, distinctly unpleasant.

It seemed as if a lot of my beautiful friendships were suddenly disintegrating. First Miranda. Now Finch. I'd never feel the same about him again, I told myself. Yet who was I to criticize, to judge, his behaviour? If only he hadn't picked on John's wife for one of his escapades! Sneaking behind John's back in flagrant abuse of hospitality and friendship! I could never forgive Finch for that.

Cottrill Street was black and empty and I was heartily relieved to see the Baileys' light shedding a warm glow across the front path, and to know that I wouldn't be alone in that big silent building. I paid the driver and raced up the steps as if the devils of hell were after me and banged on Dawn's door.

She opened it immediately. "We saw you go out earlier and wondered where on earth you were off to."

"I had an urge to see life," I told her, "but it wasn't a success. I'm dead tired and I'm going to bed."

I thrust the comics and books into her hand, and she turned her head and yelled for Blue.

He bundled me into the lift, and I wondered how much

longer he would have to go on playing this ridiculous role of bodyguard. Nevertheless, I was grateful for his presence. I didn't like the idea of entering an empty flat on my own. Not with murder and mayhem all around me.

He conducted his usual search through my rooms, and I told him in a burst of confidence that I'd hurried home because Barney would be ringing and I didn't want to miss the call.

He grinned. "That should cheer you. Sleep well. And if you're nervous, you know our 'phone number."

I shut the door after him and listened as the lift groaned on its downward journey. Then I made some tea and tidied up the flat, sorting out old papers and throwing out letters which had accumulated over the months.

The hands of the clock crawled slowly round the hour. But the 'phone remained obstinately silent. It refused to utter a single sound. I stared at it, trying to will it to burst into noisy clamour. But the room was as quiet as the grave.

I fought back the rising doubts in my mind. Barney had forgotten; he was at a party; he'd fallen for a redhead. What nonsense! He'd promised faithfully to call me. There was some perfectly simple, logical explanation. The connection was bad; he couldn't get through; there was a rush on the line tonight. But surely the line was clear by now?

Eleven o'clock . . . half past. . . . Twelve o'clock! He wouldn't ring now. Slowly I got up and prepared for bed.

The flats were very quiet and the sound of traffic was fainter and more remote as the night wore on. Once I heard a creak and I paused, with quickened breath, until I realized it had come from the floor board beneath my own foot.

Normally I never notice the hundreds of odd sounds that come by night, when a tired old building relaxes and contracts after the heat of the day. But now I heard every tiny moan and rattle. It seemed as though the house was full of eerie, ghostly noises, as though it were inhabited by a furtive, unseen presence with whom it whispered and chuckled with horrid glee.

I made sure the safety latch was on the door and then I crawled into bed and turned out the light.

I began a long imaginary conversation with Barney in which I was coldly polite and distant, refusing to acknowledge his abject apologies. It was in the midst of that conversation that I fell asleep.

CHAPTER XII

I T W A S almost dawn when I awoke. I sat up in bed, instantly alert, and every muscle taut. I was certain a noise had startled me from sleep into sudden, wide-awake awareness of my surroundings.

Then I heard it again. A queer, dull thud—followed by deep, unbroken silence. Not another sound. I was more puzzled than frightened—because I realized the noise I'd just heard had come from somewhere directly below me. From the Simpsons' flat! I put my ear to the wall, scarcely daring to breathe, in case I missed the slightest movement or sign of life from the room beneath me.

With slowly dawning panic I realized someone was moving about in the flat below! But who could it be? The Simpsons were away, and they weren't due back till next week! I waited, motionless, until my back ached, but I heard nothing more.

At last I sank back into bed, with the explanation of the noises I'd heard bursting like a flash of sunlight through my brain. What a fool I'd been! The Simpsons had arrived home sooner than expected. And Mr. Simpson, who was a notoriously early bird, was mooching about in his slippers and dressing-gown preparing the morning cup of tea, which he always swore was the best cup of the whole day.

The thought that they were home again filled me with peace and joy, and I dozed off into a dreamless, happy sleep.

It was late when I woke and there was thunder in the air— low rumbles that sounded like a dog growling—and the roofs were wet with rain. But there was still no relief from the moist, sticky heat. I longed for a cool breeze. For over a week now we'd sweltered in this breathless atmosphere.

I got up and showered and made myself tea and toast. Another day to live through. Sunday. I wondered what McLean was doing. It was difficult to understand the lives that other people lived. McLean! Simon! Clare! Tony! The pattern of their existence was so different, yet so similar. Eating, drinking, talking, laughing. But each individual a complete world unto himself, a private world in which even the closest friends and intimates had no part.

I'd known Clare for years, but how well did I really know her? In the old days we'd shared many secrets. But now she was shut off from me as if a gate had slammed in my face and I could only peep over it and catch a glimpse of what lay behind it. In the old days she would have told me about her hopes and fears. She would have confided in me. But maturity had taught her to keep her own secrets.

Oddly enough, Miranda was easier to understand than Clare, and easier to pity, too. To me, the price she paid for luxury seemed exorbitantly high, but then I suspected that Miranda and I viewed life with very different eyes. She was an expert at the slow smile, the soft word, the gentle touch that kept John happy and unsuspecting. It required little effort on her part. And always there'd be someone else in the background, someone to fill the gap which her marriage couldn't bridge. John would never know, because she was clever and because she had the face of an angel.

Finch had told me McLean knew about that episode at the Oceana Hotel. Was it the reason for his demand that we should sign our names for him? Finch seemed to think so.

But even if Lisa had recognized Miranda, it wasn't likely she'd go running to John Welch with the information. And it was even less likely that Miranda would see her walking up the long drive and lure her into the little sitting-room to murder her. Miranda wasn't the type to notice the maid who turned down her bed and tidied her room at a hotel. She had probably been telling the truth when she said, after Lisa's death, that she'd never seen the girl before. It was the mention of the Oceana Hotel that had shocked Miranda and had set her wondering whether her well-kept secret was about to be shouted from the house-top. She'd had some nasty moments— moments of doubt and fear.

I decided to go down and see Dawn. I wanted to tell her

the good news that the Simpsons were home again. I slammed the door and ran quickly down the stairs.

On the first-floor landing I hesitated, tempted to knock and welcome Mrs. Simpson back, and ask her the usual questions about her holiday. But there wasn't a sound from inside. I was puzzled.

It was queer that the flat should be so quiet. At this time of day Mrs. Simpson should be rattling pots and pans in the kitchen as she put the roast on, and her husband should be listening to the radio to discover when the experts predicted the long-awaited cool change. He was always first with the latest on the weather news. He followed the rising and falling temperatures with the avidity of an enthusiast.

I frowned and continued my journey downstairs.

Dawn opened her door to me. She was wearing a strapless sun frock that showed off the deep even tan of her skin.

In the kitchen Blue was straddling a chair, leaning backwards so that it balanced precariously on two legs. He was talking to Inspector McLean.

"You're in time for coffee," Dawn told me. "Unless you'd prefer a beer—Mac was on his way up to see you as soon as he's finished." She gave a quick grin. "I'm in the dog-house for telling you about Joey. He seems to think you've got a natural gift for giving away information even when you don't mean to."

I loathe being told I'm transparent, so I said "Good morning" rather coolly to the Inspector, and gave my warmest smile to Blue.

"I'm glad you're here. It saves me climbing the stairs." Mac waved his hand in a lazy upward movement. "I'm pleased to see you're looking well—and still in one piece, too."

He was laughing at me.

I turned to Dawn. "The Simpsons are home."

She stared at me in frank disbelief.

Blue stopped swinging his chair and rested his elbows on the table.

"Home?" Dawn repeated doubtfully. "Oh no, darling. You must be mistaken. They're not due back till Wednesday and wild horses wouldn't drag Mrs. S. away from the grand-child till the last possible moment. What made you think they were back?"

"I heard them." Doubt was beginning to creep into my voice. "I heard them this morning just as it was getting light. I thought it was Mr. Simpson up and about. In the hot weather he always gets up at the first sign of dawn."

They were looking at me queerly as if they couldn't find words. The rain outside faded away to a drizzle, then stopped, leaving the room very quiet after the gentle pit-pat of falling water on the stone path.

"You must have made a mistake," Dawn said slowly. "If they'd arrived last night or this morning, they would have left a note for the milkman. There was only your bottle out there when I went to bring ours in. I always hear Mr. Simpson when he trots down for the milk."

My doubts gave way to quickening fear. "Someone was in the flat. Who was it?"

I was scared.

"Who was it?" I asked again in a thin voice.

"I don't know," Dawn said dully. "Unless you only thought you heard a noise. There was quite a bit of thunder earlier."

She was just as jittery as I was, but determined not to show it.

"You were probably half asleep anyway, darling," she said lamely. "It's not like you to be awake in the early hours." And then, in an effort to change the subject, "Did Barney ring?"

"No," I said absently. It didn't seem quite so important this morning. There were other things on my mind—things like unexplained noises in an unoccupied flat.

I glanced across at McLean, who'd been saying nothing. I half expected him to bound up the stairs there and then. But it seemed, for all he cared, Mrs. Simpson could come home and find the silver gone!

He caught my glance and smiled. "I'm a disappointment to you, Miss Amery. You'd like some spectacular action. If I thought it would do any good, I assure you I'd go creeping up the stairs and break the door in, as I know you'd like me to. Whoever you heard, he's not there now. Don't worry, I'll investigate the matter, so you can put it out of your head. You just worry about your own flat and make sure you keep the door locked. You see and hear far too much for your own peace of mind. Tell me, where did you rush off to last night? Can't you stay in one place for longer than an hour?"

I told him, with what dignity I could muster, that I felt the desire for company, so I'd taken a taxi to the Cross. I added that it was sometimes necessary to eat, even in the midst of a murder case.

He cocked an eyebrow at me. "Meet anyone you knew at the café?"

I told him Miranda and John and Finch were there, but even as I said it I knew it was stale news. McLean already knew! He made no comment and asked no further questions.

Blue got up from his chair and wandered to the window.

"Clare and Tony are walking across the street. Simon Ashton's with them. I guess they're coming to see Gilly. They'd hardly walk in on us, after the show I put on yesterday."

Was it only yesterday that Blue had gone roaring like a lion to Coolibah?

Mac leaned on his elbows. "Oh yes! It'll be Miss Amery they want, you can bet your life. They can't do without her these days."

There was a certain amount of truth in that. For months I'd been almost a stranger to Clare and Miranda—even to John—seeing them only at social functions or reporting their latest activities in my column. But since Lisa's death I'd been embraced into the bosom of the family.

We watched them covertly from the shelter of the kitchen curtains. Mac, it appeared, was wrong, because they came straight up the path and rang the Baileys' bell. I guessed it was Clare who put her finger on the bell and kept it there until Dawn, with a doubtful, backward glance at Mac, walked through the lounge to let them in.

"They're not looking for me after all," I said.

Mac only smiled knowingly and shook his head a little.

Blue put a restraining hand on my shoulder, holding me back in case I should dart into the lounge.

"I hope you don't mind us barging in like this," Tony's voice said, "but we had to find out how Joey is and we'd like you to give him these. The Inspector won't tell us anything, and naturally we're frightfully worried and we're hoping you've had good news from the hospital. I hope Joey's well enough to read these. And I hope you'll believe me when I say how terribly sorry and upset we are about the whole business."

It was rather a pompous little speech, and Dawn replied in the same vein, very formally, very politely, "It's very kind of you. Thank you."

Perhaps Clare felt the conversation was on too stiff and stilted a plane, because she rushed in with breathless sentences, pausing now and then, but not long enough to give Tony a chance to break her flow.

"Dawn darling, I know it's most awful cheek even to dare to face you after what's happened, and I was scared Blue might kick us out and really I wouldn't blame him if what the Inspector thinks is true. But it can't be. None of us would want to hurt Joey, you must know that. And I couldn't stand it another moment and I knew I just had to come and see you and try to explain—and Simon and Tony said they'd come too, to give me moral support. Oh, I'm so sorry, you've never met Simon Ashton, have you?"

Blue and Mac and I were silent as mice in the kitchen.

We heard Dawn say, "How do you do?" and Simon's cold, expressionless voice acknowledging the introduction.

Then Clare ran on again, "Is Blue still mad at us? At one of us? Of course I know exactly how he feels, but don't you think he might've got hold of the wrong end of the stick? And that goes for the McLean man too. He's obsessed with the idea of murder and he's looking for crime where it doesn't exist. Joey's accident could easily have been caused by old brakes that had worn through. The bike was terribly ancient, you know, and it hadn't been used for ages. It could have happened that way, Dawn. But the Inspector had to drama-tize the whole thing and assume that——It's too horrible to think about and I simply don't believe it; nor does Dad. Even the police make mistakes. Everyone knows that. They make some frightful bloomers sometimes, but just because they're police no one ever hears how wrong they were or how they make innocent people go through positive hell. Dad said it was best to leave you alone until the case had been solved—the murder of that girl I mean. Did you know her name was Elizabeth Brown? It's queer the Inspector should suspect one of us, because we'd never seen the girl before—I don't mean to sound snobby, but she just wasn't that type of person. And Finch's name turns out to be Brown, and the police seem to think it's a crime to change a name by deed poll, which is what he did—— Oh God, I suppose we'll live through it. Darling, the main thing is, how is Joey? We've been so worried about him, and I kept waking up and thinking about him all last night——"

She stopped quite abruptly and waited for Dawn's reply.

I held my breath. Already they were suspicious that the whole accident had been a fake in some way, but they weren't quite sure. They were trying to find out. I could sense Dawn searching for the right words, setting her face in the right expression.

Blue sensed her hesitation too, and his hand dropped from my shoulder and he strode to the door. But McLean reached it before him, and placed himself in front of Blue's bulk, slowly surveying the faces in the room. I saw Dawn flash him a glance of thanks and relief.

"Oh, Inspector McLean! I didn't know you were here." Clare's hand flew to her face in a quick, nervous gesture.

"The Inspector can tell you whatever you want to know much better than I can," Dawn said.

"We came to ask about Joey." Tony looked anxiously at Mac and at Blue. No one seemed to have noticed me as yet.

"I hope to hear today how he is. There was no further news last night," Mac told him calmly. "But I'm sure Dawn appreciates your enquiries." I detected a hint of sarcasm behind his even tones.

Simon put his hand on Clare's arm. She was strangely flustered. "There's no point in worrying Mr. and Mrs. Bailey any further."

"No. Oh no." She made a move towards the door. "I suppose it was silly of me to come in the first place. It was all my fault. I insisted. I didn't want Blue to go on thinking awful thoughts about us——"

She looked at him. He hadn't said a word, and he didn't speak now, but something in his face must have reassured her because she gave him a small, tight smile. "Poor Blue. It's lousy for you and Dawn."

"If there's anything we can do, you must tell us," Tony said. "We'll move heaven and earth to help Joey."

"Don't keep saying it." Clare was suddenly scratchy. "Don't keep on and on when Blue knows already that we'll help if we can."

Tony gazed at her in astonishment.

"There's no need to bite my head off." His gaze found me hiding behind Blue's back. "Gilly! The very girl we want. We were coming up to see you."

Mac was right after all, I thought. Clare flew towards me as if mine was the only familiar face in a room full of strangers. I stepped into the open and she grabbed my hands in hers.

"Darling, you're coming swimming with us. You must come. Miranda's determined to spend the day on the beach and she's even talked Dad into it, and he particularly wants you to come. He said they saw you last night and he thought then that this business is getting you down and you need taking out of yourself. You can come with us in Tony's car, because poor Simon's sick of being dragged around on his own, and I was sure you'd make up a foursome. You will, won't you, darling? It's much wiser to get out and try and forget for a while."

I tried vainly to think up an excuse in the face of her persuasion, and couldn't find one quickly enough. I hoped Mac would come to my rescue, but he let me down badly by saying, "It sounds a nice idea. I wish I could take a swim too. But police have to hang about on duty, making the most awful bloomers." He grinned at Clare.

She let go my hands abruptly.

"Oh!" she said softly. "I really didn't mean—— I didn't

know you were listening when I said that. Of course I know you don't make blunders, or I hope you don't."

"I hope so too, Miss Welch. Not this time, anyway."

I threw him a look of desperate appeal. "You wanted to see me?"

He shook his head. "It can wait."

I knew then that I was sunk.

"I'm not much of a swimmer, Gillian, so I hope you'll be patient with me." Simon was trying to be friendly, but the thought of a day with him, with those pale eyes watching my every movement, sent a tiny shiver through me.

"Hurry and get your things, darling. Then we'll go back to Coolibah and pick up the others." Clare was impatient to be gone.

"But it's been raining. The weather may break."

"If it does, we'll come home. Anyway, it's the nicest time to swim, in the rain. I adore it."

"Don't worry about the weather," Tony put in. "I heard the report before I left the flat this morning and it's going to be another stinker."

I turned despondently towards the door. I could see I was doomed to a day on the beach, because for some reason they were determined to have my company. I couldn't think why.

McLean followed me out into the lobby. "I'll come up with you."

I heard Clare's surprised giggle, and her high, childish voice saying, "How peculiar! Does he make a practice of watching girls change into their bathing suits?"

Then Mac shut the door and piloted me into the lift. We rode in silence to the first floor. Dawn must have been correct when she assured me the Simpsons weren't home. If they'd returned to their flat, we would have known all about it by now. There would have been some signs of life behind that white wooden door.

"Stop worrying!" Mac's voice sounded tired. "Haven't you got any faith in me? I promise I won't let any murderous characters snoop round the Simpsons' flat. You just go for a nice swim and forget about everything, like Clare told you."

The Inspector, I thought, was a mass of contradictions.

One minute he was warning me to be careful and to watch my step, and with the next breath he was pushing me on to the very people he'd warned me against. I didn't get it! And I said so!

The lift stopped at my landing and he held the door open. "I'm not pushing you on to anyone. I'm thinking of you all the time." I could have sworn one eyelid fluttered in a wicked wink. "Quite seriously, you're much safer on a crowded beach than you are here, alone in your flat. Quit trying to work out solutions. Forget your little girl-friend was murdered, and forget about your burglar. Stop worrying about Clare Welch too. Let her sort out her own troubles. Don't try and interfere. If she's got something on her mind she can come and tell me about it, and I'll help her. You just remember those three wise monkeys and follow their example. It wouldn't be wise to let on that you'd dropped to the Oceana business. I'd keep quiet about it if I were you. Miranda Welch could be—dangerous."

"You know about her? And about Finch?" He did seem to know an awful lot.

"My God, yes! It was fairly obvious. That arty bloke's just the type she'd go for, don't you think? She didn't want me to question him, because she was scared he'd spill the beans, but she needn't have worried. He didn't. But she even managed a faint—a mistake on her part because it made me wonder why she should try to distract my attention when she'd gone through the rest of the inquisition without turning a hair. When you told me Elizabeth Brown thought she knew either Clare or Miranda Welch, the rest fell into place quite easily. It was merely a matter of checking photos at the Oceana, and quite a few members of the staff recognized Miranda . . . and I was pretty sure of Finch Martyn even before our Melbourne blokes dug up his real name for me. I got his signature—and it checked with the Brown in the hotel register, just as I knew it would."

He walked into the lounge and I followed him.

"You can't think Finch—or Miranda—had a hand in Lisa's death?" I was aching with curiosity to know where his suspicions lay.

196

"Why not? Miranda's prepared to play round on the side but she's not prepared to lose her bread and butter. She wouldn't want John Welch to find out about it. Finch Martyn wouldn't be too keen on John Welch knowing either. It'd be bad for business. One of them could easily have seen the girl coming up the path and decided to stop her mouth before she opened it too wide. And we do know she wanted to see Mr. Welch, so presumably she had something quite important to tell him."

"Finch wouldn't do that. He isn't even in love with Miranda. Not now!"

Mac seemed intent on a flight of birds through the window. He didn't speak for a moment.

"All sorts of skeletons start popping out of cupboards when it's a case of murder. Be thankful you haven't got one, because I'd drag it out. Go along and change, there's a good girl."

I was walking towards the bedroom, when his voice said softly, "I understand Finch Martyn's running after you now."

I stopped and stared at him, wondering where he'd heard that particular bit of gossip. He went on gazing at his birds, watching them wheel past in a wide circle with barely a movement of their wings.

But he knew I'd turned to look at him, because he said, "Run along. And make it snappy, Gilly!"

It was the first time he'd called me by my name, but I barely noticed the fact. After all, everyone always called me Gilly, even after a short acquaintance. Mine isn't the sort of face to inspire awe and dignity in the beholder.

I slipped into the bathroom and clambered into my bathers, grabbing a towel and zipping up my long terry gown. My rope sandals and I was ready. When I emerged, Mac was still deep in thought by the window. He seemed surprised that I'd been so quick.

"Ready?" He began walking to the door, then stopped. "You're so certain of this girl Lisa, aren't you? So certain that she wasn't out for blackmail?"

I stopped too, because I hadn't expected the conversation to revert to Lisa just as I was on my way to the beach. I could

197

feel my prickles rising at the suggestion that poor, defenceless Lisa had been a sinister, threatening character.

"If you're determined to find a blackmailer why don't you concentrate on Simon Ashton?"

"I know about him," he said wearily, "and I've got him well and truly under my eye."

I was pleased to hear it.

He appeared to forget me as a person and studied me as if I were a vase sitting on the mantelpiece, an ornament whose worth and value he was trying to assess.

"You're so often wrong, Gilly; that's the whole trouble. You don't see what's going on right under your nose half the time, and then you come out with a definite, positive statement based on pure intuition and you expect me to believe it wholeheartedly simply because you believe it yourself. Can you be wrong about so many things and right about a girl you'd barely seen?"

I tried to think of a crushing reply, because I was rather hurt to think my judgment was relegated to the realms of pure fancy. But Mac didn't give me time to reply.

"Before we go down and join the others, I want you to listen to me very carefully. When they start arguing about which beach they'll sample, you stick out for Bondi. They'll gripe like hell of course, and tell you Bondi's too crowded, and Clare will suggest a nice little spot she knows where you'll have some privacy and where people won't crawl all over you. That's exactly the sort of spot you've got to stay away from. You tell them it's Bondi or nothing for you—and they'll come round. When you get there, lead them to the centre life-saving reel and park just below it on the right-hand side."

I gaped. "What if there's no space there? I can't insist on the exact spot where we sit."

He grinned. "Nonsense! Someone'll make room for a couple of pretty girls."

He pushed me out on to the landing and shut the door.

"You're a baffling prospect for a murderer. He isn't sure how much you know, how much Lisa told you in the café. And he's trying to find out. Remember that."

I walked into the lift with knees that rattled like a pair of castanets. A happy day lay ahead, I told myself bitterly. A happy day with a murderer!

We reached the downstairs lobby and Mac held the door open for me politely.

As I slipped under his arm, he smiled down at me. "Watch out for sharks. And I don't mean the sharks in the water, either."

CHAPTER XIII

I LAY on the hot sand with my face on my towel and my eyes shut. It was heavenly to feel that heat searing through me, and although there was not much sun, I expected that tomorrow I would be as red as a lobster. But that was to-morrow and I was too lazy and too contented to think about it.

Clare and Finch and Tony were squatting beside me, and their voices floated past—words that meant nothing to me because my mind seemed incapable of taking in more than the soft white sand beneath me, the ceaseless boom of the breakers, and the buzz of humanity as children shrieked with delight and friends yelled greetings to each other. The noises mingled together into a whole, with a single word, a sentence, a scream, standing out sharply, but unrelated to the fabric of conscious-ness.

I opened one eye and looked up at Clare. She was drawing patterns on the sand, listening while Finch gave an enraptured account of the thrills of surf-skiing.

Simon was sitting beside her, but, as always, he seemed alone, on the edge of the circle, noting everything, saying nothing.

John was stretched out at Miranda's feet. She was gazing out to sea with eyes as deep and green as the water itself. I wondered what she was thinking.

The beach was crammed with people of all ages and sizes. There were lovely streamlined blondes, paunchy middle-aged men, boys with lithe brown limbs, and toddlers clad in brief seersucker bathers. There were family parties, loving couples, and even bookworms who'd brought their literature with them. It was hard to believe that this mass of bodies represented only a small part of the population of Sydney, and that other beaches were just as crowded, just as densely packed as Bondi.

I shut my eyes again and thought how queer it was that

I'd managed to persuade Clare and Miranda to come here. John, of course, hadn't cared. He'd said that one beach was much the same as another. But Clare had gazed at me with round, puzzled eyes, and Tony had laughed as if he thought the events of the last few days had turned my brain. I'd stuck to my guns, though, and when they finally realized that only Bondi held any attraction for me, they'd given in abruptly with no further opposition, and we'd clambered into the two cars and headed for the Beachcomber because Miranda felt the need of food before she faced the water.

The day had passed off much better than I'd expected, and I'd actually enjoyed a crab mayonnaise for lunch. We'd lingered over the meal, sitting beneath a huge gaudy umbrella from where we could see the big rollers curling over before they cascaded into a waterfall of white foam.

No one had mentioned murder or Joey's accident. We'd chatted gaily—just a little too gaily, perhaps—about the surf and the size of the breakers and the wonderful work the life-savers did. We'd agreed politely on the craziness of swimmers who ventured out beyond the safety line. We'd discussed the danger of undertow. Not a word, not a single remark, indicated that anything more important than swimming and sun-bathing had ever entered our lives. Just a big, happy party!

And yet the strain had been there, beneath the surface. I'd seen it in Miranda's face, despite the enormous green-rimmed sun-glasses which hid her eyes, and which she'd eventually abandoned because John insisted they spoilt her beauty.

I'd seen it, too, in Clare's fluttering hands, which seemed incapable of lying still, even when she wasn't speaking. Tony's smile had lost its old, mischievous charm and was more a concession to convention than an expression of spontaneous mirth.

Finch had fallen into his role of raconteur through sheer habit rather than from any desire to amuse or entertain us, and his stories lacked their usual bite.

Simon remained exactly the same as when I'd first met him.

After lunch I'd led the way to the beach with McLean's

instructions hammering nervously through my head, and with a dreadful moment of panic when Clare insisted we'd gone far enough and she could see a space on the closely packed beach where our little party could squeeze in. I'd pretended I didn't hear her, and had forged ahead to the centre reel, and then I'd dumped myself on the sand and looked around for the others. They followed me like lambs.

But I hadn't breathed properly till we'd settled in a group together, and then I'd flung myself full length on the sand to sun-bathe until it was too hot to bear any longer . . . and I was fast approaching that point now. I turned over on to my back, and Clare poked me with her toe.

"I believe you've been asleep. Lucky you. Sometimes I wonder whether I'll ever sleep soundly again."

Tony said sharply, "Don't be silly, Clare."

"What's silly about it? I'm not used to—murder." It was the first time the word had been mentioned. "You've seen dead people before, but I haven't. Every time I close my eyes I see that girl's face."

"Come for a swim. That'll put it out of your mind." Tony stretched out a hand to pull her to her feet, but she brushed it away brusquely.

"I can't bear it, I tell you. I can't bear the way we sit around talking about things that don't matter. It makes me sick. Who cares about whether it's a heavy sea or whether it's going to rain again? Talk. Talk. Talk. Pretending all the time. Pretending that nothing's happened. Much more of it and I'll scream my head off."

She looked as if she might, at that.

"Why don't we admit we're nearly off our heads with worry and that McLean thinks one of us is a murderer? Or a murderess! Perhaps he thinks I did it."

John had been talking to Miranda, but he lifted his head sharply as Clare's voice rose, and wriggled nearer to her on the sand.

"Be quiet, Clare! You'll have the whole beach watching you in a minute."

"I don't care. It's the truth, isn't it?" But she lowered her voice again. "It was a lousy idea to come here."

"You had no better suggestion to make." Miranda fiddled with her sun-glasses, then put them on. "We were enjoying ourselves until you started this morbid conversation. I can't think why you came if you couldn't behave like a civilized human being. It's no worse for you than it is for anyone else. In any case, I don't know what you want us to do. Sit around discussing who could have killed the girl? I have more faith in my friends than you have. I believe in their innocence."

"Then why do you carry that stupid-looking gun wherever you go?" Clare's lip curled contemptuously. "At least I don't arm myself against my friends. You thought I didn't know. But I saw you slip it into the bureau drawer in the sitting-room yesterday, and I bet you've got it with you right now. You trust your friends. Oh yes. But you won't move without a gun, will you?"

Miranda picked up her large beach bag and hurled it at Clare's feet. I couldn't see her eyes for those huge dark glasses, but her mouth was a thin red line of anger. "Look for yourself!"

Clare didn't move a muscle. "No, thank you. I wouldn't lower myself."

"Perhaps because you know it isn't there. It disappeared shortly after you saw me put it in the drawer. Strange, isn't it?" Miranda showed even white teeth in a tiny, dangerous smile. "You were the only person who knew where it was!"

Clare quivered with fury. "Are you trying to suggest I took it?"

"Someone did, darling."

I looked at her with horror rising in my throat. The comfortable, relaxed feeling had vanished. I was back in my nightmare world and there was no escape from it—not even on a crowded beach in bright daylight. For a brief fraction of time we were as remote from the hurly-burly around us as if we were on a desert island. Simon's eyes rested on Miranda, then looked out to sea, but I don't think he saw the green, translucent water any more than I did. It had ceased to exist. Only the tension which ran like a live wire around our small group seemed real at that instant.

"I don't understand," Finch said, very softly. He understood what Miranda had said, though. He knew perfectly well that an unknown hand—perhaps a murderer's hand—had removed a deadly weapon.

"Why did you carry the thing about with you in the first place?" he asked. "Wasn't it rather stupid? Like asking for trouble?"

It was John who answered him. "What harm could it do? Miranda wouldn't even know if it was loaded." He covered her hand with his. "It gave her a sense of security. McLean knew about it and he raised no objections. I told him about it myself. I also told him," he said, his eyes roving from face to face, "that it had disappeared. It's his job to find it. Suppose we leave the matter in his hands."

"Not very capable hands, I fear." Finch studied his toes. "Far be it from me to criticize the police and their methods, but they don't seem to be getting any nearer the truth."

"Don't be too sure." John sounded terse, and his eyes were hard as granite. "They probably know a lot more than they let on. They dug up your past pretty quickly."

Miranda was suddenly rigid with fear. "What do you mean?"

John pulled his hand away from hers and began sifting sand through his fingers. "It was rather smart of them to find out Finch's real name, don't you think?"

I saw the relief—the unmistakable relief—that flooded her face. She'd had a bad moment. "Oh, that! Yes, I suppose it was clever of them. But it'd be more to the point if they found out something about the girl who was killed. They don't seem to know much—apart from her name. Why should they pick on us? Why can't they leave us alone? They should find out whether she had any enemies, whether someone was following her, instead of prying into our lives. Surely there's some way of discovering what sort of girl she was, and the type of people she mixed with."

"It's difficult to trace a girl who's just arrived in a new country," Tony said, with tolerance for the slow, grinding wheels of law. "From what Gilly says, the girl's parents were killed in the blitz. But you'd think she must have other relatives who would come forward."

But she hadn't mentioned any aunt or uncle to me. Only

her parents—and her brother—and he was dead, too. With a flash of inspiration I suddenly realized that he must have had friends whom he'd brought to Lisa's home, friends who could tell the police whatever they wanted to know about her history. That was a line Mac should take.

I spoke my thoughts aloud. "Of course. Jock!"

Tony swivelled his head and looked at me with puzzled eyes. "What?" His frown cleared. "Oh, I forgot. That was her brother's name, wasn't it? But how does it help?"

I didn't enlarge on the train of thought I'd been following because at that very moment I became conscious of a man lying just a few feet away from me with his head buried in a book. He was a small dark man with crisp curling hair, and I knew, as well as I knew my own hand, that I'd seen him before. He turned over a page and looked up. Brown eyes under thick black eyebrows.

He was the man I'd seen at the Cross yesterday, the man who'd stared through the shop window while I bought Joey's comics. The man who'd sat at a nearby table while I nibbled a salad and made my startling discoveries about Finch and Miranda.

There was nothing very sinister about his appearance, but for some reason my stomach turned over. I didn't like the fact that he turned up like a bad penny wherever I went.

I realized I was staring at him, and I dragged my eyes away.

"What's the matter?" Tony asked. "You don't look well, Gilly."

I didn't feel it either. I was thinking about the information McLean had gleaned about my movements last night—about the way he seemed to know everything I'd done and said, even before I told him. I knew the reason why now. And I didn't like it.

The small dark man was a policeman and he was follow-ing me, watching every action, listening to my every word; recording his impressions carefully and faithfully to McLean. But why? Because McLean was convinced I was in danger? Or because he believed I was implicated in some way in Lisa's death?

I picked up my bathing cap and began putting it on.

"I'm going in. I've had too much sun."

I wanted to get away from those spying eyes. It's unnerving to find that you are being trailed and that every innocent sentence is being memorized and handed on to an inspector of police. I stood up.

John stretched lazily. "A swim is the answer. You're right, Gilly." He pulled Miranda up and stretched out a hand to Clare, but Simon had already heaved her to her feet.

It was queer the way they all followed my lead. If I said Bondi, they came to Bondi. If I chose a spot on the beach, they settled on it. Now, when I suggested a swim, they moved in a united front towards the water.

They ran on ahead, shouting to me to race them in. But I let them go, because I couldn't resist turning my head to see if my newly discovered spy was hot on my heels. He was still lying on the sand with his nose in the book and he seemed so innocent and harmless that I wondered whether I'd been mistaken. He looked like an ordinary citizen enjoying a day's leisure. Then I remembered McLean's insistence that we should sit right below the life-saving reel and I suddenly knew the significance behind that odd order. He'd wanted my shadow to be able to spot me easily.

Clare and Tony had reached the water and I watched them dive in together, Clare's dark hair streaming wetly behind her as she emerged, laughing, and began bobbing about on the top of the waves.

Miranda was dabbling her toes gingerly, hovering uncertainly, giving the impression that she was about to wade in sedately and timorously. I smiled. Her entrances were always spectacular—even into the water. Her timing was good. She knew eyes were on her lovely svelte figure, and she didn't disappoint them. At the unexpected moment she went into action—a graceful, arched dive that made me sigh with envy.

John and Finch hit the water with an almighty splash and swam towards her.

Funny how powerful John looked in bathers, I reflected. I'd never thought of him as a big man, but he was muscular and well built, and beside him Finch looked all arms and legs.

John certainly kept his age well, with only a slight thickening round the middle to indicate that his best years were behind him.

"They swim like fishes."

I was surprised to find Simon beside me.

I shrugged. "So they should. They're used to the water. They come down nearly every day in the summer."

I broke into my usual run which meant I was about to flop into the surf. Clare was waving to me encouragingly. Then I stopped, because one of my nicer instincts told me to wait for Simon. He wasn't used to surfing. He wouldn't know how to take a header into the waves and it would be dangerous for him to attempt to dive into the shallow if he'd never done it before. I began to wade in slowly, and he flashed me a quick smile, as though he knew exactly what was going on in my mind.

The water was icy cold at first, but it was exhilarating and pleasant to bounce about on the waves, watching for dumpers, riding in on the crest of a sea horse, hearing the shouts of dismay and delight as a distant roller curled in a magnificent sheet of clear green water and seemed to poise for a second, before crashing onward, catching the unwary in its swirling, angry foam.

I forgot about Simon and the others. I forgot about everything but the delicious thrill of judging each wave as it approached, of diving just in time to avoid a dumper, of choosing the exact moment to ride triumphantly in to shore—carried effortlessly by the charging water beneath me.

During a lull I looked about me trying to locate Clare or John or Simon. It was hard to recognize a familiar face among the hundreds of bobbing heads. Then a figure dived and came up beside me, with dark hair trailing round her face.

"Hullo, darling," Clare said, shaking a stray lock out of her eyes. "Isn't it gorgeous? Come on out a bit. Don't hug the shore."

She grabbed me and began pulling me with her. I saw Miranda then, and John and Tony.

"Where's Simon?" I asked.

She grinned. "Don't let him kid you he can't swim. He's out here with us and he knows the right ones to take too."

The fox! I thought angrily. Pretending he wasn't used to surf.

I opened my mouth to speak and a breaker caught me. I heard Clare's laugh before I went under, and then I was spinning like a ball, tossed at the mercy of the wave, carried forward against my will. And when I came to the surface, spluttering and laughing, Clare was beside me again.

"You're a dope, darling. Why don't you watch them? You'll really get dumped if you're not careful. Come on."

John was waving to us cheerfully. "Where've you been, Gilly? We've been looking for you."

I grinned and told him I'd been under a wave.

"Stay out here," Tony advised. "It's the best spot to catch them."

But I didn't like being out so far, and I said so.

"Nonsense. You can still stand, can't you?"

I tried and found I couldn't and I turned hastily for the shore.

"Dive!" John yelled at me.

I saw the breaker then—a huge mountain of water bearing down on me.

I dived. I knew I was in time, and the breaker should have passed right over me, but something had gone wrong. I seemed to be made of lead. There was a weight about my back and shoulders and it was holding me down, and I couldn't get free. I tried to struggle, but my arms had no strength and there was a steel band tightening round my head and a dreadful pounding in my ears, louder and louder. I couldn't fight against the blackness into which I was sinking and I felt my body grow limp.

The pressure of water all around me was crushing me mercilessly—crushing my temples and my breast, beating against my brain, holding me powerless in its deadly, suffocating embrace.

I didn't see my past life flashing before me. I saw a black, terrifying cavern with a tiny opening a long way off—a small aperture of light and air beyond my reach. My soul cried for air.

I felt myself slipping down and down into darkness. And then, miraculously, the tiny slit of light became larger and nearer like a wonderful shining beacon, and the bands round my chest loosened, and I found, to my surprise, that I was breathing great gulps of fresh air. I could feel myself being pulled along through the water and then firm hands held me and my feet touched sand, and I knew I was walking.

A voice that belonged to the hands said, "Take it easy, Gilly. You panicked. You shouldn't have been out so far, because you're not a strong enough swimmer."

It was strange how familiar that voice was. Blue's voice!

I knew I was dreaming, because how could Blue be here, helping me to lower myself on to the sand, sitting beside me, holding my head over between my knees, throwing my robe about my shoulders? I lifted my head. It felt dull and heavy. I could see the beach in front of me now, and the swarms of faces around me. Some of them were gazing at me with frank curiosity. I could see the children running about on the sand. And I could see Blue, studying me with anxious eyes.

He grinned when he saw I was watching him. "Buck up. You weren't anywhere near drowning, so don't tell yourself you were. You haven't even got any water to bring up. But you scared the tripe out of me, and out of yourself, too."

"What are you doing here? I didn't see you." How queer to be able to talk again.

"Mac's idea. He thought I'd better keep an eye on you, and how right he was. If you fly into a panic every time a wave hits you, you certainly need a bodyguard. Mac told me to stay out of sight. He didn't want it to be too obvious that I was keeping a watch on you. My God, what a job I had trying to stay invisible!"

"He told me to watch out for sharks," I said weakly.

Blue grinned again. "Don't mind the sharks. Just bother about the waves."

Clare came running up the beach with the others trailing after her. "Gilly, what happened? We saw Blue lugging you out and that's the first thing we realized." She was white and breathless.

Tony sat down beside me. "Let's have a look at you."

I shook my head. "I'm all right. Honestly."

John was looking at Blue curiously. "Lucky you happened to be there. I didn't know you were on the beach. I saw Gilly dive and it never occured to me that she wasn't perfectly all right. What was it? Cramp?"

"Panic mostly," Blue said calmly. "I was just going over to speak to her when she went under, and when she didn't come up again I hauled her out. There's such a team in the water she probably got tangled with someone's legs, and then she lost her head. As my son would say, 'Women!'"

"You've heard good news about Joey?" That was Miranda's voice, but it had a sharp edge to it, as though the water had washed away its lovely husky quality. "I'm so glad."

Blue shrugged. "He's a tough youngster. Takes after his Pop."

"Poor Gilly!" Clare sat down and took my hand. "What a lousy thing to happen. How do you feel, darling?"

I was conscious of Simon squatting on his heels, listening to the conversation, but contributing nothing. Not even a word of sympathy.

"I'm okay." I looked into Clare's puzzled brown eyes. "But it was horrible. I felt as though someone were trying to drown me."

She dropped my hand, and I heard her draw in her breath with a little sucking sound. I hadn't meant it when I said it, but now I thought about those terrifying moments beneath the water, I found I had unconsciously described my feelings with dreadful accuracy. I recalled that pressure on my back, that weight holding me under.

Suddenly I was frightened, desperately frightened.

But it couldn't have been that, or Blue would have known. He would have told me.

I laughed shakily. "I guess I'd better go home."

Blue was already on his feet. "I've got the rattle-trap here, so I'll take you. Dawn'll want to hear about your adventures," he added with a teasing grin.

Quite abruptly Clare said, "I'll come too."

I saw the way she clasped her hands together tightly, and

I knew she was scared. Badly scared. She was trying not to show it.

"I think you'd better let Gilly go alone with Blue. We'll follow later. Are you cold, Clare?" John picked up her gown and draped it round her. I wondered whether he knew, as I did, that Clare wasn't trembling with cold. She was shaking with fear.

Finch pulled me to one side. "Let me take you home, darling. The others can squeeze into Tony's car."

"I'm going with Blue."

"Do you still hate me?" he asked, in a gentle, conspiratorial whisper. "I don't like things to be this way between us."

I looked at his attractive faun's face and told him, quite truthfully, that I didn't hate him and never would.

"This is good-bye, Gilly."

"Don't be silly."

"I didn't tell you before but my passage is already booked. I'm off in a few days. I may not see you before then."

I was sorry, but I was glad too. It was the best decision he could have made. Cut adrift. Leave Miranda and his past life and start over again. He wouldn't alter. It would be the same pattern in England as here, but at least it would give Miranda a chance to forget him.

I wanted to wish him good luck but I didn't get the opportunity because Miranda suddenly drew attention to us by saying, sharply, "What are you two talking about?"

Finch gave his funny, crooked smile. "I was telling Gilly to take care of herself. I was advising a double whisky."

Blue grabbed me. "Come along."

No one spoke as we left. Clare was still standing with her hands clasped together and fear jumping to the surface of her shining brown eyes. John was frowning, as though his thoughts were unpleasant. Tony gave a purely automatic smile, and Miranda lifted her hand in farewell, then dropped it suddenly to her side again. Simon's face was a mask—a polite mask—that revealed nothing of the mind beneath it. They watched us go in silence. They might have been a group carved in stone.

We began threading our way through the people lying on

the beach. Once I glanced back over my shoulder to wave. Only Finch responded, with a small, caressing gesture of his hand. Unaccountably I found a lump sticking in my throat. I knew he was no more in love with me than I was with him, but it was nice to know he was fond enough to want to marry me. Especially since Barney had failed me so badly last night.

And at the thought of Barney the lump grew bigger.

Blue said, "They're nervous. It sticks out a mile, doesn't it?"

I supposed it did. It accounted for the silence, the lack of farewells, the missing phrases that usually accompany any departure.

Blue barely spoke either, on the way home, and my own flow of chatter seemed to have dried up.

As we turned off the main road, I suddenly recalled the small dark man who'd been lying so conveniently near me on the beach—near enough to hear every word I'd spoken. I told Blue about him.

"I got the idea he was watching me. It was queer that I should see him yesterday and then again today. I'm trying to work out whether it was sheer accident or design."

Blue didn't lift his eyes from the road. "He could be one of Mac's men, I suppose. But it's no good asking me because I'm only a plain bloke who doesn't know what goes on. You'd better ask Mac about him. Tell me, Gilly, who was with you when you caught that big one? Can you remember?"

"I'd just joined the others. Clare fetched me out and we were all together, and then I found it was deep and I turned back. John called out to dive and I did. That's all I remember till you dragged me on to the beach."

"Do you mind talking about it?"

"Not now. It's all over. I wouldn't have minded at the time if I'd known you were there to rescue me."

I could have sworn he shuddered. "Thank God I was! What did it feel like, when you were under?"

"I thought I was a goner. Honestly I did, Blue. Everything went black and I felt as if I were pinned down and couldn't get free." I looked down at my hand and found it was trembling. I did mind talking about it after all. It brought those

212

ugly, terrifying moments back far too clearly. I wondered if I'd ever enjoy surfing again.

Blue pulled the car to a stop outside the flats.

"I'm leaving you with Dawn for a while and if anyone calls before I get back, don't let them in. I've got to find Mac."

He took my arm and fairly rushed me up the steps and into the lobby.

He had his hand on the door when he turned to me quite abruptly and said, "Gilly, perhaps I'd better tell you. I don't think you were dumped. I think someone tried to drown you."

I leaned against the doorpost because my legs suddenly gave way beneath me and I didn't trust them to hold me.

"You think—what?" Yet I wasn't surprised. Not really. It explained so much—that weighted feeling, that dreadful struggle to escape from an iron grip, that queer sensation of being held below the water.

"Blue, who was it?" I had to know. My voice was shrill with fear at the knowledge that my life had been in danger. It was still in danger. Mac had warned me, but I'd only half believed him. I'd been frightened, yes, but deep down I'd been vain enough to think that none of my friends could want to hurt me. I'd shut my eyes to the truth. But now they were wide open. Whoever had killed Lisa and tried to murder Joey had been sitting on the beach with me today. That same person had tried to murder me too. And I hadn't the faintest idea why.

Blue was staring at me as if I could give him the answers to the questions he was asking himself.

"Who was it?" I asked again, jerkily.

"I don't know. I can't even be certain about it. But a figure brushed past me when I was under the water and I could have sworn——"

Dawn opened the door at that instant.

"Hullo." Then she saw our faces. "Blue, what is it?" Fright leaped into her eyes.

"I can't wait to tell you, darling. Ask Gilly. Make her some tea, because she's got the jitters badly. It's my fault. I shouldn't have told her."

"Told her what?" Dawn's voice, usually so calm and steady, was suddenly filled with dread.

Blue didn't answer. He slammed the door behind him and ran down the steps. I flopped into a chair before my legs gave way. It's one thing to know you nearly drowned by your own stupidity, but quite another to find it wasn't your fault at all, and that an unknown enemy had plans against your life.

Dawn didn't make tea. She poured us both a large-sized drink and we sat and sipped it and talked in whispers. I told her everything, just as it had happened, and whether it was the whisky or the relief of talking I don't know, but at the end I began to feel a little more normal. She stared at me with wide, startled eyes. She was more shattered than I'd ever seen her before—even counting the time when Joey was down with measles and running a temperature.

"Mac thought you'd be quite safe. He thought no one would attempt to touch you in the midst of thousands and thousands of people. But he asked Blue to go along in case, and he told him not to let you out of his sight when you were in the water. He said you didn't realize where your danger lay and he didn't want to tell you because he didn't want to scare you more than was absolutely necessary. Darling, you don't think Blue made a mistake? There are always such crowds diving about under the water. Anyway, I can never see a thing—just shadowy shapes."

"You know Blue better than I do."

"He doesn't imagine things. He's very practical. But surely he knows who it was?"

"He told me he didn't."

We huddled together, stubbing out our cigarettes and lighting fresh ones.

When Blue banged on the door, we both ran to let him in. We'd seen him coming up the steps because we'd been watching for him. He had no fresh news, no glimmer of hope to offer us. Mac hadn't made an arrest yet, but he was on his way to see me to get the story from my own mouth. I left shortly after that, with Blue dogging my footsteps up to my flat like a faithful hound.

"Call out when Mac rings and make sure who it is before

you let him in," he said, after he'd seen me safely installed. "If Dawn or I come up we'll give our usual signal. Nobody knows those three short rings but us."

After he'd gone I turned on the light and the radio. It wasn't dark yet, but I didn't want the evening to creep in and catch me unawares. I wanted light and the cheerful sound of voices—radio voices—to fill the room. I wanted to be alone, yet I wanted company.

I sat in a chair and listened to a mournful woman wringing the last drop of emotion from *Auf Wiedersehen*. Good-bye! It made me think of Finch and from him my mind jumped to Miranda, to poor unsuspecting John, and on to Clare with her fluttery hands and frightened eyes. She'd been badly shaken today. She'd even been snapping at Tony. I thought, too, of Simon's blank, fathomless eyes and cold English voice.

Then I realized I was still in my bathers and I hustled into the bathroom to take a shower. I was glad to have something to do. I chose my frock carefully because it gave my mind a more cheerful topic than the dark evil one of murder to dwell on. I spent an extra few minutes making up my face and brushing my hair.

I was as nervy as a cat on hot bricks and when the door-bell rang I jumped in the air as if it were a shot from a gun.

I heard Mac's voice saying, "Open up. It's me here."

I let him into the lounge, fixing him with a worried stare, hoping against hope that he'd calm my fears by telling me I could walk in peace because he'd arrested a murderer. But one look at his face and I knew he'd brought bad, not good, news.

He didn't even say hullo. He simply flew straight off the handle at me, which I thought a little unfair as it wasn't my fault someone had tried to murder me, any more than it was my fault that I'd met Lisa or that a burglar had broken into my flat.

"You've made a fine mess of things. Why couldn't you have done what I told you—and if you'll remember I particularly stressed the danger of talking."

"I wasn't aware that I had talked," I told him haughtily.

."That's the trouble with you," he said grumpily. "You don't know when you're giving yourself away." He thumped the desk with his hand, making my little typewriter bounce alarmingly. "I ought to shake you till your teeth rattle."

He didn't need to shake me. They were already chattering as if I'd been caught naked in a winter gale.

He must have taken pity on me, because he suddenly sat down and gave me a rather forced imitation of his usual friendly grin. "Let's have it," he said a little less grumpily. "What made you stumble on the truth? And once you'd shown you knew, why in God's name did you dare go in the water? You were asking to be pushed under, you know."

"I don't know what you're talking about."

"I suppose," he said witheringly, "you didn't realize you'd spoken those fatal words. Perhaps you were merely thinking aloud. But Raines heard you. He saw the look on your face when you said them, too. And so did a murderer."

"Raines? The small dark man on the sand? Then he was——"

"Yes, of course! And he ought to be sacked for letting you catch on. I've had a man watching you ever since we had that little talk yesterday morning. You told me the screwiest lot of stories I've ever heard. Almost too much to swallow."

A new panic crept up my throat. "You thought I was lying."

He looked at me steadily. "No. I believed you. I've been at this game a long time and I know quite a bit about faces. I can usually spot a good liar when I see one—or a potential liar. You show what you're thinking. But so long as you went on thinking along your own lines you were fairly safe. I wasn't taking any chances with you, though. That's why I got Blue to follow you to the beach. He's got a soft spot for you and he's a crack life-saver, so I thought you'd be well looked after with Raines and Blue both to keep an eye on you. You can thank your stars you sat where I told you to, otherwise Blue would never have found you in that mob and I doubt if you'd be sitting here now. Raines is no great shakes in the water."

I lifted a trembling hand for a cigarette. I needed some sort of nerve tonic.

Mac held a flame towards me. "What made you tumble to the truth? And why did you have to show you'd seen it?"

I could only stare at him, speechless.

He stared back at me, his eyes slowly filling with wonderment. "My God! Don't tell me Raines was wrong——" He leaned towards me and there was no mistaking the urgency in his voice when he said, "Think back to the time when Miranda told you the gun was missing. Take it from there."

I racked my brains. I was on the beach again, hearing Miranda's voice, watching Finch as he admired his toes and proclaimed the police to be fools.

"Miranda suggested Lisa might have had enemies in her past, and why didn't the police try to find out what sort of girl she was and who she mixed with. I remembered about her brother and it occurred to me that you could probably dig up some of his friends who'd known her. Then I saw Raines and I knew I'd seen him before and it suddenly hit me that he was spying on me——"

Mac's eyes never left my face. "So you decided to get away from him by going for a swim? And the others thought it a good idea and went rushing in ahead of you. Simon Ashton waited for you, though. After Blue brought you back to the beach what did Finch Martyn have to say that couldn't be spoken out loud? You must tell me."

"He only said good-bye. That's all. He's booked his passage and he leaves in a few days. He thought he mightn't see me before he sails."

"You poor child." McLean stood up. "You don't even realize what you've done. Remind me to put you in my memoirs. The girl who always jumped the wrong way. Pack your bag! You're getting out of here."

I went as cold and clammy as a wet fish.

"Then you think——" I couldn't finish it.

"I don't think. I know. The first attempt failed, but the second might be successful. It'll be better planned, more carefully thought out. But it will take place soon because time's running short. A murderer thinks—just as I thought when Raines told me about it—that you've seen the pattern for murder." He smiled like a cat sniffing at the cream jar.

"My God! When I think of it. All that shocked you was the sight of poor old Raines." The smile vanished. "You could sleep at Dawn's of course, but I'd sooner you were well out of the building. Do you know a friend who could put you up for the night?"

"I'll stay with Sandra Davis. She's one of my best friends." My voice was a mere croak, hardly recognizable as my own.

"The address?"

I gave it to him and he wrote it down. "Ring through at once and tee it up."

I dialled the number and Sandra's beery-voiced landlady answered the call. Sandra, she said, had gone swimming but was due back for dinner. Yes, she'd tell her I'd called and that I'd be visiting her in an hour's time.

I hung up with a huge sigh of relief. Tonight, at least, I would be out of the reach of murderous hands.

McLean paced up and down like an impatient tiger—a thin, rangy tiger—while I told him I could stay with Sandra indefinitely if need be. She'd be happy to have me.

"It won't be necessary. I only want you out of the way for tonight. Unless I'm mistaken you'll have a visitor to this flat and I wouldn't want you to be here when that happens."

"You know who it is?" McLean, I knew, had located his quarry. He'd singled him down to one person, and one person only.

"I've known for some time and so have you. You've been safe so far, because you've coloured every event with your imagination. You've read your own meaning into every remark. Now this is what I want you to do. Call a taxi for seven sharp and be ready to leave on the dot. At that time I'll have everyone rounded up at Coolibah, so you can be quite certain you're not followed. They're over there now," and he jerked his head towards the street, "having drinks before dinner. They've got instructions not to leave the house till I've seen them. They wouldn't dare disobey my orders at this stage. I'm going back there now, and I want you out by seven-fifteen. You understand? And don't tell a soul you're leaving."

I could only nod my head because speech had left me.

He patted me on the shoulder. "There's no need to be scared. You just put your trust in your Uncle Mac."

It was all very well for him to be cheerful, I thought bitterly. He didn't have a murderer on his trail, waiting for the right moment to strike. I watched him go to the door.

He turned to look at me. "I'd warned Dawn that you might be staying with her if we couldn't think of a better arrangement. I'll drop in and tell her you're fixed for the night."

My voice came back to me—the queer new voice I was using. "Why should anyone want to murder me?"

"Because you mentioned Jock," he said, with his hand on the knob.

I could feel my eyes popping.

"Jock?" It didn't add up to murder. Not as far as I could see.

He was opening the door now, and I couldn't bear to let him go while a thousand questions clamoured at my brain demanding answers.

"But where does Joey fit in?"

"He saw who let Lisa into the house."

The door slammed and I heard the lift rattling its way downwards and I was alone again.

Jock! Joey! Murder! Lisa! My thoughts tumbled over each other in terrified confusion.

Ring for a taxi. Pack my bag. I ran to the 'phone and ordered a cab for seven prompt, stressing the importance of time in a squeaky, frightened voice, until the girl at the other end said irritably, "I understand perfectly, thank you."

I hung up and rushed into the bedroom and began hurling my night-dress and toothbrush and small make-up case into an overnight bag.

At two minutes to seven I was sitting on the edge of a chair waiting, when Blue yelled through the door that a cab had arrived for me. I switched out the lights and hurried out, clinging to Blue's arm as if we were a couple of newly-weds who couldn't bear to be parted.

He tucked me into the car and handed in my bag. "Take care of yourself. And give Dawn a ring in the morning."

I was off.

The joy of leaving Cottrill Street behind me was so great that I could have burst into song. Instead I leaned back in a corner and contemplated a nice long evening with Sandra, telling her about the sensational life I'd been leading. I laughed aloud at the way her eyes would grow rounder and rounder and her voice higher and higher.

My driver was a matey soul who was prepared to be chatty. We discussed the weather and he told me there was still thunder in the air and tonight would see the beginning of the end.

In more ways than one, I thought happily. Tonight Mac would catch a murderer.

He'd been born and bred in Sydney, he told me with pride, and he was confident he knew more about the weather than the professionals who had to rely on scientific instruments for their forecasts. We reminisced about heat-waves we'd known, and he delighted in assuring me that we were enjoying mild days compared with spells he'd endured long before I was born!

The short journey passed quickly and pleasantly, and when we arrived at Sandra's I gave him a fat tip because he'd restored my sanity and driven away my fears.

Already Cottrill Street seemed miles and miles away.

I rang the bell and waited. Mrs. Charters, the landlady, opened the door and surrounded me with a potent aroma of gin.

"Miss Davis? You say you want Miss Davis?"

I hung on to my patience and told her I'd rung a short time ago and left a message.

"Oh yes. I remember."

I knew she didn't, and I wanted to shake her.

"Will you please tell Miss Davis I'm here?"

She peered at me glassily. "Can't do that. She isn't home."

"I'll wait for her."

She blocked the doorway—a fat untidy figure with bleary blue eyes. No wonder Sandra was looking for new accommodation.

"S'no use waiting."

"Why?" My submerged fears began rising to the surface again. Nothing must go wrong now. Not after I'd laid my plans.

" 'Cos Miss Davis won't be coming home. She's gone to stay with friends."

"Why didn't you tell me that before? When I rang you?"

" 'Cos I didn't know. Miss Davis came in and went out. In and out. Said she wouldn't be back till tomorrer night."

"Didn't you tell her I was arriving?"

She mumbled and I couldn't hear what she was saying.

"If you'll give me Miss Davis's key I'll let myself in," I said firmly. I wasn't going to be thwarted by a gin-sodden old moron who didn't even have the sense to deliver a 'phone message.

She pulled the door closer around her as though she feared I might dart past and steal the Woolworth vase from the hall table.

"I couldn't let you into Miss Davis's flat. Not when she isn't home."

"You must, Mrs. Charters." Somehow I had to make her understand that tonight wasn't just an ordinary night when I could return home and ring Sandra later. "You know me, you've seen me before. Quite often. You know I'm a friend of Miss Davis and she wouldn't mind if I used her flat for the night. I've stayed with her before, remember? You must let me in."

She drew back a bit and her face grew hostile. "Who are you to tell me what I can do and what I can't?"

I was working along the wrong lines. I tried again.

"It's terribly important that I stay here tonight. I'll take full responsibility—you needn't worry about that. I'll explain to Miss Davis tomorrow."

I saw her waver, or perhaps it was merely her curiosity coming to the fore.

I pushed on before she could think up more excuses. "It's terribly urgent. It's a matter of life and death, Mrs. Charters."

She examined my face. Obviously she didn't like it.

"Life and death?"

H   221

Oh Lord, I thought desperately, now I've said the wrong thing again.

She was eyeing me with frank suspicion. "I don't want no trouble in this house. It's always been most respeckable. And I couldn't get into Miss Davis's flat if I wanted to—not that I'd dream of it, of course—'cos I don't have a key."

It was a lie. Mrs. Charters was known to prowl round her tenants' flats when they were empty—fingering correspondence, examining private papers. Sandra always hid anything of importance before she went to work each day.

"But surely you have a master key. After all, you're in charge."

She shook her head and I knew I was beaten.

"May I use your 'phone?"

She paused. "I suppose so," she said at last, ungraciously. I followed her into the hall.

"It's sixpence a call," she said in discouraging tones, "and I hope you won't be long because I want to use the 'phone meself."

In a fever of anxiety I called Rita Leydon's number. Rita loved having friends drop in on her. She'd be glad to see me. Ping, ping. Ping, ping. I let the 'phone ring for five minutes before I gave up hope.

Who else did I know? Jane Masters! Then I remembered that Jane and her husband had gone to spend the week-end with an elderly aunt who demanded a visit at least twice a year.

So many people were out of town. Perhaps I could try a hotel.

I rang four—but the reply was the same in every case, as I had known it would be. "Sorry, but we're full up."

Mrs. Charters was sitting in a chair hanging on every word I said. She was like a fat, white toad—an evil toad—who stood between me and security. I loathed her from the bottom of my heart.

"You finished?" She stood up to indicate that I certainly was finished whether I liked it or not.

I slammed some money on the table and walked out of the door without a word, but I knew she was watching me as I stood in the street trying to hail a cab. There wasn't one in sight and I had to walk to the corner before I managed to find one.

"Where to?" the driver asked.

I gave him the Cottrill Street number.

There's no need to be frightened, I told myself, in an effort to remain calm.

There was always Dawn's flat. McLean himself had suggested I should spend the night there. He wouldn't have mentioned it if it hadn't been a good solution to my . . . difficulties. I dodged the word danger. I couldn't bear the sound of it.

It would be rather fun to stay with Dawn. She'd probably put me in Joey's room, and in the morning Blue would come round with cups of tea and we'd sit and gossip for a while before I set out for the office. By tomorrow we'd have plenty to gossip about too, if McLean got his man. Just like the mounties! Mac gets his man!

But when I reached Cottrill Street it was dark and forbidding and I wished I were safely tucked up in Sandra's flat.

The light from the lobby was reassuring, however, and it outlined the steps up to the big swing doors. I was trembling all over as I put my finger on Dawn's bell.

CHAPTER XIV

THE building was horribly silent, just the way Coolibah had been that awful afternoon when I'd stood like this, waiting for an answer to my ring. The silence of death, I thought—with fear crawling up my spine.

I heard the bell clanging loudly and urgently inside the flat.

"Dawn!" I called.

My voice floated round the empty lobby in mocking echo.

I banged at the door and called again, but still there was no answer but from my own ghostly voice, which seemed to fill the building and hover in the air with fearful expectancy.

Dawn and Blue were out! They must have gone to visit Joey!

Why did I come back here?

I ran outside again. Perhaps I could stop the taxi before it reached the main road. Too late! I saw its red tail light disappearing down the hill, leaving the street in lonely gloom, full of shadows and soft whispers.

The red-flowering gum outside the gate rustled its leaves eerily and then was silent again. Beneath the dim street light a dark shape moved, then disappeared. Only a cat, I told myself, as I flew to Dawn's french windows and tried to force them open. But they were locked.

The blackness behind me was creeping closer, surrounding me, stretching out hot, eager fingers.

I flew up the steps into the lobby again, thankful to shut the darkness out. Here at least it was light. The lift was standing at the ground floor. I shot into it and slammed the door.

I tried to steady myself, to force myself to think calmly. Flying into a panic wouldn't help matters. Firstly I must get in touch with McLean and tell him what had happened and warn him that I'd returned to the building only to find that Blue and Dawn were out. That meant getting to a 'phone, and the nearest was in my own flat. I pressed the button for the second floor.

Thank heaven the light was shining brightly outside my door! I fumbled in my bag for the key, had it ready in my hand, then a quick dash from the lift and I was inside my lounge, collapsing into a chair, panting a little, not from exhaustion, but because I'd been holding my breath in terror.

I sat thinking and listening for a minute, then I got up and tiptoed to each room, switching on the lights, assuring myself I was really alone. When I was satisfied, I returned to the lounge and picked up the 'phone book. How to get in touch with McLean? Ring through to Police Headquarters?

A soft hot wind gave a gentle moan at my windows and the curtains billowed towards me. I jumped up and threw them aside.

How silly! No one could possibly hide behind them. They were too flimsy and revealing. There was only one entrance to my flat and that was through the front door. Even a cat couldn't scale up those sheer walls and leap across the window-sill. My only danger lay in the door, and I was quite safe so long as I kept it locked. To make doubly sure I pushed a chair under the handle.

In a few minutes McLean would be over to rescue me from my plight, or perhaps before then Blue and Dawn would have returned and I could fly down to the shelter and comfort of their nice cheery kitchen.

I riffled through the pages of the 'phone book, tearing some of them in my haste. My eyes didn't seem able to focus properly. Ah! At last! I put my finger on the number and lifted my hand to the 'phone, but it froze in mid air and I felt my muscles stiffen as though I were suddenly paralysed.

My ears had caught the faint pad, pad of feet mounting the stairs. They stopped outside my door. I couldn't have moved if I tried. I sat stiffly, staring at the door in rigid fascination, and trying to quell the thunderous thudding of my heart.

The door-bell rang with startling loudness. One, two, three short rings! I sagged in my chair with overwhelming relief. My fears dropped from me like a discarded cloak and my world brightened as though the sun had burst through the clouds.

Blue! Darling Blue! Always turning up in the nick of time.

I ran to the door, thrusting aside the barricading chair, and nearly falling on to the landing with irrepressible joy.

"Blue! Thank God you've come! I'm in the most awful trouble——"

"Yes! You are in trouble, aren't you?"

Simon's pale, shallow eyes looked into mine. His face swam before me as I stepped back a pace, fighting the blind panic that swamped me.

It was a mistake to step back. It gave him the chance to put his foot in the door like a wedge. I threw my weight against the wooden panels, trying to force it shut, but he simply walked straight in and shut the door carefully and softly behind him.

He leaned against the wall with his hands in his pockets. "Blue isn't home." It was a cold flat statement based on fact. He'd checked on it!

I willed my eyes to look at him. My one faint hope of salvation lay in keeping calm, in keeping my terror under control.

"Dawn rang me a minute ago. They're on their way back now and Blue's coming up as soon as they arrive. They should be here."

I saw his eyes flicker.

I put my whole soul into a prayer. "O God, make him believe me. Please make him believe me."

Slowly he smiled. I'd won my point.

"Gilly, you are a silly girl. I believe you're frightened of me. I haven't come here to hurt you. I've come to protect you." Pretty words! The smile was friendly and the tone convincing, but I needed greater proof than that of his good intentions. I wasn't prepared to trust him an inch.

"I don't need protection." I licked my dry lips. "The Inspector has the building surrounded. He knew—a murderer —would be visiting me tonight. He knows right now that you're here. He's watching everyone who comes to this flat."

He took a step nearer. His hands were by his side, but

there was a curious bulge in one pocket that spoilt the fit of his beautifully tailored grey suit. His eyes, those blank, strange eyes, were on my face—probing for the truth, trying to decide whether or not to believe me.

"You know a lot, don't you? Far more, I fear, than is good for you."

He was coming closer and I had a wild desire to turn and run. But where could I run to?

"I don't know anything." It was scarcely more than a whisper.

He stopped suddenly and sat down in a chair, glancing at the clock on the mantel.

"We'll give Blue a few minutes and if he doesn't come by then I'll know you're not telling the truth." His voice was gently reproving. "In the meantime, let's get a few points straightened out between us. Why don't you sit down and be comfortable?"

I perched gingerly, ready to spring if he made the slightest move towards me.

"Gilly," he said, leaning forward a little. "You've been suspicious of me right from the start, haven't you?"

I couldn't answer. I could only stare at him in fearful fascination, like a bird watching a snake.

"I can't think why you always look at me as if I'm a bad smell. What've I said? What've I done? Please tell me." He shrugged his immaculate shoulders and smiled encouragingly at me.

"I don't know you, that's all. I don't know anything about you." My voice was behaving fairly well now, but I was conscious of a small pulse beating in my temple, and I found I couldn't control it. I hoped he wouldn't notice it.

"Then it's time I told you something about myself. McLean trusts me, so surely you can. I'd like to be friends, Gilly."

"Inspector McLean?" I couldn't keep the suspicion from my tone.

"Of course!" He glanced at the clock again. "He knows I'm here."

I stared, dumbfounded. "But he didn't mention you." My

mind was whirling with doubts. Perhaps I'd been wrong about Simon after all. I'd been wrong, so Mac told me, about many things. "Why didn't he tell me about you?"

He pulled his hand out of his pocket and rested it on his knee. "Because he thought I'd be more use to him if I kept my eyes and ears open and kept quiet about the fact that I happened to be a member of the Secret Intelligence during the War."

I gasped.

"Is it so surprising?" He was still looking at his hand lying on his lap.

I tried to catch my breath. I was stunned. Yet it explained a lot about Simon—the poker face, the well-modulated voice that gave no inkling of the thoughts that motivated it. A man who was used to keeping his own secrets—and other people's too.

"I can tell you about it now because it doesn't matter any more."

I began to laugh. What a fool I'd been! I'd turned him into a sinister, dangerous character who existed only in my imagination. Simon was smiling too, sharing the joke with me.

"Why on earth did you have to scare the wits out of me?" I asked him. "Why did you use Blue's three rings on the bell? I really thought it was Blue, and then the shock of finding it wasn't—how did you know, anyway?"

"You were speaking to me on the 'phone yesterday when Joey rang. Remember? And you asked Finch to let him in. I guessed then that three rings was the special Bailey signal and I knew if I used it you'd let me in. And I had to see you."

I looked at him with new respect.

"Tell me, Gilly," he said very gently, "how much do you know about this business?"

"Only what I've told McLean."

"You found out the truth about Jock this afternoon, didn't you? I watched your face on the beach. I'd been wondering how long it would be before you guessed. You see, I did hear a bit of that conversation between you and Lisa in the café, but not all of it. I told the Inspector what I'd heard. And I knew that sooner or later you'd realize Lisa had never mentioned Jock as her—brother. That was your interpretation. Once you discovered you'd been misleading yourself it was only a tiny step to the real story, wasn't it? The search in your flat for the missing wedding ring. The relief at learning Lisa had turned Catholic and was using her maiden name, because she wasn't married in the eyes of the Church. But you chose the wrong time to realize Jock was—a murderer!"

"But I didn't know—any more than I know why you said you couldn't swim and then found you swam far better than I could."

He looked rather pleased. "It's nice to beat Australians at their own game sometimes. I put in a bit of practice in the *Stratheden* swimming pool coming over."

A warning light flashed in my brain! *Stratheden!* The ship Lisa had travelled on.

"Lisa was on that ship."

He was watching me too closely. I didn't want him to see every emotion that passed across my face. I waited tensely for his answer.

"It was a shock to learn she'd been a passenger," he said calmly, putting his hand in his pocket again. "But in a way I wasn't surprised. She must have travelled tourist and I must have seen her at one of the ports. That's why her face was so familiar when I ran across her in the café. I was trying to remember if I'd ever seen her before, but I couldn't place her."

It seemed a reasonable answer, but the small pulse in my temple had resumed its steady throb.

He looked at the clock again. "Now that we're friends, Gilly, tell me honestly, because it's important I should know. Did Dawn ring?"

His hand was coming out of the pocket and it was holding a small glinting weapon that I'd seen before. I'd seen it nestling evilly at the bottom of Miranda's big bag.

I stood up and clung to the back of the chair.

"Where did you get that?" My voice was shrill because terror had risen swiftly to the surface again.

He glanced up at me. He wasn't smiling now. "Don't be

scared. It won't go off. It was quite easy to take it. I thought it would be safer with me than with Miranda."

But policemen—even in the Secret Service—don't go round armed with guns. Not in our country. Not in civilized places. Only criminals carry guns. I knew now why his suit had looked so oddly bulgy when he'd stepped inside the door. I backed away a little.

Like manna from heaven the 'phone began to ring and I stretched out a hand to lift it from the cradle, but before my fingers could close round it Simon pulled my arm away.

"Don't touch it." His voice had changed, had lost some of the friendly quality.

The sound of the 'phone clamoured through the room, then died away leaving a deathly stillness.

"You must do as I say, Gilly." He was tense and impatient now.

I put my hands behind my back and clasped them together. I couldn't afford to let him see they were shaking. I couldn't afford to let him see that, although I hadn't guessed the truth earlier, the whole pattern had suddenly blazed across my brain with dreadful clarity.

For a few seconds he'd almost had me believing his tale about the Secret Service. But now I knew it was a lie.

Secret Service agents don't blackmail their hostesses. But I'd heard Simon talking to Clare on the verandah at Coolibah.

It was all clear now. Horribly clear. Lisa had recognized Simon in the little café. She'd known he was a blackmailer and she'd gone to warn John about him. She'd known what his game was, because she'd been married to him and he'd deserted her.

He was standing looking at me queerly. I had to say something, had to keep him talking. Play for time. Surely, I told myself, in a minute or two the Inspector will come crashing through the door. I had to have some ray of hope to cling to.

"You were telling me about yourself. Tell me about your father."

I was surprised my voice came out evenly, almost calmly.

"My father?" That had caught him unawares. His eyes

seemed to be looking right through me, but I met them squarely, concentrating on keeping my face as blank, as expressionless, as his.

"My father?" he said again softly.

He couldn't answer, and I knew why. Because his name wasn't Simon Ashton and he wasn't Mark Ashton's son. He'd fooled us all—even John—because we'd taken him at his word and demanded no proof of his identity. Lisa had known his real name. The knowledge had cost her her life. His name was . . . Jock!

"You were lying when you said Blue was coming. I don't believe he is, Gilly. And it wouldn't do if he were to walk in now."

I didn't ask why. I simply prayed for a miracle. Only a miracle could save me now, because soon he'd see that I hadn't swallowed that yarn he'd spun me. He'd see the disbelief, the terror, in my face. My eyes flickered to the table. The gun was still lying where he'd left it. If only I could reach it before he did.

He took a step nearer.

He wasn't going to bother about a gun. Of course not. He couldn't risk the noise of a shot which might bring McLean flying up the stairs before he could make a get-away.

"Listen!" Fear was lending me a cunning I'd never known. "Someone's coming."

My fingers groped on the desk behind me for the ugly bronze vase Aunt Ada had given me for my twenty-first birthday. He had his head on one side, as if he were afraid I'd really heard a noise. I felt the cold base of the vase touching my hand. Now I had my fingers round it. At that second I loved Aunt Ada with an undreamed-of affection.

"I can't hear anything." But his attention was diverted. He was listening, although his eyes were still on my face.

I knew I had to choose the right moment because I was fighting for my life. I paused an instant, then I sprang at him, hurling the vase over my shoulder.

It misfired!

It caught him on the arm, and then I felt his hands grabbing me and his breath on my face. "You little fool!"

Desperation gave me strength and I kicked wildly and dug my teeth into the hand that held me. His grip grew tighter and he pressed my arms behind my back and my body went limp and I knew it was useless to struggle against him. McLean would never know that I'd found out the truth—too late. This was the end. Faces flashed before my eyes—Sandra's, Clare's, Barney's. Dear Barney! I'd never see him again.

And then an extraordinary thing happened. A miracle!

His body grew taut as though he were suddenly startled, as though he were caught in a split second of indecision. And I knew what had startled him. I could hear it myself. A faint, soft noise from down below.

I tried to summon up my breath to scream, but his hand clamped over my mouth as if he'd read my thoughts.

But a surge of hope shot through me. Help was at hand. McLean at last. Pray God he'd be in time.

Simon's breath was in my ear. "One word from you, Gilly, and someone's liable to be killed. Remember that."

He was referring to my rescuer—to the owner of those footsteps coming up the stairs. It might be Blue. It might be McLean. It might even be an innocent stranger. Simon would let the bell ring and wouldn't answer it. One single cry from me, though, and I sealed the doom of my unknown rescuer.

I didn't struggle as he half carried, half pushed me to the bathroom door, opened it and shoved me inside.

I heard the key turn in the lock and his soft whisper, "Remember, not a cheep."

He moved away on cat's feet and I was alone.

CHAPTER XV

A CHINK of light under the door showed me the gleaming white bath, the row of bottles and lotions above the hand-basin, and the small cork-topped stool where my bathers still reposed. I threw them on the floor and sat down on the stool.

Oddly, my hand wasn't shaking now. I was petrified with fear, but yet I was calmer than I'd been out there—with Simon.

I tried furiously to think. There must be something I could do, some way out. At least I was still alive, and while there was life a tiny thread of hope lingered.

The lights went out. It was pitch black now. I strained my ears, trying to hear what Simon was doing, but all was silent as the grave.

I shuddered at the word. Soon now, very soon, I might be resting peacefully in my own grave with my name embossed on a fancy headstone. Barney, of course, would come home for the funeral. Who, I wondered, would get my job on the paper? I hoped it would be Alma.

I waited for the door-bell to ring. Any minute now. Silence in a pool of darkness. Then a queer scratching noise that sent the blood pounding to my head, because I couldn't explain it, couldn't place it. A tiny whine. Now I understood! It was the whine of my front door, slowly opening.

I told myself dully that the hinge needed oiling. I tried to hang on to that mundane thought, because it helped to shut out the scene my imagination conjured up out there—in the lounge. McLean slipping quietly through my front door and Simon waiting, even more quietly, in the darkness, with a gun in his hand.

The air was suddenly stifling and I couldn't breathe, couldn't move. I was caught in a great vacuum of suspense which seemed endless as eternity itself.

"Gilly!" A mere whisper. Mac's voice? I couldn't tell, but I could hear it as clearly as if it were right in my ear.

"Gilly!" It came again, even closer, and I could place it this time. It was coming from my bedroom right next door.

Mac was making sure I wasn't in the flat—assuring himself that I'd really gone to Sandra's. In another second he'd find my bed empty and he'd go away satisfied. Simon would let him go. And then . . .?

Panic that bordered on hysteria seized me and every remaining shred of sanity fled. I had only one thought in my mind as my fingers groped along the shelf for a large bottle of hand lotion and hurled it with all my force against the wall.

I had to let Mac know I was in the flat.

The crash of falling glass was like the sudden explosion of a bomb, and before the sound had echoed away lights blazed on and the noise of voices rose in a terrible crescendo. I heard the tramp of feet, running, and then one voice rose higher than the rest in a dreadful scream—the frightful, anguished cry of a trapped animal that knows its end has come.

I put my hands over my ears and shut my eyes—and I screamed, too.

CHAPTER XVI

I DON'T know how long I sat, motionless, on the little stool with my head in my lap and my fingers pressed against my ears. It seemed like a whole lifetime. But then, time had ceased to play a part in my life.

Once I thought I heard the sound of the 'phone and voices talking, and, quite incredibly, I heard a short, sharp laugh that bubbled with quick amusement. It was a lovely joyous sound from a world that seemed foreign to me. It almost shocked me. It was such an extraordinary contrast to the silence, the crash of glass, that fearful, rending cry that had split the night air like the wail of a lost soul.

I lifted one hand from my ear, cautiously. I wasn't mistaken. Someone was laughing. Then abruptly all was quiet save for the sound of feet running down the stairs. Yet I knew I wasn't alone. I could sense a human presence in the flat with me.

Someone was walking towards the bathroom door—not with furtive, silent steps, but with the firm march of a man who doesn't care who hears him. The steps of a man who has nothing to hide. I heard the key turn in the lock, but I didn't dare look up.

The light flashed on, and that same bubbling laughter I'd heard a minute ago suddenly shook the room.

I pulled both hands away from my ears and stood up. McLean was standing in the doorway leaning against the wall with his head thrown back in a fit of apparently uncontrollable mirth. I stared at him indignantly.

His laughter, which had sounded so sweet to my ears, was suddenly as indecent and as ghoulish as if he were gloating over my corpse. It might seem funny to him that I'd been locked in the bathroom with a murderer just a few feet away from me, but personally I couldn't see the funny side. Perhaps I'd lost my sense of humour.

I told him that and a lot more. I really let go.

He put his arm across my shoulders, very gently, and tried to wipe the grin from his face, but couldn't.

I looked at the hand lotion dripping from the wall, and at the glass littering the floor, and I began to think perhaps the whole scene was rather funny—and anyway, it had ended up happily and that was the main thing. I was still on the wonderful, lovely old earth.

I began to laugh too. But it came out as a long shudder and I found I was trembling all over as if I'd developed the ague.

"You're going to lie down." Mac was sober now. "I shouldn't have laughed at you, but I couldn't help it. I was thinking I should have thought of locking you up myself, right at the start of this case. Come on."

I was too weak to argue.

I let him lead me to the bedroom and I sank blissfully on to the soft mattress and shut my eyes. Tonight, I thought, I wouldn't even bother to get undressed—I'd simply drift off to sleep as I was.

Then I thought of the mess on the bathroom wall.

I said, "How will I get it off? The hand lotion."

"Don't worry. Dawn'll be here soon and she'll fix it for you. You'll be having quite a few visitors. But you can relax and let them all come in. You don't have to be careful any longer. Everything's all right."

"You got—him?" I had to know.

"He's where he can never hurt anyone again, Gilly. I don't think he'll be able to put it across Peter at the Pearly Gates either."

I opened my eyes. "He's—dead?"

"He knew the game was up when we nabbed him in here. He was ready for it. He had the poison on him. It was all over in a matter of seconds." He grinned suddenly. "How he must have longed to slip a spot of arsenic in your tea. But that was one method he didn't dare use. I would've been on to him. He had to resort to clumsier means. I'm sorry you had to hear the rumpus tonight, Gilly, but if you'd stayed away from the building like I told you to, you would have been out of it all. What went wrong?"

I told him about my visit to Sandra and about the stubborn, horrid landlady who wouldn't let me in, and how I'd come back to stay with Dawn only to find she'd gone.

"Poor Gilly!" There was genuine sympathy in his voice. "Try not to think about it. Try and forget what you heard."

My pride wouldn't let me admit that I'd barely heard a sound because I'd been cowering on the little bathroom stool with my hands over my ears.

To cover my sense of shame I said quickly, "It didn't matter—because, you see, I already knew all about him."

He looked at me, surprised. "You worked it out eventually? When?"

"In there." I nodded towards the lounge. "His real name was Jock, wasn't it? He was married to Lisa."

Mac suddenly seemed tired, terribly tired and depressed. "Oh yes. He was married to her all right. It was one of those hurried War-time affairs. There's a lot of truth in that worn-out old saying about marrying in haste. By the time he got back to England at the end of the War, she'd disappeared. Her parents had been blitzed and the nuns at the Convent had taken care of her—so much so that she turned Catholic and reverted to her maiden name. When he couldn't locate her, I honestly think he believed she was dead—and heaved a sigh of relief. He'd had time to realize his mistake. It must have given him a nasty blow to see her walking up the drive at Coolibah—or someone so like her that he had to slip out and let her in before she was seen. He had to make sure. And once he saw her face to face he knew she was alive, standing in front of him, and in a position to wreck all his plans just when he'd found the answer to his desperate need for money. He was very ambitious, you know. Once Lisa was out of the way, his path seemed clear, until you bounced up and calmly announced that you'd met her, and that you even possessed a small article she'd dropped. Then his nightmare began all over again, because he was terrified you'd picked up a piece of incriminating evidence, and above all things, Lisa mustn't be connected with him. Certainly not by a wedding ring. He was

237

afraid that was what she'd dropped. He searched for it and realized he'd panicked unnecessarily when I showed him the little cross."

Mac paused and rubbed his hand wearily through his hair.

"But there was still the danger that you knew more than you were telling," he went on; "that you knew more, even, than you realized. Because Lisa had actually mentioned Jock to you. And then on the beach today you started to talk about Jock and gave a pretty good display of shattered nerves and he concluded only one fact could have shaken you so visibly, because he didn't know it was the sight of poor old Raines that gave you the jim-jams. He thought you'd pieced the missing links together. After that your life wasn't worth a damn. He knew he had to kill you—and quickly, before you made up your mind to tell me what you knew. Poor bloke, I almost feel sorry for him. He had to do everything in such a hurry. He married in haste and he murdered in haste. He had bad luck, too, because the one person he thought he could rely on noticed he was a hell of a time coming up from below today— when he was busy trying a spot of murder beneath the water. That person began to have doubts, and confided them in me just a few hours ago."

"It was Blue," I said confidently. "Blue really did know whom he'd seen."

"No, not Blue." He smiled. "It's over now and you don't have to think about it any more. You can go back to your round of parties and your dresses and hats."

Just another person, I thought wryly, who imagines my life is all beer and skittles.

"I've got to run along, but I'll be back," he said. "There's a pleasant surprise waiting for you. At least I think it'll be pleasant, but you never can tell with women."

He edged towards the door as though he didn't want to stay and answer my questions.

"I'll tell you anything you want to know later. By the way, I'm not leaving you alone. The whole building's teeming with people."

He was gone.

I lay staring at the ceiling and dwelling morbidly on the peculiarities of life. It goes along smoothly for a while and then comes a sharp bend and the whole vision alters. I thought of Lisa—of her sweet haunting smile as she remembered happy days with her husband. With Jock, who'd told her what a good place Australia was to live in. And I remembered the shock and bewilderment on her face when she found that Jock was not dead, as she believed, but very much alive, sitting just a few feet away from her. Poor Lisa!

I thought about myself quite a lot too, and about the miraculous way I'd emerged from the vale of death comparatively unscathed. Then I saw a shadow across the carpet and I looked up quickly to the figure standing in the doorway.

My mouth dropped open and my fingers clutched convulsively at the coverlet beneath me, before I sat bolt upright, staring, staring—unable to tear my eyes away from the eyes that looked into mine. For one wild second my thoughts flew to the supernatural, to tales I'd heard about ghosts returning to the scene of their crime.

According to Mac, this ghost should have been knocking at the Pearly Gates arguing about entrance fees.

But he wasn't. He was here in front of me, saying, "I had to see you, Gilly, before the others land in on you."

It was Simon's voice, sure enough, and it was Simon too, who was gazing at me with those oddly expressionless blue eyes.

He was very much alive!

He came towards the bed and I steeled myself not to flinch, but the old habits die hard and I found I was sitting on the very edge of the bed, carefully backing away from him.

He thought I was making room for him to sit down, and he planted himself a couple of feet away from me, and relaxed with one of my fat, blue-covered pillows behind his back.

"Gilly, I must ask you something before we're interrupted. Why did you try to bash me on the head with that vase?"

I concentrated on the chintz chair, wondering what to

say. I don't think I've ever been more embarrassed. When I looked up, still trying to find an answer, he was grinning with obvious enjoyment.

"I told you the truth, so help me God, when I confided all my trade secrets. And I thought you believed me until you tried to bash my skull in. It was a bitter blow to my pride."

I studied the chintz chair again.

"No one knows, Gilly, what happened between us in the lounge, and for my sake, I hope you won't mention it. I wouldn't want McLean to guess I couldn't even persuade a girl that my intentions were strictly honourable, and that I'd come to help her. He thinks you agreed to be locked in the bathroom for your own safety, and he wonders how the hell I got you to agree to it. He even said that I was a better man than he was, Gunga Din."

I flashed him a grateful smile, because I knew he was telling me that he'd never breathe a word to a soul that I'd made the most goddam awful fool of myself. I felt a tiny glow of warmth towards him.

"What made you come up when you did?"

"Because I saw you trying the Baileys' window and I knew Mac's plans had gone astray. I was watching the building here, and Raines was keeping an eye on Coolibah. McLean was waiting in the empty flat below you."

"The Simpsons' flat," I breathed, remembering the noises I'd heard from below, and the summary way Mac had dismissed them. It had puzzled me at the time that he'd taken them so calmly.

"Mac had the devil's own job getting in touch with the owners, but when he did, they played the game. They 'phoned the agents to let him have a key. Their flat made a perfect look-out for the job. I was supposed to be a silent partner in tonight's affair, but you altered all that. When I saw you going upstairs I followed you and dropped in at the Simpsons' for a hurried conference with McLean. He decided I should tell you my real history and take you under my wing. It was my job to get you out of there by hook or by crook before it was too late. We thought there was plenty of time. But he overestimated my powers of persuasion. And then you put me on the spot with that tale about Blue being on his way. It sounded phoney, yet I knew Dawn and Blue were out, and there was just the chance that Dawn might have rung you. And the last thing we wanted were visitors to your flat. I couldn't think why you'd make the story up if it wasn't true. You see, I thought you had a fair idea who'd murdered Lisa—I never dreamed . . ." He began to laugh. "You know, Gilly, I told you myself that I'd been out of England for the whole of the War. How could I possibly have known Lisa? I certainly couldn't have been—Jock. I thought you knew that."

An awful thought struck me. "Suppose I'd really knocked you out with that vase?"

He laughed even louder. "Suppose nothing! I've dealt with worse customers than you in the War. I saw you fumbling behind your back and I knew you were brewing something up, but I didn't have time to talk you out of it because I'd just heard Raines's signal. I knew a murderer was on his way over here."

"Signal?" I was puzzled.

"The Simpsons aren't on the 'phone, but from their flat McLean could easily hear those four rings in yours. That's why I wouldn't let you answer the call. I had to know whether it was Raines's signal, and once I knew it was, I had to act quickly—and keep you quiet."

He smiled as if the memory of locking me in the bathroom would always amuse him.

"The rest you know—I've enjoyed meeting you. I wouldn't have missed it for anything. From now on I hope we'll be friends."

After having tried to break a vase over his head, and after having been locked up in a bathroom, I doubted whether Simon and I really had a solid basis for friendship. But we could try. At the moment, I wasn't worrying about it, because a far more important question was flooding my mind.

If Simon hadn't killed Lisa, then who had?

I looked at his impassive face. It told me nothing. It assumed, just as the Inspector assumed, that I knew. And the dreadful, agonizing part of it all was that I couldn't be sure. But yet I couldn't bring myself to ask. I couldn't admit that I was still groping in the dark. Maybe I could worm it out of Simon without his knowing. Maybe pigs could fly, I added to myself.

He was making an extraordinary statement that set me back by the ears. He was saying quite calmly, "I hope you'll be bridesmaid at our wedding."

"Wedding?" I was so startled I forgot about Lisa and about murder. I was back in my own realm, my own happy world of marriages and parties and gossip. "Your wedding?"

"You're the first person to know about it. It won't be for a long time yet, I suppose, and the bride herself isn't sure about it, but I think she's coming round. I'm a single-minded chap and I know my own mind. The moment I met Clare I knew I was going to marry her and I told her so." He sighed a little as if he found his memories sweet. "We had a wonderful time together. Just one beautiful evening at a party in Melbourne. We'd never met before. I think—I hope—Clare liked me a little."

"Clare!" If I'd been standing I know I would have fallen flat on my face. "But Clare's going to marry Tony——"

Then I broke off because he was looking at me queerly.

"Gilly," he said gently. "I'm sorry. I thought you knew by now."

Suddenly I didn't want to know who had killed Lisa.

But I said, "Who was it, Simon?"

I knew the answer even before he said, briefly, "Tony."

He took out a cigarette and stuck it between my fingers with infinite understanding. I couldn't speak. I watched the flame from his lighter and in its glow I saw a fair-haired man with a charming grin, a promising young doctor from one o the best families. I heard his attractive voice telling me about his appointment with Dr. Kennedy and about his hopes and ambitions for the future. Tony Cambray! Clare's fiancé!

And then I saw another picture—poor little Lisa, who'd never hurt a soul, lying pitifully at the bottom of those wide stone steps at Coolibah. He'd crushed her as mercilessly as if she'd been a fly buzzing round his head.

I understood now why Mac had said Tony would never use poison on his victims. Who but a doctor has access to poison?

He'd picked up the poker in the little sitting-room at Coolibah and struck Lisa on the back of the head. Just one blow in the right spot.

"But why? Why?" I couldn't understand it. "He could have got a divorce. Clare would have waited."

"Would she?" Simon smiled. There was confidence in that smile. "He couldn't afford to wait for a divorce. Clare might have changed her mind. And he needed her money badly. He was never any good, you know, and his family refused to have much to do with him. They gave him an allowance, but he loved being important and he lived far, far beyond his income. He had to have the best of everything, and that costs money. He went to see his parents a couple of weeks back to try and raise a loan but they washed their hands of him. They suggested he should try and live within his means. They would have kicked him right out if they'd found he'd married a girl like Lisa. He couldn't let her walk into his life again—not with Clare's wealth in front of him, almost within reach."

"He tried to kill Joey," I said miserably. "He tried to kill me. I can't believe it."

"Joey knew Tony had left the little lounge-room when he was supposed to be listening to the Test scores. Joey was listening to those scores too, remember. He never mentioned the fact that Tony had left the room when Lisa arrived, because he didn't see the significance of it. But he shook Tony badly by giving him a vivid account of Harvey's wonderful catch. Why would Joey do that if Tony had heard it for himself? The answer was that Joey knew quite well Tony had missed that part of the commentary, and sooner or later it might reach McLean's ears. Gilly, you'll stand by Clare, won't you? This has hit her hard and she's going to need friends. I've left her with Dawn, but she'll be up in a moment to see you. It'll do her good to talk, because she's got to learn to face up to this."

There was something I was longing to know and I couldn't keep silent about it any longer.

"Simon, what did you say to Clare on the verandah at Coolibah? Remember just before you walked home with me?"

He was frowning. Then he smiled. "I was telling her I had no intention of leaving Coolibah till I took her with me. I meant it, too. Now I'll have to wait a while, but I'm prepared to be patient. It'll take time. I think she likes me a little already—she insisted, you know, that I went everywhere she and Tony went, and that suited me, because I was determined to break their engagement if I possibly could. I was quite unscrupulous about it, because I love Clare. I like to think she began to doubt whether she was in love with Tony once I arrived on the scene. Of course, I knew she was J.W.'s daughter, I knew that when I met her in Melbourne. It was because of Clare that I landed up at Coolibah and jumped at Miranda's invitation to stay."

I thought of the indecision and fear I'd seen on Clare's face. I understood it now, even though I'd misinterpreted it at the time. She'd been scared of Simon—but not in the way I imagined. She'd been scared of him because she liked him too much.

"Finch knew—about you and Clare, I mean."

Simon eyed me steadily. "Finch knows a damn sight too much about women. He's sharp. I think he had his suspicions about Tony, too, and he certainly helped to put McLean on the track. He spotted Tony's signature."

It seemed everyone had spotted something important—except me.

Simon suddenly patted my hand as if he could read my mind perfectly. "You wouldn't be expected to see it. You didn't know at that stage that McLean was trying to find the name of Jock hidden away in our signatures or in our initials. Finch didn't know that either—but after we'd signed our names he looked over the signatures and remarked that some people had sporting parents. He'd seen that Tony's initials were A.J.C.—the Australian Jockey Club. McLean saw it too, then, the obvious name a lot of Aussie pilots would fasten on

Tony. The name of Jock. In the forces, if it's possible to find a nickname for a chap, that name usually sticks. That's why Lisa knew him as Jock. Didn't you notice the way he turned and looked at you when you said his name on the beach today? He responded automatically, before he could stop himself."

I was still digesting the information when Clare came flying across the room and threw her arms round me. She'd been crying, but already I think the worst of the shock was over.

"Oh God! Don't I make the most awful mess of my life! And I thought I was being so sensible for once and everyone told me how lucky I was until I really believed it myself, and it all seemed so suitable. Even Dad was thrilled about it. Oh, Gilly."

She started to weep again, very softly.

Simon said quietly, "I'll go."

She lifted her head quickly. "No. You won't leave me, will you—not for a long time? I need someone to lean on. You do understand, don't you, Simon?"

His eyes barely altered their expression. They weren't the sort of eyes to register emotion, but his voice was strangely tender as it said, "I understand, Clare."

Somehow my heart turned over quite sentimentally.

"Lisa must have recognized his photo in the paper, of course, and she must have read that we were going to be married. God, what a shock for her, when she thought he was dead." She couldn't bring herself to say Tony's name. Not yet. "It was brave of her to come out and try and see Dad, wasn't it? You were right about her, Gilly. She wasn't a blackmailer. She was simply trying to help."

I was glad I'd been right about that, at least. I'd never doubted Lisa's integrity.

"If it hadn't been for me, if he hadn't become engaged to me, she would never have been killed. It's a horrid thought. And I never guessed. But today he tried to kill you, darling, and that's when I started to have doubts. You see, I was looking for him, and it was ages and ages before he came up and then Blue suddenly hauled you to the surface, and when

245

you spoke to me on the beach afterwards you said you'd felt as if someone had tried to drown you. I think I knew then, though I wouldn't admit it, even to myself. But I did tell McLean that he'd been right beside you when you went under."

"So it was you!" Just another shock in this devastating night.

"I'd never really considered him before—not in that role. I'd been too worried about Dad—and Miranda—to think about much else. I got the idea Miranda was keen about Finch and I was terrified Dad would see it too, and I couldn't bear him to be hurt. He adores her so. I thought if only Finch would fall for you, Miranda might lose interest." She gave a small grin. It was rather tearful, but it had a touch of imp in it. "I think he did fall too, quite hard. Anyway Dad's taking her round the world because he thinks she needs a change of scene." She studied her small brown hands. "Finch told us he was going away too, next week, and Miranda thought it might be fun if they travelled on the same ship. But Dad made it quite plain that he wanted to go on the *Himalaya*—a week later." She looked up at me. "We'll never know how much Dad guesses—and Miranda will never know either. He wouldn't let on. He's loyal to her to the last breath, and he'll always be the same. He suggested the sea trip would do me good, too, but I turned it down. I've got to stick it out and get it over. I'd only have to face it when I came back."

She'll have Simon, I thought happily. If she stays, he'll stay.

And then a lean, lanky man came rushing across the room with no apology, calling, "Gilly! Gilly darling," and Clare's problems swept right out of my mind, and I heard my voice squeaking with delight.

"Barney!" I cried incredulously, forgetting that I was furious with him and that I'd determined to be as cold as an iceberg.

I wanted to rub my eyes to make sure his long gangly figure was real. Instead I pinched him and he yelped. He was real, I decided.

"Is that a nice way to treat me? My God, I nearly broke

246

my blasted neck trying to catch a 'plane when I heard what had happened over here."

Blue and Dawn were standing in the doorway grinning at us.

"I nearly drove the air officials barmy," he said, "but I made it. I couldn't ring you last night because I was hot on the trail of a cancellation—and then it didn't come good. Anyway, what the devil have you been up to?" He sounded a little annoyed with me, as though the whole business was my fault. "I couldn't stay another minute once I heard about it."

He gave a lovely, engaging grin—a real Barney grin.

"Mac says you figured the whole thing out. It was pretty clever of you. But for God's sake, don't start joining the ranks of brainy women—I can't bear them."

I looked over at Simon, but he didn't bat an eyelid, so I sank back with a smug smile.

"I rang the flat when I landed and got no answer." Barney was gazing at me in a way that suddenly made the whole topsy-turvy world of the last few days slip back to normal. "And when I found you weren't in, I got in a hell of a flap. Then I 'phoned Dawn, and she and Blue came out and picked me up at the airport and told me the whole tale, and by the time we got here Mac had tied up the rest of it. Darling, it's not safe to leave you alone for a minute. That's why I'm here. We're going to be married tomorrow by special licence."

I wished he wouldn't spring these important matters on me in front of mobs of onlookers. He didn't seem to care. He hardly seemed to realize they were there.

Some day, I thought, I'll have to tell him the truth—if I marry him. I'll have to tell him that his wife's a dim-wit who always gets the wrong answers. But I wouldn't tell him yet.

Two proposals in two days! Awfully satisfying for the ego.

I pulled myself out of my private reverie in time to hear Barney say, "After the ceremony we'll fly straight to Melbourne." He eyed me anxiously. "You'll want to see the rest of the Test, won't you?"

Cricket scores for breakfast, batting averages for lunch, spin bowling for dinner. It wasn't exactly my idea of a honeymoon. I was thinking up a reply when Mac poked his head through the door.

"I came back to ask you whether the surprise was pleasant, Gilly?"

I hesitated, glanced at Barney, and then nodded.

"There's just one thing I want to warn you about," Mac drawled. "Never marry in haste."

THE END